A Door Into Time
An Alex Hawk Time Travel Adventure

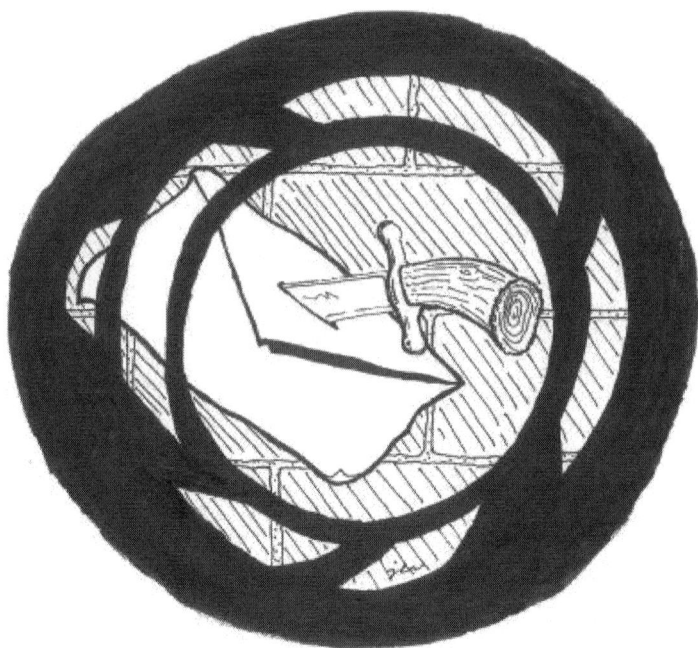

Chapter One
The Door

Alex Hawk looked from one corner of his basement to the other. He closed one eye, a puzzled expression on his face.

"Something's off," he muttered to himself.

Alex had owned the house for more than a year, but until today, he had spent little time in the basement. Now that he was here, his subconscious told him something was amiss.

He reached for the measuring tape on his workbench. He had stuck the tape in one corner when his cell phone rang.

He glanced at the screen.

Mandy. Shit.

Alex took a deep breath and said, "Hello?"

"Just want to make sure you haven't forgotten. It will crush her if you're not here."

Alex glanced at the old clock that hung above the workbench. *10:17.*

"The party is almost six hours away." He stopped, realizing that he was always on the defensive when he talked to Mandy. He started over. "I haven't forgotten. I'll be there." He thought of the massive stuffed teddy bear sitting in the living room above his head. "Why do you have to be like this?"

That was the opening Mandy had been waiting for. "Right, it's not like you miss things constantly is it? Oh, wait, it is. You missed the first two years of her life. Her first word, her first step, everything. Half the time, you don't make it here on time on days you pick her up."

The grooves of this argument were well-worn and always ended in the same place—frustration, blame, and anger.

"Mandy, I was on deployment, I—" He stopped and gathered himself. There was nothing good that would come of going one more round of that boxing match. He knew he was over-matched, and the judges' decision would inevitably favor her anyway.

"Hang on. She wants to talk to you."

A moment later, the tiny voice of his daughter came on. "Daddy? You're coming, aren't you?"

"Sweetheart." He wanted to say, 'You know I'm always there when you need me,' but that wasn't true, and he couldn't lie to her. Instead, he said, "I've got your present right in front of me. I can't wait to give it to you."

"Okay, Daddy."

There was a shuffling sound on the line, then a moment's silence followed.

"That's a dirty trick."

"Using your daughter to guilt you into showing up? I guess. All is fair, right?"

"Just—I'll be there. Okay?"

He glanced at his phone. She had hung up.

It was a lot more satisfying when we got to slam the receiver down.

Alex shook his head, took a few cleansing breaths, and returned to the problem at hand. He hooked one end of the tape into the masonry at one corner and walked to the other side. The tape showed twenty-seven feet, two inches.

He pursed his lips, calculating, then headed upstairs and out the front door into the April sunshine. Central Oregon weather was unpredictable in the spring, but it was turning out perfect for Amy's birthday party that afternoon—warm sunshine, blue skies, and just a few non-threatening clouds.

Alex stood with his face up to the warming sun—you had to take advantage of what Vitamin D was available in Oregon—then repeated the exercise he had done in the basement. One end of his fifty-foot tape hooked on the eastern corner of the house, then he stepped off to the western side, avoiding the rose bushes and rhododendrons.

The tape showed thirty feet even.

Alex let the tape roll up with a metallic snap. He ran his hands through his short hair, trying to solve the mystery.

How is the house thirty feet on the outside and twenty-seven feet on the inside?

"Because it's not. It can't be," he said to himself as he jumped up the steps of his front porch, then double-timed the stairs to the basement.

The eastern wall ended next to a window, so he could see there was nothing but open space beyond it. The western wall was blank, though.

Alex had bought the little craftsman house once he had finally accepted that he and Mandy would not work out.

He didn't want to be one of those dads who lived in a crummy run-down apartment with second-hand furniture and who took his kid out for Happy Meals every other weekend. He wanted to have a home that Amy would know was hers just as much as when she stayed with her mother.

Thus, the craftsman. He had gotten a steal on it because the owner had fallen ill and had been forced to move into assisted living. He'd let the place deteriorate over the previous ten years, which scared away a lot of potential buyers. Alex was happy to take it as-is. It gave him endless projects to fill his hours when he wasn't at work.

All of which led him to the basement on a sunny day in April, and the mystery of the missing two feet, ten inches.

The entire western wall was covered in paneling that looked like it had been there for decades. Alex peered at the paneling, looking for nail holes. There were none.

"Glued on, eh? Well, game on, then." He paused. "Is it a bad sign that I'm talking to myself more and more every day?" Another pause. "Not until you start answering yourself." He glanced around, but of course there was no one to laugh at his joke. One more downside to living completely alone. "Maybe I should get a roommate. Or a dog."

Alex grabbed his claw hammer off the bench and tried to catch the edge of the paneling and pull it down. No luck. The large pry bar gave the same result. After a few minutes of frustration, he scrabbled through his toolkit and found his small pry bar. He jammed it into the line between the ceiling and the paneling.

He tapped on the end of the pry bar with his hammer until he felt it sink in a bit, then pulled. Finally, a piece of the paneling gave way.

Alex stared at the spot where the paneling had been but couldn't see anything other than darkness. He glanced around for a flashlight, found none, then remembered the flashlight he carried with him everywhere. He thumbed his phone on, opened the flashlight app and pointed it at the corner.

Behind the paneling was red brick.

Alex slipped the phone back in his pocket and scratched his head.

Why would someone put up a false brick wall in a basement, then glue paneling over it? That doesn't make sense.

He was intrigued. Shrugging his shoulders, he said, "Only one way to find out."

With a piece of the paneling gone, it was easier to weasel the pry bar or the claw of his hammer behind it. It wasn't elegant, but after twenty minutes of steady work, he had pulled down a six-foot section of paneling, piece by piece.

There was nothing behind the paneling but a well-made brick wall.

Since his discharge, Alex had worked in construction, mostly doing drywall for a contractor putting up a new apartment building one town over. A simple brick wall wasn't going to stop him.

He grabbed his heaviest tarp off a shelf and spread it along the edge of the wall. Next, he grabbed his hammer drill and power saw.

Let's do it.

He set to work cutting along the seams of the brick, then put a wedge tip on the drill and set it to vibrate.

When he pulled down the first section onto the tarp, he was flabbergasted to see what was behind the brick wall.

It was another brick wall.

Alex laughed at the ridiculousness of it all.

I guess if you're gonna build a brick wall in your basement for no apparent reason, why not build two *brick walls?*

He glanced at the clock again. There was still plenty of time to take down both walls and have time to get cleaned up before he had to leave for the birthday party.

He went to work, taking an entire six-foot section of the first brick wall down before focusing on the second.

Soon, piles of bricks were stacked thigh-high on the tarp around him.

When he cut away the first section of the second wall, a blast of cool air hit him. He turned his head away, expecting a musty, pent-up smell, thinking that the air had been trapped for many years.

The wind was inescapable, though, and washed over and around him. It didn't smell stale or musty at all. Instead, it was an unmistakably familiar smell.

The ocean. A hundred and fifty miles inland, Alex Hawk could smell the ocean.

The breeze continued to blow, though, and it was no-doubt-about-it the smell of marine air—cold, crisp and the unmistakable scent of salt on the air.

Alex went to work taking down the rest of the wall. Patiently, one section of bricks at a time.

Soon enough, he could see what was beyond the wall. At least, he *should have been able* to see beyond the wall. Instead, there was just an inky darkness that seemed to swallow whatever feeble light reached it. Alex reached his hand into the opening. There was at least a foot of empty space between the second brick wall and the outer wall of the house.

Alex's light shone on the far wall of his house, right where it should have been. Everything looked like it should, with one exception. In the corner was a deeper blackness, delineated by a slight, shimmering outline.

He shone his phone's flashlight against that corner. There was the shimmering outline of a door, if doors were made of the darkness of the deepest sky. Next to the outline of the door was an envelope, pinned to the exterior wall by a hunting knife.

Chapter Two
The Letter

Alex tried to move the knife to see how deeply it was stuck in the wall. It didn't have any wiggle. Someone had driven it into the wall with a lot of force behind it.

Alex squinted at the envelope. There was no writing on it. The edges had curled a bit and turned slightly brown with age.

This has been here for a while.

He gripped the knife in his right hand, pulled and torqued simultaneously. The knife pulled out and the envelope dropped. Alex pinned it to the wall with his left hand before it hit the ground.

He stepped away from the dark space behind where the brick walls had been, walked to his workbench and set the knife down. It had a five-inch blade and a stag horn handle. Other than the fact that it was found in a sealed space, there was nothing unusual about it.

Alex turned his attention to the envelope, turning it left and right in the light of the window. It was business-sized, and looked like every other envelope of its type produced in the last fifty years. The flap was loose.

Whoever put it there thought that jamming a knife blade through the middle of it was sufficient to seal it.

Alex took the envelope upstairs to his office. He opened a closet and pulled a pair of thin latex gloves out of a box. He also grabbed a pair of long tweezers out of the middle drawer of his desk.

He clicked on a gooseneck lamp, sat down and peered at the envelope. He used the tweezers to open the flap. The only thing visible inside was two folded sheets of paper.

He latched on to the paper and gently pulled the pages out. They had been tri-folded. No writing was visible on the side Alex could see.

Gently, he took hold of the edges of the paper and opened them, laying them flat enough that he could see the handwriting.

The pages were filled with a scrawling handwriting in pencil.

Hey, moron!

What the hell are you doing knocking down two brick walls? Did you ever stop to think that there's an almighty good reason why those walls are there? Are you thinking at all?

I am guessing you are not, or you wouldn't be reading this.

If two brick walls didn't stop you, then probably nothing I can tell you will, either, but I'm going to try.

I bricked this space off so no one else will ever have to suffer like I have. The door that you have uncovered appeared one day in early 1977. I don't know how it got there. One day, there was just the corner of my basement. The next, there was the outline of that dark space you no doubt have seen.

I was curious. You're curious too, or you wouldn't be reading this.

Curiosity didn't just kill the cat. It killed my son. He was a good boy. He stepped through that door. A moment later, he stepped back through, telling me all kinds of unbelievable stories about what was on the other side.

I told him we needed to call the government, or just blow the whole damned house up, but he wouldn't listen. We agreed to sleep on it and decide what to do the next morning. That night, while I slept, he took our rifle and as much of our hunting gear as he could carry and walked back through that goddamned door.

He left a note saying he would be right back. Said he had to see the rest of what was there, but that he would be right back.

I haven't seen him since. I waited for him for ten years. I slept every night and ate every meal in that basement, waiting for him to come back through that door. He never did.

Finally, I faced the truth. My son is dead. Whatever is on the other side of that door killed him. If you go through it, I have no doubt it will kill you too.

If I thought it would help, I would have burned the house to the ground, but I think that would probably just bring more attention to it and more people would die.

Don't be as bull-headed as my son. You can still do the right thing. Brick that door back up before it's too late.

There was no signature, but Alex was sure Benjamin Hadaller—the old man he'd bought the house from—had written it.

Alex's first instinct was to dismiss the letter as a prank.

But who takes the time to build two brick walls on the off chance someone will take them down and find the letter? No one.

Alex leaned back in his chair and stared at the ceiling.

And how do I explain the smell of ocean air where there should be none?

When he had been a small boy, Alex's mother had told him that someday his strong streak of curiosity would get him hurt. She had been right, of course. He had spent two summers of his youth in a cast—one on his left arm, the other on his right leg—because of his insatiable curiosity.

That same drive had been what had led him to enlist in the Army. There was a big wide world out there, and Alex had known if he was going to see it, it was going to be on Uncle Sam's dollar. That enlistment, and the ten years he had given to his country, had been expensive in the end—it had cost him his marriage. At least that's what he told himself.

And now there was literally an unknown universe close enough to him that he could smell and almost taste it.

He looked at the small desk clock. 1:30. Still lots of time until Amy's party.

There was no way he could stand to do little busy work projects for the next few hours, knowing the biggest mystery of his life was waiting to be solved.

There was the letter, though. If Mr. Hadaller was right—if his son really had gone through the door and never come back, there was something dangerous on the other side.

I can just poke my head through and see what's there, if anything. If there really is something, I can go tomorrow and really explore. Today, I'll just satisfy my curiosity a little. Still, I should be prepared, even for a short peek. What if I stick my head through and someone or something is waiting for me? I've got to be ready.

Alex went to the bedroom at the back of the house, where he kept his gun safe. He spun the combination and opened the door. It wasn't a complete armory, but it was well-stocked. His .410 shotgun hung in a place of honor on the interior of the door. It was the oldest and least expensive gun in the safe, but it had been a gift from his father on his twelfth birthday, and he had been the third generation to own it. Before too many years, he would make Amy the fourth generation. In many ways, it was his favorite gun, but it wasn't appropriate for the task at hand.

He pulled the P226 Scorpion Emperor .40 caliber pistol down. With 12-round mags, it would be the right combination of reliability, capacity, and stopping power.

Gonna be a quick recon. Poke my head in, then right back home.

Alex also grabbed his Armalite AR-10 16" Tactical Rifle, chambered in .308 Winchester. With 25-round mags, it would make a formidable primary weapon.

He loaded four mags for each and slipped them into his pack, along with his flashlight, hundred-mile-an-hour tape and a few other essentials.

Most people might have felt a little over-prepared and foolish, but Alex had been trained to be prepared for any eventuality.

He went to his closet and put on his cargo pants and medium-weight jacket. He had his light pack on his back, canteen hooked to his belt, pistol holstered at his side and rifle slung over his shoulder.

Do I need all this stuff to just poke my head through the door, then step back out? No. I'd rather have it and not need it than need it and not have it.

Alex jogged lightly down the stairs to the basement and glanced in the far corner, where the stacks of bricks showed he hadn't been hallucinating earlier.

One minute. In and out. If it really is something, I'll have a better idea what's there, and I can be fully prepared to go in again tomorrow. If I want to, of course.

Alex smiled. He knew he was kidding himself. He had spent his whole life looking for adventure. If one was waiting for him in his own house, he was going to explore it.

He stepped between the bricks and glanced at the top of the pile. When he had taken down the second wall, the bricks facing him had been spotless. He had been in enough of a hurry that he hadn't bothered to look at the back side of them.

Now that he did, he noticed something odd. There were long grooves etched into the back side of the brick. He kneeled easily beside the pile and plucked a few more of the bricks up to examine. They all had the same markings.

He shucked off his rifle and pack and laid half a dozen of the bricks face down on the floor. It was a simple puzzle to put together and when he did, it made an unsettling picture. When the bricks were rearranged as they had been in the wall, Alex could see that the grooves were long claw marks, made by something with three sharp nails.

Alex stood and looked at the utter blackness of the door and the slight shimmering around the edges.

Those claw marks weren't made by anything human. Did something come in that door and find nothing but the brick wall? Was it clawing to get in?

He examined the claw marks more closely. His own hand, even spread wide, was too small to have made those marks. He tried to imagine what *could* have.

Bear? I would likely see four claw marks then, though. Can't think of anything with three claws that would have the strength to do this.

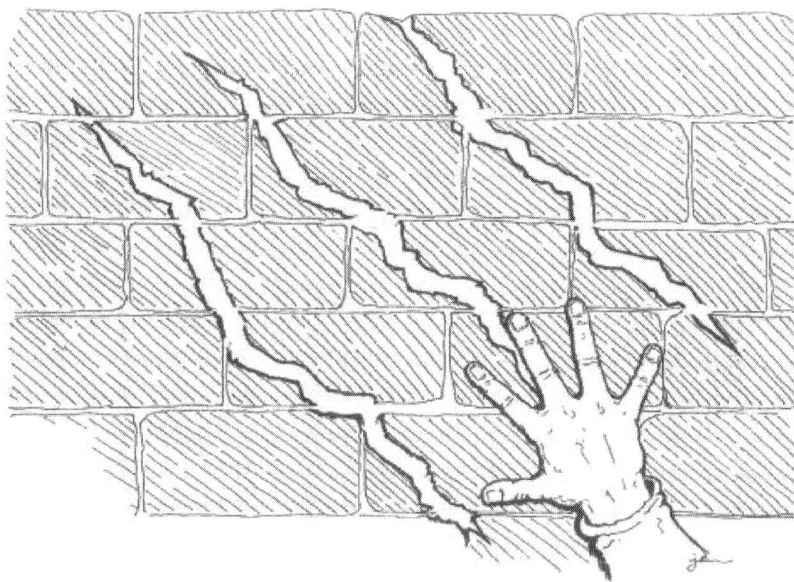

A DIFFERENT MAN, WITH a different set of drives and goals, might have let this discovery put them off. Many men might have set about rebuilding that wall before whatever made those marks decided to come back and introduce itself in a forceful way.

Alex just stood up, shouldered his rifle and pack, and stepped into the darkness where the brick wall had stood.

The ocean air greeted him once again. He filled his lungs and held his breath for thirty seconds to see if there were any deleterious effects from the air.

He let the breath out with a whoosh. No dizziness. No nausea.

He reached a hand out to touch the inky blackness of the door. Although there appeared to be something there, his hand met nothing. As he reached further into the space, Alex was disconcerted to see his hand disappear completely.

He immediately pulled it back. It was still just his hand.

Spooking myself.

Alex let a grin of anticipation spread across his face and stepped into the darkness.

Chapter Three
Kragdon-ah

And darkness there was.

Alex had anticipated stepping through the deep darkness of the door into—some unknown something.

Instead, there was an inky blackness deeper than anything he'd ever seen.

He reached his hand out, fumbling for something solid. His fingers wiggled and grasped but touched nothing.

The hairs on his arms and the back of his neck stood straight up. He quietly tapped his finger against his rifle just so there would be *some* sensory input in the void.

His ears picked up the sound, but it was more distant than it should have been—as though he tapped against the rifle's stock and found it wrapped in cotton.

He grabbed his flashlight off his belt and clicked it on. The beam emanated forth but disappeared after just a few inches.

"Shit," Alex muttered. Like the tap against the rifle, the sound of his own voice reached his ears, but sounded distant, like a third-generation echo.

His head swirled and he felt a sense of movement, but his feet were planted solidly.

With a start, he realized he was going to pass out. Instinctively, he tried to step forward and fell face-first, unconscious.

An unknown time later, he opened his eyes.

Alex realized he was face down in ground made up of tiny black rocks.

Alex tried to push quickly to his feet but only made it as far as his knees before he threw up. A ribbon of thick vomit choked him and sent him into paroxysms of coughing, trying to clear his throat.

His eyes watered. He coughed and spit, then turned and sat hard on his butt, wiping his hands across his eyes to clear them.

The sound of waves pounded in his ears. Small droplets of spray landed on his face.

He looked around. The black-pebbled sand stretched as far as he could see both left and right. An outcropping of rock pushed out into a body of water.

He managed to find his feet without further sickness and looked around him.

His jaw fell open and he closed his eyes hard before opening them again.

"What the..." Alex didn't complete the sentence. No word came to mind that was sufficient to convey what was in front of him.

How could all this be on the other side of the wall in my basement? It's impossible.

The water tossed and frothed near the shore. As the waves rolled in and out, they jangled the tiny rocks and they sounded like a giant rattle. Further out, it was steel-gray and choppy, each wave crested white. The water extended as far as he could see before it disappeared over the horizon.

Alex looked up at the sky. In his memory, he'd been outside just a few minutes earlier and the sun had been shining. Now, there was nothing but clouds and an eerie, yellowish light spread across the sky.

Aside from some faraway birds over the ocean, there was no sign of life.

Alex kneeled and picked up a handful of the dense sand, letting it trickle between his fingers, listening to the tinkling sound it made as it fell.

He remembered the door and whirled around. It was still there, a shimmering blackness standing alone on the beach. Beyond the door, dunes rose and fell, speckled by shoots of tall grass that swayed slightly in the wind.

Alex walked toward the surf, stopping just before the waves touched his boots. He drew a deep breath and the ocean air filled his lungs, pure and clean.

"Okay. There's something here," he said aloud. "I don't know what I was expecting, but certainly not this. This all feels too real." He glanced out over the water. The birds were closer than they had been a few moments earlier.

"I need to go home. I'll come back and explore soon, but I've got to get home. I can't miss Amy's party."

He inhaled a lungful of the pristine air and glanced left and right, deciding which direction he would set out when he returned.

He was snapped out of his reverie by a harsh, penetrating noise from above. He had paid no real attention to the approaching birds, but the sound from above focused his attention.

They weren't birds.

Alex had no idea *what* they were. One thing he did know was that the approaching creatures were *fast*.

He took one long look at them to freeze their image in his mind. A large heavy head that hung slightly lower than the body. Wide wings that beat hard to keep the creatures airborne. Small legs that ended in three-toed feet with dangerous-looking claws. And they were *big*. His first guess was that their wingspan was at least seven or eight feet.

Alex didn't wait to get a closer look. He whirled on his heel and sprinted back toward the shimmering door, his boots pounding against the black sand.

After the initial war cry, the onrushing creatures had silenced themselves, but the sound of leathery wings beating against the air made a terrible sound.

Alex was slowed slightly by the sand, which buried his boots with each sprinting step. If not for that, he would have likely made it back to the door.

Instead, the leading creature crashed against Alex's back, its razor-sharp claws digging through the backpack and inching toward his neck.

It wasn't as heavy as it had looked, but it still had enough impact to knock Alex face-first into the hard-packed sand.

No twenty-first century human had ever been trained to face a situation like this, but Alex had been indoctrinated to react to the situation at hand. As he fell, he pulled the Sig P226 from its holster.

He shrugged his shoulders mightily while lashing out with his left hand, which dislodged the beast. It stood on its two small legs and stepped toward Alex, as awkward on the ground as it had been powerful in the air.

Alex pulled the trigger three times in less than a second. All three hollow points found a home—the first two in the thing's breast, the third through the drooping, colossal head. The body flew six feet backward and landed in the sand, now missing most of its head.

ALEX DIDN'T HAVE A moment to savor his victory. A dark, roiling cloud of the beasts was not far behind the first and they circled around him, their cries filling the sky.

The first two to drop out of the sky landed beside the dead creature and began tearing at it with strong, sharp beaks.

The next three attacked, aiming at Alex's head. He dropped to one knee so the first one sailed just above him and landed in a heap on the sand. He took his shooter's posture and put his next shot between the eyes of the second beast.

The third had just enough time to change trajectory and hit Alex mid-chest, clawing and shredding his jacket, spreading half of his mags across the sand. Dreadfully close, the thing smelled like saltwater and decaying flesh. Its head looked like a vulture, and its wings beat at him. Its claws made short work of his jacket and shirt, and one clawed foot ripped into the flesh of his chest.

Its head rose up for a mighty blow and Alex split it neatly in two with another shot. He tossed the thing off him and saw that there were dozens more of the winged monstrosities circling over his head. Two more dove at him from behind the black, shimmering door, herding him toward the water.

He unslung his rifle, took aim, and blew them out of the air, pinwheeling gracelessly to the sand. They were immediately replaced by two more, heedless of the fate of those who had already fallen.

Alex ran, looking desperately for cover—any cover—but the beach was wide and open.

More of the creatures dive-bombed him, but he was learning their patterns, and managed to avoid being hit and knocked down.

Alex sprinted full out, zigzagging along the shore and working his way back toward the dunes. Finally, he spotted a massive log resting at the edge of a rise. His heart skipped a beat when he saw that one end of it had been hollowed out.

He juked left, then ran straight toward the log, first tossing his rifle, then throwing himself headlong into the hollowed portion.

Immediately the thud of the predators sounded on the sand outside of the log.

Alex wriggled himself further into the log, but his boots remained outside.

The first creature waddled over, raised its head and delivered a sharp jab with its beak, striking the sole of his left boot. It didn't penetrate to skin, but it was obvious it wouldn't take many more strikes to do so.

Alex pulled himself deeper in, simultaneously turning on his back and sighting his pistol down the length of his body. He turned his feet outward to give him a good firing angle and fired as the beast dropped its head for another slash at his boots.

The creature flopped over backwards, its leathery wings flapping spasmodically.

Immediately, two more of the creatures fell on the first and began devouring it.

No honor among thieves or nightmare creatures, eh?

Alex repeated this process twice more. The sand outside the log looked like a scene from a horror movie—covered in grayish blood and a mound of half-devoured creatures.

Alex grabbed another magazine from the front pocket of his pants, slammed it home, and took out three more of the winged predators. He took a mental inventory of the bullets he had for his pistol and tried to count how many of the winged beasts he had seen approaching him. He didn't like the way the math came out.

After he had killed another ten of the creatures, the pile of carcasses grew high enough that the remaining vulture creatures could not see him. They pecked and clawed at the heap of fallen comrades, then one by one, flew off.

Alex reached inside his jacket and his fingers came away sticky with his blood.

I need to deal with that, but I think I'll do that back home. If this is the welcoming committee, I'm not sure I want to see what the rest of this place has to offer.

He started to wriggle out of the log when he stopped cold.

A large human hand waved at him from the open end of the log.

Chapter Four
Hobbled

The hand withdrew and Alex was left in a world of uncertainty. He was head-first in the log, so coming out was going to be awkward and leave him exposed to danger. He didn't know the intentions of the person attached to that hand, so he didn't want to do that. At the same time, there wasn't room in the log to turn around and even if he pulled his feet in, he was still vulnerable to a slash attack.

A deep voice reached Alex's ears.

"Kanyama! Ama danten fenken tol."

Auntie Em, I'm not in Kansas anymore. Or Oregon, for that matter.

Even though he knew it was a long shot that he would be understood, Alex said, "Okay, okay, I'm coming out. I mean you no harm."

Alex wiggled out feet-first, a tingling of nerves spreading along his body as his lower half was exposed to attack. He was blinded by his position and wriggled as fast as he could.

As his shoulders popped out of the log, many hands grabbed him, pulled him the rest of the way and stood him upright.

Alex took in their number and strength, considering his options. He hadn't put a new mag in and knew he was down to only two shots. Also, although the men did not look friendly, they were not attacking him and beyond knives and spears, they were not armed.

Am I capable of unslinging my rifle and shooting them? They haven't done anything to me. But, they could just be confident because they have me outnumbered and surrounded.

Alex holstered his pistol and raised his hand in a gesture of peace.

He was surrounded by a dozen men, all of whom were at least half a head taller than his own 6'2".

The man directly in front of him had dark skin, brown eyes, and long hair that hung nearly to his waist. Alex judged him to be nearly seven feet tall. He was well muscled, but lean, with the build of an athlete. He had an old scar that started above his left eye and ran across his cheek. His left eye was clouded over.

The others around him were similar in build and skin color.

The scarred man stared at Alex and said, "Camin pa tol?"

Alex shrugged and said, "Sorry. Whatever it is you're speaking; I don't understand." Alex had at least a few words of Spanish, Arabic, and Farsi, but whatever this language was, it didn't resemble any of those.

Alex shook his head from side to side, then shrugged his shoulders, knowing the risk that either of those gestures could be the equivalent of "up yours" in whatever culture he had come face to face with.

Most of the men wore loose shirts and pants made from what looked like spun cotton. They all wore belts slung low on their hips with a knife stuck in a sheath or a club dangling from a leather cord.

The man who had spoken reached for Alex's pistol.

Alex moved half a step back, grabbed the bigger man's wrist using a pressure point and turned the hand away.

Like lightning, the scarred man's other hand struck out toward Alex's head. Alex was prepared for that, slid to the left, grabbed the man's other wrist and turned, flipping him to the ground. The man sprang lightly back to his feet almost before he hit the ground and half a dozen other men smothered Alex.

This wasn't like the movies, where a single man was able to take on a dozen others because they politely waited their turn to attack. These men moved as one. They were strong, fast, and didn't hesitate. They all carried weapons but did not draw them. Instead, they simply used their superior numbers and strength to overwhelm Alex, driving him first to his knees, then onto his face. Two of the tall men put their knees on Alex's back. Another put a heavy foot on the back of his head, pushing him deeper into the sand.

A moment later, he had been stripped of his pistol, rifle, and shredded backpack. He was forcibly rolled over onto his back and many hands searched him, retrieving his compass, flashlight, ammunition, canteen and both knives.

When he was stripped of everything but his clothing, one of the men opened Alex's coat and shirt and pushed it away from his wounds. He said, "Mamor tenk hason di," and two of the men who had subdued Alex stepped forward to hold his clothes away from his wounds.

Alex looked at his chest. There were three ragged tears oozing blood. They weren't deep, but they were already turning red around the edges.

The man conducted a quick and efficient exam of the wounds. He turned to the youngest-looking of the men—not more than a boy, really, although taller than Alex—and quietly said a few words. The boy moved away and rustled through a bag. He hurried back with what looked like a hollowed-out animal hoof covered with hide.

The man untied a string with his teeth, then dipped his fingers inside. He pulled out a brownish-red substance and applied it to Alex's open wounds.

Alex tried to stay still but the ointment the man was applying burned.

The man looked at him sternly, laid one hand firmly on his shoulder and held the other in front of Alex's face. The message was clear—stay still.

Alex closed his eyes and did his best to not move.

The medic was thorough in applying the paste but was not unnecessarily rough. The young boy took the container back and reattached the cover, tying it shut with the string. Without being told, he returned to the bag, put the hoof inside, and retrieved a ball of cloth, handing it to the medic.

The man raised his hands above his head and nodded at Alex, who mimicked him.

The medic held on to the end of the cloth and dropped the ball, unraveling a few feet of it. The boy caught it before it hit the ground and fed it out to the man as needed.

The man reached the end around Alex's back, then wound it around and around him until the wounds were covered. He tore the cloth and tucked it inside the wrapping.

The men who had been holding Alex's clothes away from the wound dropped them and stepped away.

No idea what their intentions are. If they had wanted to kill me, they would have tried to do so while I was stuck in the log. It seems like they are interested in having me stick around, and I can't have that. I've got to get home.

An image of Amy sitting on the steps of her mother's house, waiting for him, sprang unbidden into his mind.

Ignoring the burning wounds in his chest, Alex ran straight toward one of the older men. He slammed his shoulder into him pushing him aside. He looked ahead, where the shimmering outline of the door was, not more than seventy yards away.

It won't matter if I hit it at full speed. Gotta remember to keep my feet moving once I get through it, so I come out at home. Will they fol-

low me through? Either way, I should come out on the other side, then they'll be on my turf.

A nagging thought in the back of his brain told him that he didn't know that was the case. For all he knew, the door was a one-way trip. It could be a solid wall on this side. He was already moving, though, and the time for thought had passed.

He sprinted directly at the door, not wasting any time or energy on zigzagging or looking back to see if the men were chasing him.

They did not run after him in one big group. Instead two men split off and ran one on each side, trailing him, but not trying to take him down.

Another man gripped a heavy piece of wood shaped like a baton. He took a step to his right and stood for a moment, judging the distance and Alex's speed. He pulled his arm back and released it in a sidearm throw with a grunt. The weapon slammed into Alex's legs just below his knees.

Again, Alex collapsed in a heap. He tried to spring to his feet, but his left leg didn't work properly. He looked at the door, tantalizingly close.

He took one limping step toward it when the two men who had been trailing Alex launched themselves at him, knocking him back to the sand. Alex struggled to throw them off, but they smothered him.

Two more men grabbed him roughly and stood him up. The man who had bandaged his wounds approached him, whistling tunelessly under his breath. He checked the bandages, then looked reproachfully at Alex.

"Gunta menka han wika brid, dolam," he said as though he expected Alex to understand. He reached his hand out and the same boy as before handed him a length of softly braided rope. He moved swiftly and tied a knot around Alex's hands. Alex recognized it as a handcuff knot.

THE MAN KNEELED AND did the same around Alex's ankles, leaving enough rope that Alex would be able to walk, but not sprint. He was effectively hobbled.

Alex's shoulders slumped and he turned and looked with longing at the shimmering door to home.

Chapter Five
Captured

Alex heard shouts from further up the shore and tore his eyes away from the door to see four more figures approaching.

More of this group? Or someone to attack them? If there's a battle, I might be able to get to the door, even hobbled.

As the figures drew closer, Alex saw that they were dressed the same as the men that had taken him hostage and his captors waved to them.

Alex's heart sank. Another opportunity to get home gone.

Alex considered making another dash for the door while they were at least slightly distracted, but one of the men—older and with streaks of gray in his hair—laid an arm on Alex's shoulder, letting him know he was not forgotten.

For a moment, the dozen men simply watched the approaching figures, then the shouts of the four became clear, and the cries sounded a warning.

Behind them, a swirling flock of the nightmarish vulture-creatures were flying toward them.

The older man grasped Alex's arm firmly and led him away from the beach as fast as his hobbled legs would allow. Even so, they fell behind the other men, who sprinted ahead of them without looking back. They hurried over the dunes and Alex could see that beyond that, there was a stretch of flat land that led into a forested area.

The four figures caught Alex and his guide and passed them by. As they did, Alex noticed that they were all young, too, although each was at least as tall as he was. They were still chattering loudly, but to Alex's surprise, they were laughing as they ran.

"Benda de Tralen ha," the man said quietly to Alex, arching his eyebrows.

What does that mean? 'Kids these days?' Is that one of those universal things?

Alex glanced over his shoulder and saw the approaching cloud of creatures was gaining on them rapidly. He looked at the tree line ahead, then back at the creatures again.

It's going to be close.

He picked up his pace until he was going as fast as he could with his limited gait.

When they closed in on the trees, one of the creatures screamed a rattling, hollow screech. The older man pushed Alex ahead and turned to face the oncoming attack. The first creature dove at the man, who side-stepped neatly at the last moment while he drew a long cudgel attached to his belt. The beast missed the man but adjusted and flew straight at Alex.

The man swung the club smoothly, letting the weight of it do the work. It slammed into the crooked neck of the thing as it flew by him, and the beast crumpled to the ground.

Moments later, they made it through the tree line. The winged creatures circled and screamed. After a few moments, they turned and flapped lazily back toward the ocean.

"Karak-ta," the older man said, smiling, as though that explained everything.

Alex wasn't sure if "karak-ta" was the name of the creatures, or if it meant, "Damn, we nearly died right there."

Alex looked around at what he had at first thought to be a normal forest, and saw that every tree was dead. They stood tall as though they were all still vital, but there were no leaves or needles. There was live undergrowth of vines and brambles surrounding them, but the trees themselves were nothing more than giant toothpicks jammed into the ground.

Alex's captors moved deeper into the woods, then stopped in a small clearing. They broke into groups of two or three and spoke in their strange language. Strange to Alex at least, though he supposed English sounded equally odd to them. The men grinned, gestured, and seemed to be telling each other stories. Alex half-expected one of them to hold his hands wide apart, showing how big the one was that got away.

Alex recognized what he was seeing. It was the post-stress blow off after a successful operation. Death had been in the air, but it hadn't visited any of them, and now they all seemed to feel that sense of rebirth.

Alex wouldn't have been surprised if one of them had pulled the equivalent of a case of beer out of one of the bags and passed them around. They didn't, of course, but the four young men who had come screaming up the beach did kneel and open the bags they'd carried on their backs.

Carefully, they each reached inside and pulled out several large blue eggs. Each was speckled with yellow and gray dots, and the other men stood around admiring them.

Alex began to think he might be able to quietly sneak away and risk his life with the leather-winged beasts at the sea, when the older man who had guided him away once again laid his hand on his shoulder and shrugged.

The gesture was so human, so seemingly universal, that it almost made Alex laugh.

I guess that could mean, 'Sorry, dude, but you're still our prisoner,' or 'You will make a delicious stew for us tonight.' It could go either way.

After a few minutes of rest and celebration, the men shrugged their backpacks onto their shoulders. The man who had carried Alex's rifle took it off, walked to a nearby rock formation, lifted the rifle by the barrel and smashed it into the granite.

Alex winced.

Why?!?!?!

Chips of the rock flew everywhere, but the AR-10 held together.

"Stop!" Alex cried. He rushed toward the man, but strong hands again grabbed and held him.

The man who held the rifle did not look angry. He seemed bent on its destruction, but he was business-like about the process.

The man examined the rifle, saw that it was still straight and true, and lifted it far above his head, slamming it on the rock again and again and again. The handguard, the scope and the buttstock separated and flew in different directions. As soon as the parts hit the forest floor, the young men of the group scrambled, plucked them up, and stuck them in their bags like souvenirs.

Why? They already had it. Why destroy it? If those beast-birds are any indication, a rifle would come in very damn handy around here.

Finally, the man jammed the barrel between two rocks and torqued on it with all his strength.

Alex winced as he saw the barrel bend, then return mostly to true.

Finally, the man turned the damaged weapon over to another, younger man, who slung it over his shoulders.

The man with the scarred face, who Alex had begun to think of as the leader of the group, said, "Dalen ka trent. Mala ne daka."

The group fell into a marching formation, putting Alex in the middle, and set off at a very healthy pace.

Alex was in excellent condition—he'd never been in anything else since basic training—and he was thankful for that fact.

The men took long, steady strides and didn't stop for rest.

They soon left the dead-tree forest behind and emerged into a long flat stretch of land that served as a canyon floor, where tall hills covered with thick growth rose above them. The lower section was covered in trees that were as dead as the ones in the forest. Higher up were living trees that swayed slightly in the wind.

They walked through the canyon for hours, finally emerging onto a broad plain that went on far enough to disappear beyond the curvature of the earth.

To Alex's eye, the unending level plain looked unsafe. If there were creatures like the oversized vultures at the ocean, he believed there would be other, even more dangerous threats. On that open plain, there would be no place to hide.

The scarred man seemed to agree. He turned to his right and hiked up through the dead trees and the other men followed him. Halfway up the hill, he stopped and dropped his pack.

All around him, the other men sprang to what seemed to be pre-ordained duties. Some gathered rocks to build a small fire pit. Others went in search of firewood. A group of young men disappeared into the trees above them.

The older man who had apparently been assigned to ensure Alex didn't try to get away pointed to the ground next to a tree, then sat down himself. Alex was happy to do the same.

The old man's brown eyes bore into Alex's as though looking for answers. He put his hand over his throat and said, "Doken-ak."

Alex mimicked the gesture and said, "Alex." Then, he pointed to the man and repeated, "Doken-ak."

The man's eyes twinkled in the way someone might when a pet learns a new trick. He pointed to Alex and said, "Aleks," with an intonation that showed he wasn't completely sure he had gotten it right. The old man leaned back against the tree, seemingly satisfied that he had taught Alex—and himself—enough for one day.

Alex watched as a fire pit was built, with a fire immediately following. Wood from the dead trees was used as dry tinder, then other fuel was added until the flames leaped three feet high. Once that burned down, a pot was hung just above the hot coals and filled with water produced by another group who emerged from higher up the hill.

It was all organized and accomplished with a minimum of conversation.

The sun went down and temperatures dropped. The older man, who Alex now thought of as *Doken-ak* awoke from his brief nap and motioned for Alex to move closer to the fire. One of the young men presented Alex with his backpack—now empty. Another gave him a carved wooden bowl filled with a steaming helping of whatever had been cooked in the pot.

Alex sniffed it.

The young man mimed putting a bowl to his lips and drinking.

Alex did and although the flavor was strange to him, it wasn't bad. He took a second drink of the thick liquid, which seemed to have some sort of beans and green herb in it, then smiled at the boy who had brought it to him.

At least it's not the stew pot for me tonight. Maybe tomorrow, but not tonight.

A dozen of the men and boys stretched out on the ground to sleep while four others set up a perimeter watch.

I won't make the mistake of writing these people off as backward. They are organized and every man knows his job. If there's dissent in the ranks, I'm not seeing it.

Alex stood. Doken-ak groaned a little as he stood beside him. Alex gestured off toward the woods, putting one hand in front of his groin, hoping it was a universal sign for 'I have to pee.'

Doken-ak also pointed to the woods and they set off in that direction. They walked just a few paces beyond the glow of the fire and Doken-ak stopped Alex.

Alex thanked the gods he didn't have a nervous bladder, unzipped and let forth a stream of urine. Without a thought, he peed on the base of the closest tree.

Doken-ak said, "Ment!" but it was too late, the pee had already sent vibrations up the tree. Doken-ak grabbed his cudgel and looked up. A black form the size of a Chihuahua came scuttling down the tree at an alarming speed. When it was just a few feet away, Alex recognized it as a form of cockroach, blown up to many times the normal size.

The black roach sprang from the tree while it was still several feet above their heads, spreading dark wings and making a chittering sound that might have made Alex lose control of his bladder if he hadn't already been peeing.

As he had with the creature at the edge of the forest, Doken-ak timed his cudgel's swing perfectly, knocking the creature out of the air. The frightening thing was, as mighty as the blow was, it didn't disable the bug.

The thing continued to chitter as its antenna—as long as a man's hand—waved from the center of its compound eyes.

"Holy shit!" Alex cried as he jumped back, hoping to clear the jumping range of whatever the thing was.

Doken-ak calmly stepped forward and slammed his club into the body of the bug, spreading its insides over the forest floor. Then, he firmly took Alex's shoulders and turned him away from the base of the tree.

Alex found that he didn't need to pee anymore.

They walked back to the campfire and Alex noticed that the others were grinning but trying not to look at him.

That's fine. Come to my neck of the woods and I'll make fun of you. Of course, we don't have vulture-dinosaurs the size of a compact car or bugs that could be mistaken for a small dog.

He shuddered involuntarily.

Alex did his best to maintain his dignity and tried not to look to see if he had peed down his leg.

He found his spot by the campfire and laid his head down on his backpack.

He stared up at the night stars, which glowed brighter than he had ever seen in his life.

Home—and Amy—felt very far away.

Chapter Six
Dire Wolves

Alex had the habit of keeping his eyes closed when he first came awake. The first thing he noticed was there was no light hitting his eyelids, so he knew it was early. He heard soft rustling and movements, but nothing more.

He might have woken confused, hoping the day before was a dream—that he wasn't really trapped in a place so far from home, but he wasn't confused at all. He knew he was sleeping on the ground of a forest in a strange land. He knew he was a prisoner and that he was hobbled so he couldn't get away.

He also knew that the ropes that held him were not strong. They couldn't be expected to hold him for too long. Given just a few minutes of freedom, he could have found something to use as a tool to saw through them. So, they were either not traveling very far, or they would soon replace them with heavier rope or even chains.

When he finally opened his eyes, he saw that Doken-ak was sitting, leaned against a tree, watching him. Around the camp, men moved quietly, packing up, throwing dirt on the fire, preparing to leave. Four young men emerged from the trees above them, carrying the eggs they had stolen the day before. The eggs were in a net and water dripped off them.

They must have kept them in a stream somewhere nearby to keep them cooler. Whatever exercise these people are doing, they've done it before, many times. The question is, where do I fit in?

The stars were dimmer in the sky and the first pale light of day lit the east—the direction they had been walking the day before.

Alex had many questions, none of which could be answered at that moment. Or at all, at least until he learned to speak the language.

Doken-ak stood and stretched his arms above his head then touched his toes. He smiled at Alex as if to say, 'I am old, but not dead.' He gestured at Alex and led him away from the camp.

Alex followed, making sure he didn't bump into any of the trees. He didn't want to repeat his meeting with the giant cockroach again.

After just a few hundred yards, the melodic tinkling of a small creek reached his ears. A moment later they found it. It was a runoff stream that meandered down from the top of the hill. Doken-ak pointed at Alex, then at the water.

He happily dropped on his belly and put his head underwater.

"Whoo!" Alex said, popping up from the icy-cold water. "That's better than any shower first thing in the morning." He cupped his hands and drank deeply from the clear water.

Doken-ak did the same, then they walked a few yards away from the water, turned their backs to each other and peed.

This dude is probably thirty years older than me, but why do I have the feeling that if I ran for it, he could still catch me. Or whip that club off his belt and hit me behind the knees again. I hate that we are walking directly away from the ocean—and the door—but what can I do? Try to remember the landmarks as best I can, so when I find a way to break free, I can find my way back.

Doken-ak led Alex back to the campsite, which was already broken down. Men stood in casual groups talking quietly. Doken-ak grabbed his own bag and reached inside. He pulled a dark blob out of the pack, tore it down the middle and gave half to Alex.

He sniffed it and watched Doken-ak bite into his portion with his strong teeth. Alex did the same.

It was delicious.

Like pemmican. Lots of protein, easy to make, easy to carry.

Alex nodded his thanks at Doken-ak, who didn't acknowledge him.

The group formed into the marching formation they had used the day before and wound their way down the hill. At the bottom, they once again faced the broad, open plain.

The man with the scar and clouded eye pointed to various men and seemed to give them their assignments. Four of the men, who each carried a long, heavy spear, went to the four points of the group and moved twenty yards away. The others formed up in the same formation they had used the day before, walking along the valley floor.

Alex thought they had set a good pace the day before, but he saw that was slow compared to the way they took off today. All the men had longer legs than Alex and were able to keep it to a fast walk, but in order to keep up, Alex found he needed to lightly jog at least part of the time.

In just a few minutes, the valley and the hills that rose above it grew smaller, and the fast-moving group was in a sea of open space with nothing to protect them. They walked through long fields of golden hay that reached above their hips.

Well tall enough, Alex calculated, to hide any number of nefarious creatures. Alex kept his head on a swivel, looking forward, left, right, and skyward, but didn't see anything but more miles of waving grain on all sides of them.

By the time the sun loomed high in the sky, Alex estimated that they had traveled ten or twelve miles. The scarred man showed no inclination to stop or rest, though. Men pulled bags of water from their bags and drank as they walked. Alex did the same from his canteen he had filled that morning.

Alex had been trained to stay alert for extended times on marches, so he didn't lapse into daydreaming. Still, the suddenness of the change in his circumstance, combined with walking mile after mile over an unchanging terrain did relax his vigilance.

He was brought back to sharp focus by a piercing whistle ahead and to his right. He squinted through the bright sunlight and saw one of the men who was walking farthest away from the group sending hand signals back.

Alex stood on his tiptoes as he walked, straining to see if there was danger afoot.

Slowly, the man who had whistled angled his path so that he drew nearer to the main body of the group.

When he was only about ten yards away from the right-hand column of the group, Alex saw what had caused the excitement.

He couldn't get a perfect view of what was out in the grass, but he could see a slightly arched gray and silver back cutting through the golden grass like a shark's fin in water.

Wolf. That moves like a wolf.

Alex's mind did some unwanted math, wondering that if a cockroach was a foot and a half long, how big might a wolf be?

The creature stopped, and lifted a mighty head, sniffing the wind. It was a hundred yards away from the men and let out a series of short yowls, which, disconcertingly, were echoed back from half a dozen other locations around the men.

We're surrounded.

Alex surveyed the whole circumference around the group. The other scouts had moved closer to the group, closing ranks. Everyone was alert, but there was no panic in them. The other wolves which were hunting them were not visible, obviously hunched down in the tall grass until they were ready to reveal themselves.

The men moved on at the same steady double time pace.

Doken-ak gestured for Alex to look in front of them. A few hundred yards ahead was a tree line—tall pines and firs, dotted with larger oak trees.

Don't know what good that does us. Wolves won't be turned away from the trees like the vultures were. They can just separate us and tear us to shreds. If I had my rifle, we would at least have a chance.

Without stopping, Doken-ak fell in behind Alex, pulled his knife and cut the rope attached to his ankles.

At least I'll be able to sprint before one of those damned things makes lunch out of me.

The men who carried the long, thick spears moved to the outside of the group and raised their spears into an easy throwing position.

The wolf who had shown itself lifted its nose to the sky and howled, which sent a primal shiver up and down Alex's spine. As one, the other wolves stood at their full height, revealing themselves. They didn't sprint toward the group at once, but instead, slowly closed ranks on them.

With a clear view, Alex realized that although these animals were larger than any wolf he had ever seen, they weren't as supersized as the vultures and cockroach. The leader of the pack turned its mighty head toward them, and Alex realized there was an unsettling intelligence in its eyes.

THE SCARRED MAN, WHO had moved to the front of the men, whistled twice—two short, sharp retorts. The men picked up their pace. Not yet a run for them, but a fast jog. For Alex, he was glad he was untethered and could stretch out his legs to keep up.

Beside him, Doken-ak loped easily along until his foot stepped in a small hole and he tumbled forward.

The men in front of him moved on, unaware that one of them had fallen.

Alex and the others who were trailing behind stopped and hurried to Doken-ak.

As a group, they might have a chance to survive, but one man alone would be lost.

Doken-ak picked himself up and motioned the others to go on. He took two steps and stumbled, nearly falling again. Alex scanned the surrounding grass. No wolves to be seen anywhere, which was worse than seeing them approach.

Two of the young and strong men put Doken-ak's arms around their shoulders and they ran for the trees.

Alex saw that the cudgel that Doken-ak had used so effectively the day before had dropped, jarred loose when he had fallen. Alex retrieved it and took up a position at the back of the now-smaller pack of men.

The leading group noticed that some of them had fallen behind and slowed.

Now all the group was at risk.

Slowly, the two groups merged together. Two of the spear-carriers joined Alex at the back of the pack just as one of the wolves showed itself.

One man cast his spear at that wolf, but it buried itself in the dirt in front of it.

From the left, another wolf leaped at them, fangs bared and a guttural growl coming from its throat.

There was no time to throw the second spear, but the man did manage to raise it up and deflect the jumping attack, ripping fur and flesh from its throat.

At the same moment, the first wolf charged the man who had thrown the spear. The wolf attacked headfirst, slamming its head into the man's groin, tumbling him to the ground. Its sharp claws tore at his legs while its fangs sought his throat for a killing blow.

Alex ran forward, silent except for the pad of his boots against the grass. Before he reached the wolf, he raised the heavy club above his head. His momentum carried him into the animal, but not before he slammed the cudgel down on its hindquarters.

The sound of splintering bones mixed with the cries of the man trying to scramble away from the teeth of the wolf.

Alex tumbled over both of them, rolled on his back and jumped to his feet, ready to attack again.

There was no need. The rest of the men had fallen on the wolf with knives, clubs, and spears. Its heart was still beating, and blood spurted from its wounds, but it was mortally wounded.

Many hands reached for the wounded man and as a group, they turned and ran for the trees.

Losing one of their number slowed the wolves and added caution to their attack, but they did not retreat completely. As the men ran, long silver-gray backs broke the surface of the group alongside them.

When they were fifty yards from the trees, the scarred man yelled, "Monto!"

As if by magic, arrows flew through the air from high up in the trees. One hit a wolf in its front shoulder, and it disappeared beneath the tops of the grass. Other arrows zipped over the heads of the oncoming men and pierced the earth in front of the running wolves.

Whoever was firing from the trees could see the wolves clearly in the grass and had the best angle possible to fire on them.

The largest of the wolves stopped and howled in frustration.

The group of men made it to the trees, half carrying Doken-ak and the other wounded man.

Alex saw crude ladders attached to the tall trees and small platforms high up.

I guess if the wolves attack in the open plain, they stand and fight. But if they're close enough, they run for the tree stands, knowing they have archers here who can take out whatever predator is after them.

Four men came swinging and jumping down from the trees. They didn't seem to notice Alex but conferred with the scarred man while the man who had dressed Alex's wounds the day before examined the man who had been mauled by the wolf.

Alex approached Doken-ak and knelt to look at his ankle. He had obviously twisted it when he had fallen, and it was swollen. But there was no blood and it appeared that he could put some weight on it, albeit with a substantial limp.

The scarred man said, "Mena tu, kan," and everyone once again fell into formation, with two of the archers partially holding up the injured man.

There was a path that wound through the trees that was wide enough for four men to walk on side-by-side. It curved this way and that through the forest for several miles before it opened out onto another smaller flat area.

This plain was surrounded by rock walls that rose several hundred feet in the air.

More paths led up the lower reaches of the walls. Halfway up, the paths ended and long ladders were extended from one ledge to another. Three-quarters of the way up the wall, deep ledges were indented, forming long overhangs and caves.

There were men, women, and children in the space of the overhangs, as well as scattered around the open area. On the far right, a small waterfall flowed into a pool in the rock below.

The traveling group emerged into the clearing, and a horn sounded from above. Women ran to them and relieved the young men of the bags that held the eggs. More men hurried to help Doken-ak and the injured man.

Alex felt almost forgotten, but escape didn't seem likely.

How can I make it across that open plain alone? Maybe if I had my rifle and pistol, I could make it, but alone, there's no chance.

A strange looking man broke from the others and approached Alex. He was strange looking, but only compared to everyone else here. He was the first man Alex had seen since he'd come through the door who was shorter than he was.

He was older, too, with crazy white hair sticking out at all angles and a long white beard. Alex hadn't thought of it before, but none of the other men had any hair on their faces.

The white-haired man gawked at Alex like he was a museum piece, even reaching out to touch his chin and turn his face from side to side. He looked deeply into Alex's blue eyes, then stood straight and raised his right hand in a dramatic greeting.

Alex expected a barrage of the language he did not recognize.

Instead, the man grinned and said, "What's up, man?"

Chapter Seven
Winten-ah

Alex blinked. Stared. Blinked again. His brain appeared to be stuck in neutral.

"I have seen some passing strange things in the last twenty-four hours. An entire world where the corner of my basement should be. Giant cockroaches that fall from trees if you piss on them. Death from above in the form of dinosaur vultures."

The bearded man just listened, nodding. A slight smile played on his face.

"But seeing you here, and hearing English again, when I thought I might never hear it again? Well, I think my mind is blown."

The smile slowly disappeared from the man's face.

"Wait," he said. "Did you say, 'an entire world where the corner of your basement should be?' Is that what I heard?"

Alex nodded, still marveling at someone speaking his own language in this strange new world.

The bearded man looked at the ground, lost in thought, then said, "Shit."

"What?" Alex asked.

"That means you got here through the same door I did. And that probably means my dad is dead."

"Is Benjamin Hadaller your father?"

The man's eyes lit up. "Yes! Yes! Do you know my father? Is he still alive?"

"I never met your father. I just bought the house from him. He was still alive the last time I heard."

"Whoa," the man said in a decent imitation of Keanu Reeves. After a long moment of silence, he stuck his hand out and said, "Dan. Dan Hadaller."

Alex shook his hand as if in a dream, and said, "Alex Hawk."

"They call me 'Vanda-ak,' here, though."

"You speak their language, then?"

"I have to, or I never would have survived. There are dozens of languages here. Each group of people has their own language and there's one simpler universal language that everyone can speak. It's like the Tower of Babel around here!"

"Can you help me learn?"

"That will be my job from day one. Ganku-eh doesn't like the idea of having someone around that can't communicate. She will have questions for you and some of them, she will want to be able to ask directly."

"Ganku-eh?"

"She runs things around here. Chief of all this," Dan said, circling his arm to include the rock wall and open area. "No need for women's lib around here. Our last three chiefs have all been female."

"Is she the one I can talk to about getting home?"

Dan looked at the ground. "Yes, sure, but I wouldn't get my hopes up. They're not going to want to let you go. They'll think you might be the answer to an old prophecy. They thought the same about me, until I disappointed them." He looked skyward, as though settling something in his mind. "I'll bet dad wouldn't have wanted to sell the house too quickly after I disappeared. He'd have wanted to wait to see if I came back like I promised. What year was it when you stepped through the door?"

"2019."

Dan took a step back and whistled. "Holeee shit. Forty years. I have been here forty years. I thought so, but I was hoping I was wrong. What's it like there? The war in Vietnam was over when I stepped through. Hopefully, we've been at peace since then." He smiled and flashed a hopeful peace sign.

Alex laughed bitterly. "We've been at war as long as I can remember. Iraq, Kuwait, Somalia, Bosnia, Afghanistan..."

Dan shook his head. "I thought we might have learned something by getting our butts kicked in Southeast Asia."

Alex shrugged. "I spent years deployed in the Middle East. Same shit, different war. Technology is different, but for the boots on the ground, it's mostly the same. Did you fight in Vietnam?"

Dan nodded. "I had no choice. My grades weren't good enough to get me into college, and my dad wasn't rich enough to buy my way out. He and I talked about Canada, but we couldn't see doing that. So, I went. I was lucky. I came home with all my fingers and toes." He tapped his head, "Maybe not so much up here, though. That's probably why I stepped through that door when I found it. It felt like everything back home had gone to shit, and I just wanted to get away."

"I'm sorry you've spent so long here, but I've got to get home. I've got a four-year-old daughter waiting for me. Yesterday was her birthday. I can't have her thinking that I abandoned her. I've got to get back."

Dan's expression was sorrowful, but he didn't say anything more. He wasn't one to stomp on a man's dreams.

Alex had a hundred other questions lined up for Dan, but he was cut off by a young woman who sprinted up to them. She rattled off a long spew of words, all the while pointing at Alex.

Dan listened, a smile slowly spreading across his face again. While the woman was still speaking, he turned to Alex and said,

"Looks like you made a good first impression. Did you rescue some-one from one of the wolves?"

"No, I don't think so."

The woman continued excitedly, still pointing at Alex.

"She sure thinks you did. Says a wolf was attacking her husband and you rushed it with just a club and got it off him."

"Oh, no, I think she's confused. A wolf attacked us, but it was everybody who saved him. I just hit him with a club. Other men rushed it and killed it."

"Uh-huh," Dan said. He turned to the woman, who was at least six inches taller than him, and answered her in the same language.

Tears filled her eyes and she stepped toward Alex and wrapped him in an embrace, holding him tightly against her. Alex's head fit neatly in the crook of her neck. He hadn't felt so small since he was a child and his mother held him.

"Tekan din, mata dak," the woman said.

"She says, 'Thank you, stranger.' You're never going to convince her you're not a hero, so you might as well go with it."

"Can you tell her, 'it was nothing' and ask her how he is?"

Dan conferred with her for several long moments, then said, "He is okay. He'll live, but he might have a limp. She says that if you hadn't attacked the wolf when you did, his wounds would have been much worse, and he probably would have lost too much blood to make it home. She would have been a widow by nightfall."

The woman, so tall and lovely, stepped away from Alex, held her hand against her throat and said, "Malen-eh."

Alex did the same, and said, "Alex."

The woman turned to Dan again and spoke for some time.

"She says your name is too funny. 'Aleks' are what they call the mules they use to carry things from place to place. She doesn't think it is dignified enough for you. She says she will bring it up at the council and they will pick a new name."

Malen-eh turned and hurried away.

Alex leaned close to Dan. "I'd really rather not be around long enough to need a new name. What are the chances I can escape and make my way back to the door?"

Dan shrugged and said, "You're not likely to escape from here in the first place. They have guards posted every few yards, day and night. If you do manage to get by them, how would you pass the great plain to the shore? You saw the wolves and the way they attacked a caravan of men. What would they do to you? And, you were lucky. You didn't cross paths with godat-ta, the king of the beasts around here. You and I might call him a grizzly, but that's like comparing a rowboat to the Titanic. Same idea, different scale. The problem with godat-ta is that once he's on your trail, there's no way to escape him. He's twice as fast as you are, he can climb better than you, and he's like a seal in the water. Whatever he wants to kill, he kills."

Alex stuck his chin out. "Thanks for telling me. I can't give up, though. I can't be stuck here for forty years while my little girl grows up and forgets about me."

Alex glanced at Dan and saw that his unintentional barb had hit home. "Sorry. I don't know what your deal is, Dan. I don't know if you ever wanted to get away from here or not."

Dan looked over Alex's shoulder into the distance and said, "I did. I tried so often they stopped having the guards tackle me. They just let me go, figuring that Kragdon-ah would teach me my lesson."

"Who's Kragdon-ah?"

"Not who—what. Kragdon-ah is what all the people call this world. They were right. They let me go and I nearly died trying to get back to the door to let dad know I was all right. I was lucky—it was Ronit-ta, the wolves, who came after me. I escaped them by climbing and stayed in the tree for two nights, waiting for them to leave. Finally, they came and rescued me. That was more than forty years ago now and I haven't tried since."

Alex thought of spending two nights treed by those massive wolves and understood.

Dan and Alex had been standing on the edge of the clearing, lost in conversation, but they were again interrupted by the man who had first inspected Alex's wounds after he had been injured by the vulture birds.

Without preamble, he lifted Alex's shirt and unwound the bandages, dropping them on the ground.

"Holy cow, man. What got a hold of you?" Dan asked.

"One of those big freaking ugly birds that look like a vulture crossed with a pterodactyl. Did you see them when you came through?"

"Yeah, sure did. I was luckier than you, though, and stayed one step ahead. I had a rifle, too."

"So did I," Alex said, trying not to wince as the medic poked and prodded at his wounds. "I took down a dozen of them, but one of them got to me first. That's how I met these guys."

"Right, of course. They were after karak-ta eggs, and they heard your gunshots. I'm glad you didn't try to get in a battle with these guys. They might have just subdued you, but they might have been forced to kill you. By the way, did they get some of the eggs?"

"Sure looked like it."

"Cool. We'll have a feast tonight. You'll want to try some. If they got enough, we'll be able to restock the things we need. Karak-ta eggs are sought after, but we're the only ones that can get them consistently. A word of warning, though—when they pass you the egg, don't eat too much. You need to build up a little resistance to it."

That made no sense to Alex—*build up resistance to an egg?*—but he had so many other questions that he put that one on the back burner.

"Listen, Dan, I was wondering—"

Dan held his hand up to cut off Alex as two men came hurrying up. Dan listened for a minute, then said, "Sorry. I know you've got a million questions. I'll do my best to answer them all, but I've got to go with these guys." Dan turned and hustled away toward the tall rock face.

Alex watched as he scrambled up the inclines, then a ladder, then disappeared into one of the caves.

Pretty spry for an old guy.

As he watched, an old woman with a bent back and long gray hair twisted into a braid did the same.

Guess they're all pretty spry. Maybe it's from eating karak-ta eggs.

Alex looked around. No one seemed to be watching him or paying him any attention at all.

No way I can make a run for it, not yet. Maybe I can get my rifle back and see if it's still operational. If not that, at least my pistol. I need firepower to get across that plain.

He thought of a book by Jules Verne that he had read as a teenager—*The Mysterious Island.*

Maybe I can build a hot air balloon and float across, then land right by the door. He rolled that around in his mind a bit. *Of course, I have no idea how to build a hot air balloon, and I don't think anyone else here is going to help me.*

Alex gave himself a guided tour of his new and, he hoped, temporary, home. He walked to the waterfall and looked at the pool beneath it. Several young girls were there, filling bags with water. As he watched, they slung them over their shoulders, whispered to each other, giggled, then walked up the trail and ladder to the cave.

No wonder they've made this their home. It's perfect. Protected on three sides and all your basic needs taken care of without needing to leave the area. If anyone tried to attack them, they'd hold the high ground. Even if an attacker brought their own ladders, there's nothing worse than trying to climb and fight uphill while an enemy rains pain on you from above.

Alex looked at the top of the granite walls. There were small platforms built into the top every forty feet and a guard sat, looking down the flank of their home.

No one is going to sneak up on these guys.

A BOY ALEX RECOGNIZED approached him. He was caught in that vast wasteland between boyhood and adulthood—large in body but obviously still seeking maturity. He had a serious expression on his face, as though carrying out a responsibility he wasn't sure he was up to.

"Nanta bu tenta," he said, as though Alex would understand. When it was obvious that Alex did not, in fact, understand, the boy pointed up the face of the cliff.

"Ganku-eh kala nin."

Alex had no idea what 'Kala nin' meant, but he did recognize 'Ganku-eh' as the name of the chieftain. He could guess the rest.

"Lead on then, soldier."

The boy seemed to grasp the meaning by context, turned and headed toward the main path that led up the granite face.

Alex followed him. There were switchbacks every twenty paces and that got them halfway up the vertical wall. When they came to a ladder, the boy scrambled up it as though born to it, which he probably had been.

Alex examined the ladder, touching it, lifting it a bit to test its heft. It was surprisingly light but had no give and was obviously constructed by a craftsman. Alex followed the boy up the ladder, then two more switchbacks and onto a path that went all the way from one side of the wall to another.

Finally, the boy pointed to another ladder.

"As far as you go, huh? Got it. Dismissed."

Alex scrambled up the ladder and was surprised to see a space that had been carved out well back into the rock, forming a semi-private cave with an overhang.

Half a dozen people sat around a fire, waiting for him.

Chapter Eight
Alex's Decision

At the mouth of the opening, Dan Hadaller waited for Alex. "I'll introduce you to everyone, but the most important person is Ganku-eh. She makes the final decisions."

"Final decisions about what? Like whether she'll help me get back to the door?"

"I wouldn't ask about that right now."

"Okay, that's fine, but what other final decisions will she be making?"

A troubled look flashed on Dan's face, soon replaced by his normal *hang loose* expression.

"I should have told you when I first met you, but there's a chance they'll put you out."

"Out?" Alex asked, shocked. He pointed to the great open plain that could be seen from this vantage point. "Out there?"

Dan nodded.

"That would be a death sentence. I mean, I would make a run for the door, but I don't think there's any chance I would make it."

Dan glanced over his shoulder at the figures around the fire. Ganku-eh shifted impatiently.

"Don't worry about it. Just tell them the truth and you'll be fine. Oh, one other thing. I'll be translating for you, but I've been teaching Ganku-eh English, so don't assume she won't understand you."

"Great," Alex said, dazed. "I don't even know why I'm here, but I might be sentenced to death in a court martial where I don't know the rules and have no representation."

"You worry too much, man. Just go with the flow and you'll be fine. When I got here, I went through the same thing and I didn't have anyone to translate for me..."

Dan put a hand on Alex's shoulder and led him toward the fire.

There were six low-slung wooden chairs arranged in a semi-circle on the far side of the fire. Alex looked up and saw that the smoke was drawn up to a hole in the ceiling above.

They may not like technology, but they are not stupid.

Dan started by introducing Alex to the people in front of him.

He started by pointing to a man in the middle with a scarred face and a milk-white left eye.

"Banda-ak, who you've already met. He is the mate of Ganku-eh."

Banda-ak did not acknowledge Alex, but sat upright, patiently waiting. He had a regal air about him. He may not have been chief, but he knew his place in the hierarchy.

Dan pointed far to the left and for the first time, Alex noticed a very young girl.

She can't be more than a few years older than Amy. What's she do-ing sitting in on something like this?

"This is Lanta-eh, which means *chosen.*"

Alex had no idea why such a young girl was called 'chosen', but calculated that this was not the proper time for him to be asking questions.

In turn, Dan introduced Malen-eh, the wife of the man who had been injured by the wolf, Doken-ak, who had already befriended Alex on the trip from the shore, and Sekun-ak, a powerful-looking man who did not look happy to see Alex.

Finally, he pointed to the tallest woman Alex had ever seen, and said, "This is our leader, Ganku-eh."

Ganku-eh nodded at Alex, a gesture he hadn't seen used by anyone but Dan since he arrived. "Welcome, Alex," she said with evident pride in being able to speak Alex and Dan's language.

She turned to Dan and spoke for a long moment in her native tongue.

Dan turned to Alex and said, "Ganku-eh says we will continue in their own tongue, so that the others can fully understand."

Again, Ganku-eh spoke.

Dan turned to Alex and said, "She would like to know what you are doing here, invading their land."

"That makes two of us," Alex muttered.

A sharp look from Ganku-eh silenced him.

Alex saw her expression and said, "Sorry. I don't know. I didn't intend to come here. I jumped when I should have thought, and ended up here. I didn't know this was my destination. One moment I was inside my own house, the next I was here."

Dan nodded, then relayed Alex's answer, occasionally pointing to himself.

Sekun-ak, the warrior with the angry expression, spoke up, his voice harsh and tinged with anger.

Dan again translated. "Sekun-ak wants to know if you agree to destroy all technology you brought with you and pledge to never create any more?" Under his breath, so quietly that only Alex could hear it, Dan whispered, "You need to agree."

Alex was caught completely off guard. *Why would they want me to destroy everything I brought? It could help them. And I could help them more by showing them how to build things themselves.*

He looked at Dan, whose eyebrows were raised, as if to say, *this is not the time to hesitate.*

Alex drew a deep breath. He saw two paths before him. Agree, or fail to make the pledge and very likely be put out on his own, knowing he would not be able to survive.

He looked at each of their faces. Lanta-eh, the young girl, who could have been expected to have no interest in a proceeding like this, sat placidly, staring at him with unblinking dark brown eyes. Alex had to admit that she didn't carry herself like a normal child.

Doken-ak and Malen-eh, leaned forward slightly as if willing Alex to do the right thing.

Sekun-ak's face clouded over and grew darker with every second that passed.

"I swear it," Alex said.

Dan let a small whoosh of breath out, as if he hadn't been aware he had been holding it. He translated Alex's words, though it was obvious what he had said.

Ganku-eh spoke and Dan translated as, "That's it then. She says you cannot be a member of the tribe, but you can find safety here and you will be expected to work as everyone does."

Ganku-eh leaned forward and spoke quietly with Doken-ak and Malen-eh. Malen-eh answered her and Ganku-eh turned and spoke to Dan Hadaller.

Dan listened, then said, "Your new name here will be Manta-ak, which means fighter. You should be honored. Vanda-ak, my name here, means runner, because I ran from them when I first came through the door, and they had to tackle me."

"If I hadn't already been on the run from the birds—wait, the *Karak-ta*—I'm sure I would have run from them, too. Not that I *could* outrun them. They're all a foot taller than me and run like Olympic athletes."

"The hard part of the day is done, now. The sun is setting, and it is time for our feast. You can sit next to me, and I will do my best to answer all your questions."

Dan turned and hurried along a series of ladders, pathways and switchbacks as confidently as Alex walked through his own house.

Eventually, they emerged into the largest room Alex had seen yet. It was like a massively expanded version of the room he had just come from. There wasn't just a single fire burning here, but eight—all feeding their smoke into a central chimney system above. Along the edges of the room—the side that faced the open space—there were a dozen torches, casting an inviting glow.

A sudden realization hit Alex. "It's a world lit only by fire," he said.

"That it is. You get used to it—the smoke, the shadows. It's been so long, if I saw an electric light, it would look almost as strange to me as it would to them."

"But, is it like this everywhere in this world?"

"I can't answer that for sure because I haven't been everywhere, but as far as I know, yes. Travel is difficult because death tends to wait around every bend in the trail, but I've seen a lot. There was a time when a faraway tribe began to create new technologies. It wasn't much, but all the other tribes asked them to stop. When they wouldn't, we sent people from all over to stop it for them. We destroyed their village, and their people were dispersed to other tribes. That is *kunta*, the death of a tribe."

"You say, 'A faraway tribe.' How far is faraway?"

"I don't know. We were recruited and I was volunteered to go. We walked for months to get there, although we joined up with other groups like ourselves. How far is it from what you know as central Oregon to South Dakota?"

Alex's jaw dropped.

"You walked that far?"

"Walked is a kind word for it. Forced march is closer. But I got to see something that told me when I had stepped out of the door, at least in a way."

"I've thought about that constantly. Are we in the past? Is this just some time so distant that all records of it have been lost?"

"Definitely not. We are in the future. Way, way, *way* in the future."

The two of them walked into the open cave, chose one of the fires, and sat in two of the low-slung chairs. Alex admired the handcraft that had created them. They were made from a polished white wood with some sort of canvas for the seat and backrest. They were surprisingly comfortable.

The rest of the cave was slowly filling up with more people, all of whom looked curiously at Alex. It was obvious that a new arrival wasn't an everyday occurrence.

"How do you know? If we're that far in the future, are there any remnants of our world left?"

"Not really. But there is one exception, and I saw it."

"Don't tell me you rode to New York on a horse and saw the Statue of Liberty buried in the sand."

Dan laughed. "Ha! No, nothing quite that dramatic. I have a feeling if I got there, that statue would be long lost to the world."

"What did you see, then."

"I saw *mendada*, which means *faces*. That's what they call it, anyway. It's a holy spot to them. You and I would call it Mt. Rushmore. The faces are worn away, but they're still recognizable. They've survived the centuries."

Alex sat quietly, chewing on that.

"It's going to take a while for me to wrap my brain around that. Let's change questions. *Where* are we?"

"I'd say we're about fifteen miles away from where you popped your head out of the door."

"Sure, but where is *that*?"

"Your position on the planet didn't change—just the time."

"No, sorry, that can't be. That's impossible."

"You use that word pretty confidently for a man who just stepped through a door in one world and into another. Do you mean we can't be in the same place because of the ocean?"

"Of course, because of the ocean. When I stepped through that door, the ocean was maybe fifty yards away. But we live in central Oregon. The ocean is at least a hundred and fifty miles away."

"Or at least it was, the last time you went to sleep in your house."

Alex opened his mouth to argue, but Dan held a hand up. "I thought the same thing when I first got here. 'If the ocean is here, that door took me to some*place* else. Not just another time, but another place, right?"

Alex nodded his assent.

"Do you remember Saddleback Mountain?"

A nostalgic look spread across Alex's face. "Of course. I went horseback camping with my dad there twenty years ago."

"Good. It's an easy landmark to remember. Sometime soon, I can show you exactly where Saddleback Mountain is. It's right where it's supposed to be, even though the ocean is not."

"Are you really saying that the Pacific Ocean is in the middle of Oregon? What about Washington? California?"

"The big cities of the West Coast—Seattle, Portland, San Francisco, Los Angeles—are all gone." Dan paused, decided that wasn't dramatic enough, then added, "Not just gone. They might as well have never been there. There's nothing but churning green ocean where they once stood. But that's not all. I said I've traveled a lot, and I have. All signs that our civilization ever existed are gone. The geography is essentially the same, just changed by many centuries passing."

Alex stared into the fire, drawing obvious conclusions.

"So, we destroyed everything, then?"

Dan shrugged. "I don't know if it was us, or the San Andreas just let go one day, or what, but it's all gone. It's so far back in history from where we are now that there isn't any record of it."

"So, we're here in this completely changed world and we have no idea how we got here?"

"That's about the size of it. I think we walked through the door so far into the future that no one here has any memory that our civilization ever existed."

"But, even if we stepped out of the door fifty, sixty, a hundred thousand years later, does that explain how the animals evolved? Cockroaches as long as my arm, vultures that look more like dinosaurs than birds, a grizzly bear that might stand twenty feet tall. How did that happen?"

"No idea. Nuclear war? Radiation? A plague that wiped out ninety-nine percent of humanity? Some sort of hybrid experiment that went wrong? I've thought about it for forty years and I still have no idea. These people know nothing about us or our time. There aren't even many legends. The most ancient memory they have is called "The Leaving." It's a story about how people climbed on a giant bird and left for the stars."

Alex whistled. "Maybe things got so bad, people left, looking for a better place."

Dan nodded. "That's what I think. The people who could, left, and these are the people who were left behind."

"Does that explain why they hate tech so much? They destroyed my rifle as soon as they could, even though it would have helped a lot when those wolves attacked us."

"Absolutely. No doubt. They would rather die than use something like your rifle to save them. They're going to ask you to finish destroying anything technological that you brought with you."

"And they made me promise not to build anything else. What if I had fallen in with a different group of people? Would it have been different?"

"No. It's consistent. Every group I've ever met hates anything that resembles technology. If a tribe ever tries to go against that, all the other tribes band together to destroy them, like I said before."

"I guess somewhere along the line, everyone who was left behind decided that everything bad that had happened had come from technology."

"Wouldn't you, if you felt something was responsible for the destruction of your world?"

Alex looked around and saw that the room had filled up with people. He tried to get a count, but everyone was moving about, talking, and he couldn't manage it. He gave up and asked.

"How many people are there in this tribe?"

"A little over two hundred. The population hasn't changed much since I got here. Most of the Winten-ah will be right here for the feast, except for the guards out in the woods and up top."

"I saw the guard stations above. How often does this place get attacked?"

"It doesn't, at least not very often. Would you want to put an attack plan together against this place?"

Alex thought about it. Alert guards in protected blinds in the trees. The open space in front of the granite walls. The challenge of having to be constantly attacking uphill against a well-fortified position. More guards at the top to alert and protect the community from a flanked attack.

"It would take an overwhelming force to do any real damage, I think. A lot of grunts would have to be willing to die just to get close to a real attack."

"Exactly. And that's why we haven't been attacked in a very long time. There are no overwhelming forces here."

"Why not? Couldn't a tribe just grow and grow until they were big enough to absorb the losses necessary to attack a place like this?"

"You're still thinking with a technological mind. These tribes never get big populations. Something that resembles a city requires people that don't do anything useful to a tribe's survival. Planners. People to pass new laws. People to enforce those laws. Lawyers to twist the laws into things they were never meant to be."

"And so," Alex took over, "you've soon got people doing the real work of survival—hunting, fishing, farming—just to support that infrastructure of non-productive people."

Dan nodded. "On the nose. That keeps populations low. I don't know of any tribes with more than five hundred people in them. This tribe is called Winten-ah, which translated, just means 'The People.' All the tribes tend to have names that translate the same way. Each one believes they are the true people of the earth."

"Pretty much just like it was in the twentieth century."

"Some things never change," Alex agreed.

Alex saw that Ganku-eh and Banta-ak had entered with the young girl, Lanta-eh.

"What's the deal with this young girl? She's just a kid, but she walks like a queen."

"The Winten-ah believe she is the fulfillment of an ancient prophecy. For as many years as anyone can remember, the tribe has waited for a baby girl to be born on the summer solstice with a birthmark of a moon." Dan nodded at Lanta-eh. "Then she came along. Born on the solstice, with a moon-shaped birthmark on her shoulder."

"What's the rest of the prophecy?"

"Like most ancient prophecies, that's where things get a little fuzzy. She is supposed to be the person who leads the tribe in a time of great need. *She will have the wisdom of the ages*, and all that stuff."

"A lot to put on a little kid's shoulders."

"Yeah, but she seems to have taken to it. Look at her."

Lanta-ah moved through the room, touching people lightly, smiling at them, and offering her blessing.

"I don't know," Alex said. "Being a messiah seems like an awful gig."

A voice, throaty and deep, echoed a chant through the room. Another voice, this one high and crystal-clear, cut through the babble of conversation around them.

Dan leaned over to Alex, lowered his voice, and said, "The show's about to begin."

Chapter Nine
The World Spins

A dozen children—taller than any children Alex had ever seen, but children nonetheless—paraded onto a slightly raised stone platform at the back of the room. Torches burned behind them so that as they began to dance, undulating shadows rose and fell around the room.

Alex peered through the semi-darkness, and saw that the two voices came from Banda-ak and Ganku-eh. The children danced in an odd, herky-jerky motion, lifting their left foot and slamming it down, then doing the same with their right. They established a rhythm and soon the others in the room—including Dan—began to chant.

Alex felt like he'd wandered into a play where everyone else knew their roles and he was clueless. Although he could not understand a single word being chanted or sung, the voices touched him somewhere deep inside. The ritual brought everyone together into a single stomping, chanting entity.

As the song reached a crescendo, more tribe members came out, managing to walk gracefully in the same rhythm while carrying carved-out logs heaped with food. A young girl appeared over Alex's shoulder and dropped a large, smooth wooden plate in front of him. Immediately behind her, a man dropped food on it. There was some sort of roasted meat, a vegetable that Alex had never seen, and something that looked like a salad.

Alex looked around for silverware but saw that Dan and everyone else were already eating, albeit with their fingers.

When in Rome, I guess.

Alex lifted the meat to his mouth, wondering what he was about to eat. He needn't have worried. Whatever it was, it tasted like a savory pot roast flavored with a sauce that was different from anything Alex had ever experienced—sweet, yet tangy.

Dan noticed his expression and smiled. "Don't get the idea that we eat like this every night. This is a feast because the expedition to the shore was a success. Tomorrow we go back to normal."

Alex wanted to ask what normal looked like, but the singing and chanting swelled so he knew his question wouldn't be heard.

In perfect synchronization, the dancing children made one last leap and stomp, and both the singers and chanters stopped. For a moment, silence ruled, broken only by the sound of faraway frogs and crickets. Then everyone in the room slapped the table in front of them and hooted and cheered.

"Finish that," Dan said to Alex, pointing at his plate, "the highlight of the evening is coming next."

Alex hurriedly ate the vegetable, which reminded him of a potato, but with more richness of flavor, and his salad, which was tossed with an earthy seasoning that he hoped he would get to taste again.

A tall man—tall even, relative to these other giants, entered the room holding one of the karak-ta eggs like a holy offering. The top of the egg had been cut off smoothly and steam issued from inside. The man walked directly to Ganku-eh and offered the egg. She waved the steam into her face, then reached in and removed a small piece of something.

The tall man moved to Banda-ak, who repeated the small ritual. The tall man moved around the room, offering the egg to each person in turn, who waved the steam like an oenophile at a wine tasting, then reached inside and took a small bite.

Each person placed the food inside their mouth, but didn't chew, instead letting it melt as much as it would, then sliding it whole down their throat, a joyous expression on their face.

Alex cast a glance at Dan.

Dan leaned closer and said, "Just do what I do, but don't take a very big bite. You don't want to pass, because that will bring suspicion on you. Just take a small morsel and they will be happy."

Eventually, the tall, graceful man arrived at their fire and offered the egg to Dan, who waved the vapor toward him, then reached inside and removed a piece the size of a quarter. He put it on his tongue and a blissful expression overtook him.

Calmly, the tall man turned to Alex who did a fair mimicry of the ceremony. The rising steam had a strong odor, but it was nothing he could identify. He reached into the egg and pulled lose a piece the size of a dime. All the other people at their fire kept their eye on Alex until he put the piece on his tongue.

The flavor of the egg was buttery and filled with herbs, but there was a definite egg-like taste to it as well. Eventually, Alex swallowed and felt nothing.

Dan was too cautious. I should have taken more.

And then, the world began to spin. Alex tilted and fell out of the low chair. The ground seemed the safest place to be. The spinning, swirling world went on as though he was laying on a piece of playground equipment. He lifted his head a bit so he could see outside the room. The stars were closer than he had ever seen them. He opened his eyes wide and the stars themselves began to twirl and dance.

No one paid him any attention. Everyone was in their own world.

Conscious thought stopped for Alex and he stopped trying to control the flow of his brain. He let go of the banks of consciousness and slipped into a stream he had not known existed. Time was meaningless. Only a moment passed, but at the same time the seasons changed, and the earth rotated. He could not have told which of those conflicting ideas were the truest.

Some unknown time later, he opened his eyes, but the world still didn't make any sense. The logic of life still escaped him. He blissfully shut his eyes and let eons pass.

When Alex opened his eyes a second time, it was daylight, and both Dan and Malen-eh were hovering around him. He made an effort to sit up, but hands held him down. Malen-eh wiped his face with a cool cloth.

Dan smiled and said, "I told you to not take too much your first time."

"I didn't. Or at least, I didn't think I did."

"It's okay. It won't hurt you, no matter what. Until you build up a resistance to it, though, it *will* take you on a powerful trip. I guess I don't have to tell you that, though."

Malen-eh had a concerned expression on her face, but Alex thought he detected a humorous expression behind it.

"How long was I out? It seemed like just a few minutes. But it also seemed like a few years."

"That's part of the magic—it dissolves time. We've been watching over you for two days."

"Two days? Holy shit, that's some powerful stuff."

"Don't worry, we don't have feasts very often. It'll take a little more time before it's completely out of your system, but Malen-eh brought you something to chew. It will help the effects pass."

"It was just egg, right?"

"Don't ask questions you don't want the answer to."

"Fine, but I want to know."

"It *is* the egg of the karak-ta, but when they prepare it, they mix in some special herbs and..." Dan hesitated.

"Go on, tell me what I ate."

"Along with the egg and herbs, they add in droppings of the karak-ta. Guano. Get it?"

Alex closed his eyes. "Yeah, I get it. Remind me not to ask questions I don't want the answer to."

"I just did," Dan said. "But you asked anyway."

"Right," Alex answered. "How is Malen-eh's husband?"

"Let's start our language lessons right now. There are no possessives in this tongue. It would just be 'Malen-eh bukti.' Context would show that it is her husband."

Malen-eh heard the words she knew, and ran her hands along her left leg where her husband had been injured. Then, she touched her heart lightly and pointed at Alex.

"If you didn't get that, Janta-ak, her husband, is recovering, thanks to you. It will take more time for his wounds to heal, but they have strong medicine they apply in poultices to animal wounds that almost always lead to healing."

"Almost?"

"Kragdon-ah is a harsh world."

"What's in those eggs that make them so trippy?"

"The karak-ta nest in the rocks above the seashore. The cliffs are sharp and almost impossible to climb. In the highest rocks above their nests, a certain plant grows that has highly hallucinogenic qualities. The karak-ta protect their nests fanatically, so they are the only creatures that manage to eat that plant. It passes through them and into their egg, which is why they are so highly sought after."

"If the karak-ta nest in an area that is impossible to get to, how does this tribe manage to get them?"

"I said the rocks are *almost* impossible to climb. That's why only the youngest, fastest, most agile members of the tribe are sent on the quest for the eggs. They work in small groups—two boys approach the nesting ground and cause a commotion, firing arrows or spears up to the nests. The karak-ta all lose their mind and chase after those boys, who lead them away from the nests as fast as they can. The remaining boys climb the rocks and grab as many of the eggs as they can, then try to disappear before the karak-ta return."

"Isn't that dangerous?"

"Yes, of course," Dan said. "The tribe loses three or four of our best young warriors every year. If one of them injures themselves—twists an ankle, say, jumping from the rocks, that's it. No one can help them."

An image of being attacked by those monstrous creatures, nearly helpless to defend yourself, flashed through Alex's mind. He gave an involuntary shudder.

I had a hard time dealing with them when I was fully armed. That is not how I would choose to die.

"But, it's worth it to the tribe. Surrounding tribes will pay almost any price for the eggs."

"It's worth it for the tribe, but how about the poor boys that die trying?"

"Really?" Dan asked. "I thought you were a grunt like me. Was it any different for us when we were sent off to 'Nam or Afghanistan, or wherever you were deployed?"

Alex was silent for a few seconds.

"Never thought about it that way."

"I've had forty years to think about things."

"When does the tribe send another expedition to the karak-ta?" Alex asked, wondering if that might be the best way to get back near the door again.

"Not for months. The tribe is careful to not take too many eggs or harm too many of the karak-ta. They want them to maintain a stable population."

The image of a huge pile of karak-ta falling dead at his feet flitted through Alex's mind.

I might have set their conservation plan back a few years.

Alex sat up, found that the room wasn't spinning, and accepted a bright green leaf from Malen-eh.

"Attaboy," Dan said. "Chew on that for sixty seconds or so and you'll be feeling better than ever."

Alex bit into the leaf and made a face. It was so bitter, he almost choked.

"I never said it tasted good, did I? Be a good boy, or she'll wrestle you to the ground and make you chew it. Believe me, she could do it."

Alex looked Malen-eh over from head to toe. "I believe she could." He forced himself to chew on the sour bitterness until he couldn't take it anymore. Finally, he spit it out and looked at Dan.

"Is that good enough?"

Malen-eh laughed and said, "Dora bin conta la."

"That's good enough," Dan said. "She says she's never seen anyone chew it that long."

Chapter Ten
Near Death

Alex spent the next few days in long huddles with Dan, trying to learn the language of the tribe. Since he had already learned several other languages in the Army, and since this was a relatively simple language, he picked things up quickly.

When he wasn't spending long hours learning the language, he prowled around his new home, learning the best ways up and down the cave system, finding the guard stations above the openings and in the trees. He wasn't thinking of escaping—Dan had convinced him of the uselessness of that plan—but he was a trained military man. In a world where an attack from either man or beast could come at any moment, he was driven to understand his environment.

The tribe had a communal toilet. Several levels up the granite face, there was a room where there were large holes in the floor. Men and women alike hovered over the holes, hanging on to grips built into the surrounding walls. Twice a day, adolescents carried bags of water up to the holes and rinsed them. The holes had cracks in the bottom which leeched the water and detritus away over time.

That had been a hard adjustment for Alex. He had been raised to shut the bathroom door behind him. When he and Dan were in the middle of a lesson, he asked, "Why can't we just sneak off in the woods and do our business?"

"That is strongly discouraged. First, I've heard that you found out the hard way what happens when you pee on a tree with a tree roach living in it."

Alex remembered the massive bug skittering down the trunk at him and shuddered.

"But," Dan continued, "it's just an overall bad idea. It attracts predators that we don't need. Even the mighty Godat-ta would have trouble reaching us in the caves, but how many might die before everyone got to safety?"

Alex could see the wisdom in that, but still had a hard time using the stone toilets when women were present.

On his fourth day in Karak-ta, his modesty was tested and ultimately cast aside.

He woke up in one of the communal sleeping chambers—where unattached men and women slept on mattresses stuffed with hay. As always, he kept his eyes closed for several moments, listening to the movements of people around him and acclimating himself to the new day.

That was when the first disturbing rumble in his stomach presented itself.

He sat upright on his mattress. One second later, he was hurrying along the corridors and ladders to the stone toilets. All of them were occupied, but not full. There was room for five or six people at each hole, but he had always waited until one was empty to use it. This morning, he did not have that luxury.

Alex ran into the last hole, where an old man and woman were speaking in low tones.

"Sorry to interrupt, but it's an emergency," Alex said, knowing they would not understand him.

He pulled his pants and underwear down, grasped the stone grip and lowered himself over the hole. He voided his bowels with a push so mighty that the old couple, who had seen it all, looked over their shoulders at him in distress.

Alex stayed in that position until his quivering legs threatened to give out on him. He reached for some of the leaves the tribe used for toilet paper and cleaned himself.

"Wooh," he said out loud. "Wonder what caused that?"

He had no more pulled his pants up than he was again pushing them down around his ankles and repeating the same exercise.

The old couple did their best to keep a straight face, but Alex heard the quiet giggles as they walked away.

"Some things are funny no matter where you are, I guess," Alex said ruefully.

Half an hour later, after he had voided more diarrhea than he would have thought possible, he finally managed to get his pants up and belt buckled.

Whatever that was, I never want to do it again.

He hobbled his way to where there would be food for breakfast, still not liking the way his stomach felt. When he got there, he looked at the cold meat left over from the night before and immediately turned back to the toilets.

He made it there before vomiting, but it was only through sheer strength of will. When he had thrown up more than he would have thought possible, he started back to the sleeping chamber, but ran into Dan halfway there.

"Not sure I'm gonna make my language lesson today, Teach."

"Oh," Dan said, laying a hand against Alex's clammy face, then touching the glands in his throat. "I was hoping you would get a pass on this, but you look like death."

"Death would be a major improvement. A free pass on what?"

"There's no name for it, because it's possible you and I are the only ones who have had it. I suffered with it right after I first got here. I didn't mention it to you because I hoped it was just me. Diarrhea?"

"If you want to call cleansing your insides with a firehose 'diarrhea,' yeah."

"Have you vomited, too?"

"I think I saw my toenails come up in the last round. I am wiped out. I'm going to go lay down."

"That's a good idea, but don't go back to the communal room. It's too far from the toilets."

"Oh, I don't think I have anything left to throw up or crap out."

"You'd think that, wouldn't you? Unfortunately, the human body is capable of handling extremes. If your case is anything like mine, you've still got several days of this ahead of you."

"Days? No way. I don't have anything left inside me."

Dan threw Alex's arm around him and led him to a small, clean chamber with a sleeping mattress, a jar full of water, and shelves filled with small pots and bags.

Alex laid down on the bed and Dan scooped out a ladle of water. "Drink this. Any time you're not throwing up or on the pot, you need to be drinking something. It's the only way to stay ahead of it."

Alex drank half of it, then waved it away.

"I'll be back with Niten-eh. She nursed me through this forty years ago. She'll have some idea what to do for you."

Alex collapsed back on the mattress in complete misery. He tossed and turned, searching for an elusive, comfortable position.

Finally, Dan returned with a woman half a head taller than him, her long gray hair twisted into one long braid down her back. She looked Alex over, poked and prodded him, then spoke quietly to Dan.

"Niten-eh says she will stay with you until you are either better or have died."

"That's quite a bedside manner she's got," Alex said.

"She's going to make up a potion of herbs and roots for you. It will taste so bad, you might think dying is preferable, but force it down. It will give you the best chance to get through this."

"I don't think it's that bad. I must have eaten something that didn't agree with me."

The thought of food was too much for his stomach, so he immediately rolled onto his side and threw up again. Niten-eh was prepared, though, and had a large wooden bowl ready to catch it. When Alex was done, she handed the bowl to Dan, who carried it away.

Alex collapsed back on the bed, suddenly feverish. He gave in to the sickness. It washed over him in waves, overwhelming him.

Alex slept, more in a coma than a normal sleep.

Malen-eh, who had just finished nursing her husband back to health from the wolf attack, came and stayed. They turned Alex over, cleaned him up after he soiled himself again and again, and forced water and the medicine down him in whatever amounts they could.

After lapsing in and out of consciousness for two days, Alex woke up and seemed to have his wits about him. Dan was standing at his feet, with Niten-eh and Malen-eh on either side of him.

"Dan, I don't know. I think I might be done for. I don't think I've got the strength to make it."

"Knock it off, soldier," Dan said intently. He looked at Alex, who was haggard, had a gray complexion, and needed a shave. He softened. He kneeled close to Alex. "Listen, I felt the same as you. I was asking them to just kill me to put me out of my misery, but luckily no one could understand me."

"Did you get better on your third day?"

"I can't lie to you, man. I didn't."

"Fourth?"

Slowly, Dan shook his head.

Alex started to curse but lapsed back into his coma.

For two more days, it was more of the same. His body rejected everything Niten-eh tried. Malen-eh turned to dipping a rag into the water and dribbling it down his throat a few drops at a time to keep ahead of the horrible dehydration he was suffering.

On the fifth night, Alex tossed and turned, throwing off his blanket and anyone who tried to hold him down. Malen-eh's husband was summoned to hold him quiet and keep him from hurting himself. He held him down through the night until the first rays of light showed in the east.

Lanta-eh, the young girl of the prophecy, came into the room and kneeled gracefully beside Alex. She held her hands palm down over him and chanted. They were not words in any known language, just sounds. Nearly a song, with a cadence that rose and fell.

Slowly, she lowered her hands until she touched Alex's sweaty, feverish chest. She quieted, kept her eyes closed, but nodded to herself.

A moment later, she smiled at Malen-eh and Niten-eh and slipped away.

Alex stopped fighting, his thrashing relaxed, and he slipped into a normal sleep. He slept through the entire day almost without moving. When the sun dipped below the horizon, Niten-eh found that she could get a few drops of water past his chapped lips.

Alex sat up again, looking around but seeing nothing.

"Mindy? I'm sorry I'm late. I'll be there soon." He laid down, rolled over, and was out again.

The night was much quieter. Niten-eh was sent to her own bed, as was Malen-eh. Dan sat alone with Alex, watching him.

In the deepest quiet of the night, when even the frogs had quieted, Dan realized that Alex was looking at him and that his eyes were clear.

"I'm still here," Alex said.

"I never had any doubt," Dan answered quietly.

"That makes one of us. What the hell was all that?"

"No idea, really. All I can think is that during whatever time has passed between our time and this, new strains of viruses and super-bugs have been created. Maybe it's even part of what killed off most of the world's population."

"*That* I can believe," Alex said, trying to sit up.

"Whoa, brother. Not yet. You were close enough to death to smell its fetid breath. It's going to take you some time." Dan pulled a ladle of clear water from the jar and handed it to Alex. He tried to drink it too fast and ended up choking himself.

"Slowly, right? There are no hit times here. Nothing that needs to be done *right now*. Relax. Take it easy. Let Niten-eh take care of you. She's been with you since the beginning, almost never leaving. She'll nurse you the rest of the way back to health."

"I had nightmares, but every time I woke up, there were people here. Why would they do that for me?"

"They say you and I aren't part of the tribe, but they treat us like we are. Maybe we're like pets to them. Ugly, short, white-skinned pets."

"You make us sound so appealing. How could they resist us?"

"One thing, though. Your clothes were ruined. They burned them to get whatever bad juju you might be carrying with you."

Alex lifted the blanket and peered at his nakedness.

Dan reached behind him and gave him a set of clothing like the tribe wore—a cotton shirt and kilt that dropped below the knee.

"Your boots are still in good shape, if you want them, but they made you a pair of moccasins. I wore my old army boots around here for two years after I got here, but once I tried on a pair of mocs, I wondered why I had bothered."

Alex's eyelids grew heavy and his head started to nod.

"Listen. Just lay back and do what Niten-eh says for the next few days. For now, get some rest."

That last was unnecessary. Alex was already asleep.

Chapter Eleven
The Oath

Alex was slow to earn back his strength. He had never been truly sick before and so expected to jump right up and go back to life as normal.

There were no mirrors in the caves, but when Alex first looked down at himself, he reeled. His knees were knobby, his hip bones stuck out, and he could have played the xylophone on his ribs. He had never been heavy, but he found himself emaciated. He guessed he had lost thirty or more pounds in less than a week.

For a few days, he stayed close to home. Dan continued their interrupted language lessons, and Malen-eh brought him more food at each meal than he could eat. Slowly, he recovered from having spent an extended time living on death's door.

Malen-eh showed him a special place to spend time while he got his strength back. It was the highest of the caves inset in the rock wall. It was small—barely ten feet across. It was a spot often occupied by the oldest members of the tribe. When Malen-eh led him up the ladder, she spoke to the grayest-haired members of the tribe, who pushed aside and shoved a chair to the front for Alex.

When he sat in the chair, the most astonishing view revealed itself. He could see the open field directly below him, but also the ring of trees where the blinds hid the guards around the clock. Beyond that, the grass of the open field rippled like waves in the wind. Before the geography faded beyond the curvature of the earth, he saw hills rise on the left and right.

If I've got to be a patient for a while, this is a good place for it.

While he sat and watched the beauty and drama of this wild earth, he also saw visitors who didn't appear to be from Winten-ah. Something about them—the weapons they carried, the way they dressed, the way they moved—told him that these were outsiders.

When Dan came for his lessons that afternoon, Alex asked about them.

"Those are our trading partners, seeking the karak-ta eggs."

"Still? How long do the eggs stay good?"

"They know how to process them and keep them good for almost two weeks. There's no instant communication like a telephone here, so they find ways to extend their shelf life."

"Or the Internet."

"The what?"

"Oh. Right. 1980. Sorry. Never mind. What kind of things do we trade for?"

It went unnoticed by both of them that Alex had already begun to think of the tribe as *we.*

"Sometimes it's raw materials that we can't find around here. Other times it's a finished product that we don't make. Sometimes it's an animal we might use as livestock." He pointed to a man and woman emerging from the woods hauling a small wooden cart behind them. "Today, it's dogs. Or, at least, what you might think of as dogs."

Alex strained forward to see what might be evident in the back of the cart, but there was nothing visible.

"Let's go look!"

"Niten-eh will have your hide. You're supposed to be resting."

"I've been resting for days. I'm going stir crazy. Even this view isn't enough to keep me immobile forever."

Dan sighed, shook his head at Alex's stubbornness, and said, "Let me go down the ladders in front of you, so if you faint and fall, I can catch you. Or, more likely, we can both tumble to our deaths or at least a few broken bones far below."

"You're such a downer," Alex said, struggling slightly to rise from the chair.

"One other thing," Dan said. "I call these creatures 'dogs,' and they are pretty close, but if you're expecting a tail-wagging Labrador or cute little Pomeranian, you need to adjust your expectations. These animals have evolved quickly. They are built to survive in this world. And, they're intelligent."

"Like a border collie? Those are so damned smart."

"No, that's not what I'm saying. They've evolved. They're not smart like a breed was in our time. They're intelligent like a five-year-old kid."

They had been walking along the ledge toward a ladder, but that stopped Alex cold.

Dan turned to face him. "It's not like they can speak, or anything like that, but they do understand hand signals and they can problem-solve. Plus, they bind themselves to their human for life. They are a big responsibility. Kinda like adopting a kid."

"I gotta see these things. Lead on."

They arrived at the bottom of the wall just as the wagon rolled up to it. Kids who had been playing a rough and tumble game of tag recognized the traders and came running and screaming up to them like they were the ice cream truck in the neighborhood Alex grew up in.

Alex, meanwhile, had expended what little strength he had to get to the bottom and leaned against the wall, huffing and puffing.

Niten-eh approached him, raised her voice, and let loose what sounded like a string of invectives while shaking her fist at him.

Dan started to translate, but Alex held up his hand. "No need. I get it. She thinks I'm an idiot."

"Oh, it's much worse than that. Idiot would be complimentary compared to what she's calling you. She thinks you have a death wish."

"Can you tell her I just wanted to see what the trader was bringing in?"

"Tell her yourself. That's what all these lessons are for."

Alex turned to Niten-eh and stumbled through an explanation using his limited vocabulary in the language of the Winten-ah.

Dan nodded, pleased, but Niten-eh was not so easily assuaged. She rattled off another long, angry sentence, then turned on her heel and left. She stopped after a few steps and directed another tirade at Dan before stomping off.

"See what you've done? You've got me in trouble with her, too."

"Let's go look at the dogs, then we can rest for a while before we go back up," Alex said.

Adults had come to the traders and scattered the kids with mild cuffs to the back of the head.

Everyone was speaking in the universal language of Kragdon-ah, so Alex was once again lost. He had no idea if they were already bickering over prices or talking about the weather.

Finally, the man who had arrived with the cart grabbed the cover and flung it back dramatically. Alex knew he was in the presence of a salesman, Kragdon-ah-style.

Everyone took a step or two forward and surrounded the cart. Curled up under the tarp was a creature that somewhat resembled a dog—if that dog was a mastiff crossed with a bulldog, crossed with a newfoundland that had wandered over into prehistoric territory.

Alex's mouth fell open as he estimated that the dog must have weighed in at two-hundred and fifty pounds or more.

The massive creature was fast asleep, totally oblivious to the attention being paid to her.

Attached to each of her teats was a suckling pup, small only by comparison to their massive mother. They were a wide variety of colors, but their curved-spine shape was all the same.

"Just don't reach out to touch one of them," Dan cautioned. "She looks asleep, but you'd be amazed how fast she comes awake when a hand is near her pups."

Alex raised his hands to indicate he hadn't considered it. It was then that he noticed a smaller pup nearly hidden in the long grass the mother laid on. It didn't have a teat to suckle and instead mewled pitifully.

Without getting his hand too close, Alex pointed to the smallest pup.

Dan shrugged. "Looks like she had too many and that's the runt. Maybe once they sell one or two, it'll have a place at the buffet, too." Dan touched the trader on the arm and asked a question in the universal language.

The man's answer was short and curt. He obviously had bigger fish to fry and had no interest in this short, wild-haired white man.

Dan leaned into Alex and said, "He says that's the runt. She's already abandoned it. Even after the other dogs are sold, she won't feed it. He'd sell it if anyone would buy it, but he knows no one will. Without enough of its mother's milk to get started, it won't make it."

Alex nodded, but his eyes kept returning to that mewling little face, chewing the air, asking for a chance to survive.

Serious bickering began and the conversation between the trader and Banda-ak, who had taken the lead in negotiating for the Winten-eh, became heated.

Alex watched, fascinated, as the two giant men got into each other's faces, spittle flying as they angrily exchanged words. Alex was sure they would come to blows at any moment. If that happened,

Alex liked Banda-ak's chances. He was older and only had one eye, but the trader didn't have the same lean, hard look of a warrior.

Just when their noses were almost touching, they both acted surprised, stepped back, and laughed, then reached out and put a hand on their opponent's shoulder.

"Holy shit, is that how this always goes?" Alex asked.

"Yep. Starts out friendly, looks like they're going to go to war, then suddenly, they agree and they're the best of friends. It's like a ritual."

The wife of the trader took one of the dogs away from the teat and it also began to mewl as if it was starving, even though its pink underbelly was distended with milk. She stepped forward and handed it to a warrior Alex didn't recognize, who held it tight to his chest. Almost instantly, the crying stopped, and the dog was asleep.

Banta-ak turned and received two of the karak-ta eggs and ceremoniously handed them to the trader, who in turn gave them to the woman with him, who slipped them inside a bag.

Alex turned to Dan. "Ask him how much he wants for the runt."

"You don't have anything to trade with. If you were a craftsman, you could offer something you've made, but you aren't."

"How about my guns? My pistol will still work fine. Will he accept that?"

Dan shook his head vehemently. "No way. You promised to destroy them. You don't want to go back on that oath, believe me."

Alex looked at the pup in frustration. "Isn't there anything I can do?"

"No, there isn't. You're as poor as a church mouse in this world."

Dan looked at Alex for a long moment, then stepped to Banda-ak and spoke quietly to him. Banda-ak looked surprised then stared at Alex. He was silent for several seconds, then spoke just as quietly back to Dan.

Dan stepped back to Alex and said, "Banda-ak says he will negotiate for you, pay the price, and give you the runt. But he wants a new oath from you that you will perform a service for him when he asks it, no matter how dangerous it will be. He also warns you it will be for nothing. The animal will die, but you will still owe the oath. It's a terrible offer, because he's right. The animal will die, and you will have nothing but a new debt."

Alex didn't hesitate. "I'll do it."

"Think it over."

"I don't need to. I'll pledge the oath right now."

Dan shrugged and returned to Banda-ak, who raised his voice and spoke to the trader.

The trader looked shocked but covered that expression quickly and entered into a new negotiation. This time, neither side could summon as much energy in the service of such a minor bargain. Within moments, they came to an agreement and Banda-ak had dispatched a runner to get one of the baskets the Winten-ah were justifiably famous for making.

Onlookers stood open-mouthed, unable to believe that Banda-ak had made such a poor deal. Their baskets were their second-most valuable trading commodity. They found it hard to reckon why he had given one away for nothing. A basket was a low price for one of the animals who would serve the tribe for many years, but a far-too-rich price for an animal that would likely not live to see the next sunrise.

The woman trader picked up the runt, who was perhaps half the size of the first dog they had purchased and held it out to Banda-ak. It was obvious that she felt they had by far gotten the best end of this trade, but she did her best to mask that expression.

Banda-ak pointed to Alex. The woman, who towered over Alex, handed the animal to him with a slight smile playing on her lips.

Without a further word, the two traders picked up the cart's handles and headed toward the forest. The warrior guards of Winten-ah would see them safely through the forestland and then they would be on their own. Neither trader was young, though, indicating that they had many tricks to survive these treacherous journeys.

Dan looked at the squirming, undernourished animal in Alex's arms and said, "Now what, mama?"

Alex had no idea what was next. He'd grown up in a small town in central Oregon, but it hadn't been on a farm. He hadn't even been a member of the Future Farmers of America, which might have taught him to care for a cow or a sheep. He'd had a dog—a white German shepherd—from the time he was eight until she had died ten years later. That didn't do him much good for saving a near-dead distant cousin of that dog, who was genetically different in almost every way.

The squeaking, mewling animal had quieted against him. Alex put a hand against its chest to make sure it was still alive. He was rewarded with a steady thump-thump-thump against his fingers.

"I've just got a feeling about this guy. Is there anyone in the tribe who can give me some advice?"

Just a few minutes before, Alex had been leaning against a wall, trying to catch his breath, so exhausted he didn't want to move. Now, looking down on a face so homely only a mother could love it, he felt filled with energy.

Dan sighed, laughed a little and shook his head. "You are one of those people who jumps, hoping a net will appear before you hit the ground, aren't you?"

"Always have been," Alex said, rubbing behind the ears of the strange creature he held against him. The dog-hybrid snuggled deeper into his arms.

"Okay," Dan said. "Follow me. Luckily, we shouldn't have to climb to find him. He lives and works here on the ground."

"Who are we looking for?"

"Karga-ak. He's trained two of these beasts since I've been here. He also takes care of the work animals we have here." Dan glanced at Alex and said, "He's not a miracle worker, though. I should probably take you to Benka-eh, the priestess. I think this little guy needs last rites more than anything else."

Alex was oblivious to Dan's criticism. In his heart, he felt like he'd done the right thing, even if it might cost him terribly in the long run.

On the cliff's edge opposite the waterfall, there was a small area fenced off with sharply pointed logs that pointed skyward. They were tall enough that anything short of Godat-ta, the legendary bear that Alex had yet to see, would have an impossible time getting over them.

Inside the fence, a grassy area was divided up by wooden fencing—this time not so menacing. The animals inside each pen were not menacing, either, although they were large. Some of the creatures resembled cows, though they dwarfed the bovines Alex had driven by every day in Oregon.

Dan pointed to several tall, black creatures with ears so long, they looked like a caricature. "That is an alecs-ah," he said, barely stifling a laugh. "You and I would call them an ass."

"Yeah, yeah, I get it," Alex answered.

A tall, slightly bent man came around the corner carrying a rudimentary pitchfork with hay. He effortlessly flicked it over the fence to one of the bovines, who happily chewed it. His eye caught the dog that Alex was holding, and he approached and plucked him away.

He pulled back the dog's eyelids, opened his mouth and looked down his throat and palpitated its stomach. He handed it back to Alex and said, "Korin denta min."

"He says it's gonna die," Dan said helpfully.

"Yeah, I get that. That's what everyone says. It's still breathing right now, though, so what can I do until it dies?"

Dan and Karga-ak engaged in a long back and forth. Finally, Karga-ak turned and went into a lean-to against the cliff. He returned a moment later with two clay pots—one half again as big as the other—and a piece of woven fabric. He handed these to Dan and gave him a set of long, detailed instructions.

Dan thanked him and led Alex back out to the first level of the inset caves.

"I know you're focused on this right now, but I also know you're supposed to be doing nothing but resting. We'll stop here and you can try your hand at being nursemaid to this little monster."

It wasn't a little monster, of course. At least, not yet. It was just a pup hanging on to the knife's edge between life and death.

Alex found a chair in a quiet corner of the room and settled himself in. He set the two clay pots and cloth on the ground, crossed his leg to make a perfect cradle and laid the little animal into that space.

Alex's heart sank. He laid his hand on the pup's chest. There was no movement. No heartbeat. On the walk up, the little thing had given up and finally stopped breathing. It was possible that being taken away from the warmth of the mother who had otherwise rejected it had been the final straw, and now it was gone.

Alex let his head fall on his chest and fought back tears. It was ridiculous, he knew. He didn't even know this creature had existed an hour before. Now he was grieving it as though he had lost an old friend.

He felt a hand touch his arm. It was Niten-ah, kneeling beside him. She looked at his anguished face and held out her hands for the dog.

Alex lifted it up to her, then turned his face away, unable to watch.

Niten-ah examined the dog, then began rhythmically pushing on its chest. She counted her compressions of the chest and every thirty times, she stopped and blew down its throat, forcing oxygen into its lungs.

After five long minutes, Alex looked at the two of them, the regal woman with her long hair braided down her back and the pitiful animal that had never had a chance.

Niten-ah did not give up, but continued to patiently compress the chest, breathe air in, then start over, chanting the same words over and over.

That was when the miracle of life and a will to live took over. The dog's pink tongue, which had been motionless, poked out, then lolled to the right. The chest began to rise and fall rhythmically.

Niten-ah smiled and pointed at the milk in the bigger pitcher and the towel beside it. Alex picked it up and attempted to hand it to her, but she pointed at him. Alex dipped the cloth in the milk and took the dog back. He dipped the end of the cloth into its mouth and nearly cried when he sucked on it anxiously.

Instead, he laughed and dipped the cloth again. Again, the hungry mouth sucked on it until there was no milk left.

Niten-ah laid a hand on Alex's shoulder and said, "Stay here. Rest."

Alex was shocked to realize that she had spoken in her own language and he had understood. He said, "Yes. I will," also in her own tongue.

Happiness swelled inside him, and he found himself rocking back and forth in the chair, dipping the cloth and letting him drink as much as he was able.

The pup soon closed his gray eyes, but now his chest rose and fell more strongly. It seemed he had let go of the knife's edge and had fallen on the side of life. The pup cuddled into Alex and slept, but Alex did not. He laid his hand on its chest and felt the comforting in and out movement all through the night, until the first light of dawn.

A few hours later, Dan showed up with a plate of food for Alex and more milk for the pup.

"What are you gonna call the little bugger now that a miracle has happened?"

Alex hadn't given that idea any thought.

He looked down at the sleeping lump of puppy, scratched gently under its chin, then said, "What's the Winten-ah word for 'survivor.'"

Dan smiled, nodded, and said, "It's very close to your own tribal name, Manta. The word for survivor is monda."

"That's it, then. His name is Monda-ak."

Chapter Twelve
A Quest

In the following weeks, both Alex and Monda-ak recovered. Alex put most of the weight back on that he had lost, though he stayed a little leaner than he had been before. Monda-ak ate like there was a hole in him that would never be filled.

Alex went to Karga-ak, the animal trainer and asked him for food, but began to feel guilty at how much the ravenous dog ate.

At the end of another of his endless language lessons—they had begun to add in words from the universal language as well—Alex said, "I can't rely on Karga-ak for food forever. What can I do?"

"I should have mentioned that before you gave a life oath to get him. These dogs eat like they'll never see another meal. But look at him! I'd swear he's doubled in size in only a few weeks."

"He sleeps on top of me every night, I think he's done more than that. I have dreams I am being smothered by a pack of animals, and when I wake up, it's just him laying across my chest."

"It's only going to get worse. If he sleeps on your chest six months from now, he will smother you. I don't think Karga-ak resents the food too much yet, though. He sent you this." Dan handed over a piece of leather that had been knotted and twisted. "I think he soaked it in bone broth. Said it'll be good for the runt's teeth."

Monda-ak stirred himself from a nap in the corner and toddled over to Alex. He stood on his hind legs and sniffed earnestly at the leather. Alex dangled it just a few inches above his nose and the puppy, who most resembled a beer barrel with legs, tried to jump up and bite it. That resulted in him landing flat on his back with an 'ooof.'

"Not the most graceful thing, is he?" Dan observed.

"Not yet. Give him time. He'll be... he'll be... hell I don't even know what these guys are supposed to do. What *are* they supposed to do?"

"They are warriors in battle and in the hunt. They're not all that fast, but they can still outrun a man, and they have incredible stamina. Plus, their loyalty is insane. They'll never leave your side unless you give them the command. And, if you fall in battle, he will stand over your body and protect it until he's killed himself."

Alex kneeled and looked at the homely face of Monda-ak. One ear stood straight up and the other flopped comically forward. "Would you do that for me?"

Monda-ak saw his chance to grab the leather and jumped forward, putting all his weight into bowling over Alex. He grabbed the strip between his teeth and jumped away. He threw his head left and right as though he was snapping the neck of the leather twist, then dropped it in front of him and growled ferociously. He laid down beside it and started chewing it vigorously.

Dan and Alex both watched him, laughing.

"I am going to need to take care of his upkeep very soon. Can I go on one of the hunting trips and help bring the meat in?"

"Maybe, but it takes more than just asking. Being one of the hunters is a position of honor in the tribe. Most Winten-ah train for it from the time they are children."

"I can't claim that, but I hunted with my dad from the time I was ten or so. We took down just about anything you can name—grouse, pheasants, mule deer, even squirrels when I was learning to hunt."

"That helps, but when you were hunting grouse, what were the odds that some other carnivore like a dire wolf or a bear as big as your house were going to be hunting you at the same time? And, these hunters use spears, clubs, atlatls, and knives, not shotguns and rifles with hi-tech scopes."

"True enough, but now that I'm feeling better, I'll go stir crazy staying around here all the time. Who can I talk to about joining the hunters?"

"You'll need to talk to Sekun-ak. He's the chief hunter."

"Who's that? Have I met him?"

"Of course you did—at the ceremony where you promised to help destroy your guns."

Alex flashed back on the huge warrior who seemed to hate Alex before he even knew him.

"Oh, great. Him."

Dan laughed at the expression on Alex's face. "Hey, don't worry about it. If you don't want to talk to him, I can talk to Malen-eh. She can get you on with the housekeeping crew. They change the bedding, wash clothes down at the creek, that sort of thing."

"You know, you can really be an asshole sometimes, right?"

Dan continued to laugh, but said, "You're not the first person who's told me that. Now, do you want me to take you to him, or not?"

Dan and Alex found Sekun-ak at the armory. It wasn't much by twentieth century standards—there wasn't a long-distance weapon or tin of gunpowder in sight—but it was what they had.

Sekun-ak was sitting at a table, attaching an arrowhead to the shaft of an arrow. When Dan and Alex walked in, he didn't bother to look up.

"Gunta," Dan said.

Still, Sekun-ak did not turn his attention from the arrow.

Ah, Dan doesn't exactly get along with this dude, either. Interesting. Maybe he just doesn't like our type.

"Sekun-ak, Manta-ak wants to be part of the next hunting expedition."

That finally got the man's attention. He delicately set the arrow down, then stood and stepped in front of Alex. He looked down on him from his full 7'4" frame and smirked.

Alex thought of his first hand-to-hand combat instructor, who was only 5'2", but made Alex look foolish every time they met on the mat.

The bigger man is not always the best fighter.

Sekun-ak smirked down at Alex, then said, "Nunta den."

Alex knew enough of that language to be surprised. *Nunta den* meant *no problem.* Dan turned to interpret, but Alex waved him off.

"That's great," Alex said. "Can you ask him when the next hunting expedition leaves? I'd like to go."

Sekun-ak blurted out a long litany of Winten-ah that Alex lost track of after the first few words.

When he finished, Dan turned to Alex and said, "Well, the gist of it is, you can become a hunter, but first you have to complete three tasks that all hunters must perform to prove they belong."

"Is that true? Do all hunters have to prove themselves with these tasks? If so, that's completely fair."

"I have no idea," Dan answered. "I never tried to join the hunters, and I'm not privy to all their goings-on."

"So it could be a trap, intended to hurt or embarrass me."

"I'd bet on it."

Alex couldn't prevent his chest from puffing out a little or the fact that his chin jutted up toward Sekun-ak. He had never backed down from a challenge.

"Great. Tell him I'll do it."

Dan shook his head. "I'm surprised you've managed to live this long."

"Like you said earlier, you're not the first person to tell me that."

"OKAY," DAN SAID, EARLY the next morning. They stood out-side the armory. A group of Sekun-ak's hunters had joined him to watch the fun. "These tasks are supposed to get progressively more difficult, so this one should be a piece of cake."

"I like the way you think," Alex said, scratching Monda-ak be-hind the ears.

"You stay here. I don't want your fractured Winten-ah to get you in trouble. I'll talk to him and ask him as many questions as I can."

Dan and Sekun-ak conferenced and went back and forth for sev-eral minutes. It looked to Alex like Dan was trying to determine the finer points of the challenge.

Finally, Dan came back to Alex.

"It's fair. It's not like you have to pull one of Godat-ta's teeth and bring it back."

"Don't even say that," Alex said, but he saw that Dan was only trying to loosen him up.

"What you have to do is bring back a pinecone."

Alex looked flabbergasted. "Seriously? That should take what, about five minutes? Maybe we can knock out all three of these chal-lenges today."

"Hold on there, Hercules. It's going to be a little harder than that. The pinecone must be as long as your arm, and it has to come with a bit of the branch attached to it, so he knows you didn't just pick it up off the ground. He wants to test your ability to climb. The only trees in the forest that have pinecones that big are the sugar pines, which are at the far southern end of the forest. The good news is, you'll be in our forest, which means you'll be relatively safe on the trip there and back. Our guards keep the forest trail pretty clear of predators."

Alex swallowed hard. "How about tree roaches?"

"Can't make any promises there, bud. Sorry."

"Can I at least get a club or something to fight them off with?" Dan turned to Sekun-ak and asked.

Sekun-ak smirked and said, "Fen." He turned to one of his men and barked an order. The man hesitated, obviously not wanting to comply. Sekun-ak repeated himself, much more quietly this time. The man's face clouded, but he grabbed his cudgel off his belt and handed it to Alex, who hung it off his own belt. It was too big for him and banged against his calf when he moved.

"REMIND ME TO FIND WHOEVER makes these and learn how to do it myself, so I don't look so much like I'm playing with Dad's weapon."

"Don't worry about it now, you've got more important things to think about. Do you know what a sugar pine looks like?"

"No idea."

"It'll be easy to spot. When you come to the end of the forest, look up. They are the tallest trees within ten days travel."

"Ah, that's it," Alex said. "It's to see if I have a fear of heights or not. Doesn't have much to do with being a hunter, but okay. Whatever. Let's get this over with."

Without another word, Alex set off at a fast march. He walked past the children playing in front of the cliff and was soon at the cool edge of the forest. He turned south and less than a hundred yards later, saw the first guard in his blind.

Alex waved and said, "Gunta!"

The guard waved back and offered "Gunta!" back to Alex.

That word had been an easy one to pick up. 'Gunta' was a heavy-duty, all-purpose word in Winten-ah, like 'aloha' in the Hawaiian Islands. It could mean 'hello,' 'goodbye,' or 'May the wind be at your back,' all depending on context.

There was a small trail through the forest—not much more than a game trail, but Dan had told him to stick to it.

Alex broke into a light jog, anxious to get to the sugar pines and see what new challenge waited for him.

It was a beautiful day and slanting beams of sunlight cut through the trees as his footfalls were muffled by the pine needle carpet on the ground. On any other day, Alex would have slowed and enjoyed nature.

Instead, he moved quickly, carefully avoiding brushing into any of the trees he passed. He hoped he wouldn't see any of the giant roaches on his first challenge.

After an hour, he stopped to catch his breath and drink from the water bag he had brought with him. When he tilted his head back to drink, his eyes fell on one of the tallest trees he had ever seen. It rose above those around it like a mountain set amidst foothills. He choked on the water, then lowered the bag and gaped at the tree.

Holy mother.

Alex closed one eye and tried to estimate how tall the tree might be. It was so out of whack with the surrounding trees that he could only guess.

Two hundred feet? Maybe three hundred.

He didn't have a fear of heights but looking up at the top branches of the tree, which were swaying magnificently in the wind, he felt his stomach tighten.

This is the easy one, huh? Can't wait to see what he's dreamed up for the next two.

Alex approached the tree as one does any worthy opponent. Slowly, sizing it up, seeing what tricks it might have in store for him.

At least it has low branches. That will make it a little easier to climb.

He arrived at the bottom of the tree and spread his arms around the trunk to measure it. He had to use three of his own wingspans to measure around it. When he stood at the bottom and looked up, he couldn't begin to see the top.

Alex checked his equipment, which was sparse. A Winten-ah backpack which Dan had loaned him, his water bag, the too-long club, and his wits. Always his wits.

Alex kicked the tree several times to send vibrations up it, then stepped back and waited with his club drawn. If he was going to face one of those monstrous roaches, he wanted to do it here, on solid ground.

Seconds passed and the only sound came from the whispering of the trees as they swayed in the wind. Alex hadn't noticed it before, but here at the edge of the forest, the wind had picked up substantially.

I don't have to climb clear to the top, anyway. Just high enough to pull off a pinecone. Wait. Correct that. A pinecone as long as my arm. Damn.

Alex jumped slightly, grabbed hold of the lowest limb and pulled himself up. Again, he paused, waiting for the appearance of the giant cockroach. None came.

Alex had been a tree climber all his life. That was how he had come to wear a cast the summer between sixth and seventh grade. He had recovered enough from his bout of Winten-ah Flu to be almost back to one hundred percent. Confidence flowed back into him.

C'mon, Hawk. You've got this.

Alex looked at tree climbing the same way he did chess. The problem isn't the move at hand. The problem is the move seven or eight turns down the road. Or, in this case, the limbs twenty feet above him.

Soon, everything but the climb passed from his mind. Amy and what she was thinking about him was normally never far from his mind. Formulating an escape plan was also constantly rolling around his brain. But now, pulling himself from one branch to another, occasionally making a calculated leap, all those thoughts dissipated.

After ten minutes of hard climbing, Alex looked down. He was surprised to see the treetops of all the other trees. For the first time, he had a perfect view of the surrounding area. He squinted and tried to eliminate all the landmarks he took for granted—roads, bridges, and buildings.

As he strove to remove the trappings of civilization from his mind, he began to see that Dan had been correct. The land was the same. He hadn't moved in space. Only in time.

After a brief rest, Alex looked at the pinecones around him. Sugar pines had massive cones and they hung all around him. Big as they were, they didn't measure as long as his arm.

He climbed on.

The higher he got, the more the wind became a factor. One gust hit him so hard that he had to throw his arms around the trunk and dig his fingers into the bark to hang on.

Even when the wind wasn't gusting, it blew steadily and the tree swayed unnervingly.

Alex put the swaying out of his mind—it was one of the many things in his life that he had no ability to control.

Up he climbed, the trunk of the tree narrowing, which made it easier to get a grip as the whipping action increased.

Finally, he saw what he had been looking for—the biggest pinecone he had ever seen.

It hung on a limb over his head and was a few feet beyond his grasp. In order to reach it, he needed to let go of the trunk, balance on the lower limb, and stretch well above his head. It was either that, or climb up another limb, hunker down, and try to get it that way. That might have been the easiest way.

Alex so rarely took the easy way in anything.

He shuffled his feet along the lower limb, praying that another big gust didn't choose that moment to sweep him off. He kept his left hand touching the trunk of the tree as long as he could, but soon realized he was going to have to let go and balance on the limb.

The wind pushed the tree to the right, then see-sawed it back to the left. Alex half-kneeled, like a tightrope walker that almost lost his balance. He recovered and stretched upward. It was easy enough to touch the pinecone, but if he just grabbed the bottom and pulled, he might not get the required piece of the limb.

Alex gathered his equilibrium, took a deep breath, and jumped up. He grabbed the upper limb with both hands, smashing his face into the massive pinecone. It wavered but did not fall.

He let go with his left hand and swung one-handed in the breeze for two long seconds while he waited to see if his right hand would hold him.

It did.

He reached up and tore the pinecone away, making sure to bring a piece of the branch with it. The pinecone was huge—well longer than his arm—but it wasn't heavy. He cradled it in his left arm and craned his neck to look at the branch below him.

This was the tricky part—letting go with his right arm, landing on the limb below, and holding his balance long enough to step back to the trunk of the tree.

All without dropping the pinecone.

Alex's grip made the decision quick. It released and he fell. His feet hit the branch below and he pinwheeled his right arm, seeking a precarious balance.

He realized he was going to fall, so he leaped toward the trunk.

He made it, although barely. His left leg slipped off the limb and scraped viciously against the ragged wood, drawing blood. He kept his left arm gripped around the pinecone but managed to grab the main trunk with his right arm.

Alex took a deep, shaky breath, knowing how lucky he had been to not plummet several hundred feet to the ground. The pinecone would win the challenge but would have made a terrible parachute.

Okay. I'll rest up for just a minute, then climb down.

Alex had planned to use the backpack to carry the cone down, but now that he had it in his arms, he realized it was far too big to fit into that. He would need to climb with only one arm.

While he rested, he glanced up to see how close to the top of the tree he had gotten. He noticed a dark, shadowy area in the limbs at the very top of the tree. When he focused, he realized what it was—a nest. A nest by definition, but larger than any he could remember seeing.

What now? The karak-ta nest in the rocks by the ocean. What fresh hell can this be?

That thought no more than passed through his mind than he heard an urgent chirping coming from the nest.

Alex looked around in a panic and saw the single largest bird he had ever seen in his life. It was circling overhead with a small animal dangling lifelessly from its claws. It was even larger than the karak-ta. Where the karak-ta looked almost comical in a horrifying way, this animal looked like death on two wings. It was apparently an eagle, or some distant relative thereof. It had the same hooked beak, sharp claws and predator's gaze.

It fell out of its circling flight path and dove straight at Alex.

Alex didn't panic but picked the fastest and most dangerous path down, which was to jump from limb to limb. He jumped twice and landed perfectly.

On his third jump, he miscalculated. His right foot landed properly but his left slipped off.

With no chance to check himself, Alex's right foot also slipped.

He fell, plummeting toward the ground.

Chapter Thirteen
A Quest II

Alex instinctively dropped the pinecone so he could have both hands free to save his life.

The good news was that the tree was heavily limbed, so he didn't just free fall to the ground. Instead, he hit branch after branch on the way down. That slowed him down, but since he landed awkwardly on each one, it also served to beat and bruise him.

Less than fifty feet from the ground, he was still tumbling, but managed to grab an offshoot of a branch, which slowed him enough that he could right himself and aim his feet at the branch below. He was still moving too fast, but finding a momentary foothold allowed him to jump again and land more solidly.

He hugged the trunk of the tree, sweat pouring off him, breath coming in ragged bursts. He looked upward to see if the giant eagle had followed him down, but there was no sign of her. Perhaps the fact that he had tumbled several hundred feet away from her nest neutralized him as a threat.

Alex held onto the tree trunk and waited until his breathing and heartbeat stabilized. Only then did he remember that he had dropped the cone he had fought so hard to get.

If it's lost the attaching branch, I don't know what I'll do. What is worse? Admitting I failed the challenge, or trying to climb back up there again?

Alex knew the answer, but he dreaded the thought of another climb. He was not only exhausted, but his out of control tumble had battered him so badly he secretly doubted his ability to successfully manage it.

He gingerly made his way down the last forty feet of the tree, wincing with each small jump. His leg was bleeding, he'd wrenched his left arm trying to grab a branch, and he had more cuts and bruises than he could count.

He hopped down onto the thick carpet of pine needles and immediately saw the giant cone. The top was turned away, but when he picked it up, his heart leapt.

It's intact!

Alex felt such relief that he plopped down on the trail and let himself rest for five minutes. That's rarely a good idea in Kragdon-ah. If you're not moving, something is typically moving toward you. In this case it wasn't anything fatal, like Godat-ta the bear, but something annoying. Ants.

Like so many other things in Kragdon-ah, the ants weren't the annoyances found at picnics, but were each an inch long, with a fire-red warning on their abdomen. When the first one climbed up the back of Alex's shirt, it was heavy enough to attract his attention. Before he could swipe it away, ten more climbed aboard to investigate.

Alex would have thought that he couldn't jump off the ground to save his life, but he was wrong. In an instant, he was up gyrating, jumping, slapping at himself. He grabbed the pinecone off the ground, shook it to make sure it wasn't also carrying ants, and hustled up the trail.

The trip back was uneventful. As he passed each lookout's blind, they shouted down, "Gunta!"

Alex wasn't enthusiastic in his replies, but he did manage a tired, "Gunta," to each of them as he marched by at double-time.

He emerged into the clearing, and the children—who were only a few inches taller than he was—ran to him, laughing. They tried to touch and grab the giant pinecone, but Alex held it away from them, saying, 'Kel!' which was Winten-ah for 'No!'

At the base of the cliff, Alex saw Dan. Monda-ak also saw him and sprinted toward him. When he got close, Alex began to back up, saying, "Whoa, whoa, whoa!" but it didn't matter. The pup had all the grace of a hippo on ice skates and hit Alex at a full gallop, almost knocking him over. Alex looked down at the dog, whose entire posterior was wagging, not just its tail, and couldn't manage to be even slightly angry.

Dan looked over his wounds and said, "Good thing this is the easy one, eh? It looks like you've been shot at and missed but shit at and hit."

"You're hilarious. Let's get this to Sekun-ak. I can hardly wait to see what he's got for me tomorrow."

When they tracked Sekun-ak down in one of the upper caves, he looked slightly surprised to see Alex lugging his giant pinecone. He recovered quickly though, saying in Winten-ah, "Tomorrow will be harder. Find me at apex." Alex was pleased to realize he understood. He was adapting, learning.

Apex was what the Winten-ah called noon, or a close proximity. It was the time when the sun was at its highest point each day.

Alex did his best not to limp as he walked away, but when they were down several levels, he said, "Maybe I should go see Niten-eh. I don't want all these cuts to get infected."

An hour later, Niten-eh had bandaged him up, laughing a bit while Alex told the story of recovering the pinecone and how he almost died.

"These people have a morbid sense of humor," Alex said.

"It's the image of you tumbling ass over teakettle, holding on to that giant pinecone that got her. You'll be the talk of the tribe by tonight."

"Great. At least I'm still alive to be gossiped about."

Alex was too tired to even eat, and he and Monda-ak retired to one of the communal sleeping chambers. He was asleep almost before he laid down.

⚔

ALEX, MONDA-AK AND Dan met just outside the armory at midday. Alex still looked like he was on the losing end of a heavyweight boxing match, but Monda-ak was full of puppyish joy, bouncing ahead of Alex, then retreating to make sure he was still coming, then tripping over nothing and falling face-first.

"Come on, great white hunter," Dan laughed.

Inside the armory, Sekun-ak stood over a large shallow box. Inside the box was sand—the same dark sand that Alex had seen at the beach when he stepped through the door. Again, he was surrounded by his hunters—six men and two women. None of them looked happy to see them.

Guess they thought they'd get rid of me yesterday.

Dan and Sekun-ak convened at the table and had a long conversation with Alex looking on and eavesdropping as best he could. As they spoke, Sekun-ak used a piece of wood to draw lines in the sandbox.

After a few minutes of rapid conversation, Dan turned to Alex.

"I don't know what trick he's got up his sleeve this time. It seems pretty simple and straight-forward."

"Which makes me nervous," Alex said.

"Right. I mean, they didn't exactly cheat yesterday, but it wasn't as easy as we thought."

"Nothing we can solve by worrying about it. What's the task?"

"Sekun-ak says he wants to test your stamina and endurance. That's the method they use most often in their hunting. They form huge rings around whatever they're hunting and chase it toward each other until the animal is exhausted."

"Got it," Alex said, nodding.

"He says he sent a hunter to a specific spot today and placed a household item—a simple wooden plate. All you have to do is run to the location, retrieve the plate, and bring it back here. The rub is that it is more than seven miles each way. So, a fifteen-mile round trip, over some dangerous, uneven ground, and you have to be back here before the sun disappears over the hills."

"That gives me what, seven hours? That's barely a two-mile an hour pace. No problem."

"I seem to remember you feeling this confident yesterday, then you were mostly dead when you stumbled back into camp."

"Whatever. Just show me where I need to go."

Dan showed Alex the route Sekun-ak had drawn in the sand. "Into the forest once more, then at the northern end, where the trees give out, turn east and run along a game path until it ends at a river. It's a big river, you can't miss it. He says the plate is sitting on a flat rock right by the river. All you've got to do is grab it and bring it back here before sundown."

Alex knew the clock was ticking, so he leaned down and patted Monda-ak on the head and said, "Stay with Dan. I'll be right back."

"You're going to have the only multi-lingual dog in the world."

Monda-ak whined when Alex moved away. He was already completely bound to him and hated to be separated.

Alex came back, scratched his ears again, then turned and jogged toward the forest. He had done dozens of long marches in Special Forces training, so he knew what he was doing. Don't start too fast. Stay hydrated.

He was equipped the same way he had been the day before—nothing but the carry-bag on his back, his water bag, and the same borrowed cudgel. That meant he was light. By the time he had gone half a mile in the forest, the stiffness and soreness from the previous day had mostly left him.

He set a metronome in his head—tic, tic, tic, tic—and matched his steps to it.

Again, he greeted each guard sitting in the trees, although he might have been a little less cocky about it this time.

He made great time to the end of the forest and found the game trail easily. If this really was an endurance test and didn't have any hidden issues, he was confident he would be back long before the sun touched the hilltops.

Alex kept his head on a swivel as he marched. He had asked Dan about what wildlife he might run into on the journey, but he hadn't known. He was on a game trail, though, and where there is game, there are predators. If they were lying in wait for whatever came along, he had not seen them.

Two hours after he left, the trail widened out and he could hear the burbling of a running river. He slowed his pace and approached the river carefully.

Water sources were often great hunting grounds, and he wanted to determine as best he could that he would not be on the menu.

Alex had known that there would be water at the river, so he hadn't conserved his water bag on the trip. It was a hot day, and he wanted to avoid dehydration, which might lead to cramping.

He laid on his belly and dunked his head in the water. When he came up for breath, he stuck his face back down into the cold water and drank. Not his fill—he also didn't want to risk a side-ache on the march back—but enough to slake his thirst.

He filled his water bag, then turned his attention to finding the plate. He was ready to return to camp.

It didn't take him long to find the first wrinkle in the quest. There was only one flat rock in the area, and it was perched precariously on top of a pile of rubble that was over his head.

Bastards can't make anything too easy, can they?

Alex approached the rubble cautiously, looking for any other tricks they might be playing on him. None were in evidence, so he put one foot a few feet up the pile of rocks. As he did, the shale shifted under his feet and he found himself back on solid ground.

This is going to take a lighter touch.

He stepped again, but more cautiously this time. He made it two steps before everything shifted and he once again found himself where he had started.

He calmed his breathing and closed his eyes for several long moments. He stepped as lightly as he possibly could, holding each step for several seconds before shifting his weight and taking another. This method worked, as he worked his way higher and higher up the rubble pile.

Another challenge was that the flat rock was large—maybe ten feet across. If he had climbed up on the wrong side, he would also have to work his way around the pile to reach the plate, which might be in the very middle.

Tentatively, he touched the edge of the flat rock and looked up over the edge.

He could see the wooden plate.

He could also see a western diamondback rattlesnake curled up around it, rattling a warning.

Chapter Fourteen
A Quest III

"Gah!" Alex was so surprised by the appearance of the snake that he forgot about his tenuous foothold on the shale. He jerked backward, lost his balance, and tumbled down the small hill. He wasn't high up—no more than twelve feet—so nothing was hurt but his pride.

He sat at the bottom of the hill and tried to calm his heart, which was racing at the sudden appearance of the deadly threat.

Holy shit. That thing must be twelve feet long. I didn't think rattlers grew that big. But of course they do. I am in Kragdon-ah where everything that is deadly is bigger and badder than you expect. I was lucky it didn't strike when I poked my head up there. Does this heat make it sluggish? I don't think I want to count on that.

Alex stood, dusted himself off, and paced back and forth.

Now *what do I do? That massive thing was curled up around the plate. There's no way it got up there itself, so Sekun-ak or one of his hunters must have put it up there. How? That's a problem for another time. I've got more urgent concerns.*

Alex walked away from the flat rock, hoping a new perspective would help him solve the puzzle. He racked his brain for ideas and came up blank. Eventually, he remembered a show he had seen on the National Geographic channel. It had been about snake handlers.

Most of it had been about people who handled snakes with their bare hands, but he wasn't about to try to do that with the monster up on the rock.

While he contemplated, the sun moved inexorably toward the horizon. Whatever he was going to do, he needed to do it fast.

That show had also shown someone in India corralling a huge poisonous snake using a long piece of wood with a forked end.

That's it. That's what I can do.

Alex looked around desperately. The woods had thinned out to just a few scrub trees near the river, so he hurried back the way he came, looking for a tree with a limb that could work. After a quarter mile of stopping and starting, examining each tree, he found an elm tree that looked like it might serve his purpose.

The next challenge was that he was only equipped with his cudgel, which wasn't much use in cutting off a limb. He searched around the trail until he found a sharp-edged rock. He used that to hack at the limb until he was able to break it free. It had a forked end like he wanted, but the tree was green and the limb was springy. Once he held it in his hands, though, the springiness made him wonder if it would lift the behemoth he had just seen on that rock without dropping it. The last thing he wanted to do was try to lift it and have it fall.

A twelve-foot rattlesnake was bad enough. He couldn't imagine what a twelve-foot *pissed off* rattlesnake would be like.

Alex looked up and saw another limb, thicker than the first, that was a little higher up the tree. He weighed the time it would take to retrieve it now versus the time it would take to run to the rock, try the other limb and run back here if it failed.

He glanced at the sun and decided to play it conservatively for once.

He climbed up the tree a few branches—an activity he had hoped to avoid for a long time after what he'd gone through the day before—and again hacked at the limb until he was able to tear it free.

He climbed quickly down, gathered up the stronger limb and ran for the flat rock.

Back at the rock, he hurriedly plucked the stray small limbs and leaves from it until he had a reasonable facsimile of the forked stick he remembered.

He moved around so that he was behind where he remembered the snake's head had been and climbed the shale. He was impatient. He could feel time ticking away. Halfway up, he slipped back to the bottom.

Slow is smooth. Smooth is fast.

He patiently put one foot after the other until he again got close enough to the top that he could peer over the edge of the flat rock. The snake was facing away from Alex.

Perfect.

He lifted the stick up and held it parallel to the flat rock. As he extended it, it got heavier, and he was worried he would scrape it against the rock and alert the snake. His muscles quivered, but he managed to keep it aloft.

When the forked end of the limb was just a few inches from the thick body of the rattler, he gathered his strength and simultaneously lowered the stick and jabbed it forward.

The snake immediately raised its head and tail and twisted around toward Alex. Its rattles echoed like a deadly warning that Alex knew he had no choice but to ignore. Muscles bulging, Alex leveraged the branch against the edge of the rock and leaned his weight into it.

That lifted the snake up, up, up. Alex had *over*estimated how much force was required. The rattler flew straight toward his face.

For the second time, Alex jumped backward in surprise, fear, and shock. He stumbled down the shale hill and this time fell face first onto the hard ground. A split-second later, he pushed himself to his feet and backpedaled with lightning speed. The flight and fall had momentarily stunned the rattler, but it recovered quickly, coiled itself and prepared to strike. A rattlesnake can strike at a distance between one-third and one-half its body length—quite a distance for a snake this size. By the time it sprang, Alex was out of range.

The snake recoiled itself, lifted its magnificent rattles into the air and shook them in frustration.

Alex hurried around to the other side of the hill and slowly climbed back up, keeping one wary eye on the snake.

This time when he peeked over the edge, there was nothing but the plate sitting there. He reached out, grabbed it, and jumped down, landing on his feet for once.

He glanced at the sun, which seemed perilously low in the sky.

No time to think. I've gotta move.

Alex slipped the plate into his pack and took off. He set the pace he had long ago learned was the fastest he could move without dropping from exhaustion after a mile or two.

His moccasin-clad feet pounded against the game trail. After just a quarter mile, he slowed a little. His optimal pace was based on starting at full health and not already being exhausted. After his adventure with the sugar pine the previous day, neither of those things was true. He was tempted to keep one eye on the sun's progress but decided instead to blank everything out of his mind except for the mechanical motion of putting one foot in front of the other.

He made steady progress. After a mile, he saw a long, thick stick lying across the path in front of him, twenty-five yards away.

Don't remember that being there on the way to the river.

Rather than maneuver around it, he decided to just jump over it. It wasn't until he was right on top of it that he saw that it was no stick. It was another western diamondback rattler, sunning itself. This one wasn't as immense as the specimen he had encountered at the flat rock, but it no doubt had fangs and venom.

Alex had competed in both the long jump and the triple jump in high school. That served him well. He planted his right foot, sprang off his left, and soared above the snake. It saw him coming and struck upward, but Alex's leap carried him well over it.

Mental note: don't jump over any more long sticks.

That turned out to be a good strategy. Where the path had been clear on his trip to the river, he came across four more rattlers of various sizes before he reached the forest. Once he knew what they were, they were easy to avoid. Only the first one had posed any real danger to him.

When he reached the forest, Alex knew that he would be almost completely out of sight of the sun for the rest of the trip. He stopped, measured where it hung in the sky and estimated how long it would take him to reach the cliffs. He didn't like the answer he came up with.

A steady pace has to go out the window. I've gotta give it all I've got. Be all that I can be, *like the old ad used to say.*

He took one long drink from his water bag and ran—not jogged—toward the settlement. He moved so fast that he didn't have time to exchange any kind of greeting with the lookouts as he ran past them.

When he reached the cutoff toward the cliffs, he turned left and glanced up, but couldn't see the sun, which was blocked by the tall trees to the west. It was possible he had already lost.

It didn't matter. Alex sprinted toward what he had already come to think of as home. He had been a jumper in high school because he wasn't fast enough to run any of the sprints or middle distances. On this occasion, though, he ran like he had a stiff wind pushing him along.

He was dirty, beyond exhausted, and hurt in a hundred places. And he ran on.

When he hit the meadow, he saw something completely unexpected. The children of the tribe were lined up, waiting for him. When he reached them, they turned and ran alongside him, cheering for him with the wild abandon of children of any era.

Alex had thought his tank was empty, but the cheers of the children gave him one last spark. He increased his speed again and sprinted straight toward the armory.

Sekun-ak, his hunters, and Alex's small rooting section—Dan, Malen-eh and Janta-ak—waited there for him. Alex skidded to a stop, too out of breath to speak. Instead, he simply handed over the backpack that contained the plate. He turned and looked west.

The sun was still an eyelash above the hills.

He had done it.

He fell to one knee, too exhausted to be jubilant. The children were not. They raised their hands above their heads, jumped, whooped and hollered.

Monda-ak took advantage of Alex being more at his height and attacked him with wet kisses from his magnificent tongue, which was already five inches long and resembled a head of cauliflower at the tip.

Dan, Malen-eh, and Janta-ak gathered around Alex, lifting him up, smiling and laughing.

Sekun-ak reached inside the pack and pulled out the plate. This time, his face showed a certain grudging respect.

"Final test tomorrow," he said. "Same time."

Alex looked at Dan and said, "There were snakes. The biggest rattler I've ever seen in my life was curled up around that plate. How the hell did they do that?"

Dan smiled ruefully. "I guess I should have told you. Balta-ak, the hunter with the scars on his arms, is a snake-charmer. He has a magic touch with them. It's like he hypnotizes them and makes them do his will. Damnedest thing I've ever seen."

"It was almost the end of me. The rattler missed me, but I nearly died of a heart attack when I saw it."

Dan glanced at Sekun-ak's retreating back. "Let's get you some food, water, and a bed. After these first two, I hate to think what he's got lined up for the last one."

Chapter Fifteen
A Quest IV

At apex the next day Alex and Dan met Sekun-ak at the armory once again. Monda-ak nipped playfully at their heels as they walked.

Whatever cockiness Alex might have felt the first two days was gone. He knew that instead of simply questing for a position in the tribe, he might be fighting for his life.

Sekun-ak stood in front of the armory; arms crossed against his chest.

"Gunta," Alex said to him.

"Gunta," Sekun-ak mumbled, then looked down at Dan. Unlike the first two days, when his instructions were complicated, today he was brief.

"He says all you have to do is capture a desma-ta and bring it back. You can stay out as long as you want, but I think you need to return before it gets dark. The area where the desma-ta lives is not dangerous in the daytime, but I don't think you'd survive out there after dark. If you return to camp without one, you have failed at the task."

"I'm afraid to ask, but what is a desma-ta? Some poisonous lizard? A badger the size of a grizzly?"

"No, the danger is not in the capture, but in the likelihood that you won't be able to do it. You would probably call a desma-ta a prairie dog, but unlike what you might remember from our time, this is much larger."

"Of course it is. Why does he think I can't catch one?"

"Like prairie dogs, they live in a community of tunnels. They are also lightning quick. It's easy to find them, but damn hard to get your hands on them. And even if you do, you'll be surprised how hard they are to subdue. They have teeth and claws and will fight when forced to."

"And he says he wants it alive? That seems odd for a hunting challenge."

"It's so much harder to deliver a live desma-ta than a dead one. To bring in a dead one, you could find their tunnels and take one out with a bow and arrow when it pops its head up."

"Okay. I get it. This isn't supposed to be easy. Where can I find them?"

Dan quickly gave Alex directions to find the desma-ta tunnel system, then said, "Stay here. I need to get you something."

Dan hurried away, then returned with a large, empty leather bag. "Use this to carry the thing back if you actually grab one. You don't want to have to wrestle it all the way home."

Alex folded the bag and slipped it inside his backpack. "Thank you. I'll be back with a desma-ta or die trying."

"That's what I'm afraid of."

Alex kneeled and held Monda-ak's face in his hands. "This is the last time, okay? After today, I won't leave you anymore."

The dog whined as though he didn't believe him.

"Hold onto him, will ya? I don't want him following me and getting devoured by Ronit-ta or being a small snack for Godat-ta."

"You got it brother," Dan said nervously. "Don't be a hero out there, all right? If you can't catch one, you can't catch one. Come back and we'll find you something else to do."

"I know, I know. Malen-eh can always use help with the laundry, right?"

"I can be such an asshole sometimes."

"As we've discussed. No worries. I'll be back."

Alex left the compound at a more leisurely pace than he had the day before. He didn't have the same strict timer on him, and he didn't have as far to travel. He didn't want to dawdle, but he also didn't want to exhaust himself before he got there.

The children didn't seem as excited by today's quest as they had been the day before, ignoring him as he passed through the field toward the forest.

Alex turned left onto the game trail and walked south for a few hundred yards. He came to a tree that had been hit by lightning and was mostly charred, but still stood. He slowed and continued for a few yards until he saw a barely visible game trail that shot off from the main path. He pushed through the forest, using his cudgel to push barbed vines out of his way. Dan had warned him that these vines not only tore at the skin, but also were tipped with low-grade poison.

He came to the edge of the forest and his view opened onto the large plain. He knew he wasn't far from where the tribe was attacked by the Ronit-ta, so he paused. He didn't see any sign of the wolves' backs cutting through the grass like a great white shark's dorsal fin.

That doesn't mean they're not out there, though, does it?

He looked left and right and found a tree that was ripe for climbing. He climbed up forty feet and had a much superior view of the open plain.

A little reconnoitering never hurt anybody.

He peered out at the swaying grass, staring at each section for several long minutes.

If they're there, they're disguised as grass.

As quietly as possible—it was never a good idea to make noise when you could just as easily be the prey as the hunter—he climbed down.

He continued south along the edge of the forest, constantly casting a cautious eye out over the open plain.

Just as Dan said he would, he came upon an area where the grass stopped. There was a clearing a hundred yards square where there was only dirt, holes, and a few mounds with holes in the top.

Alex had seen prairie dogs before. He and his parents had stopped and watched them on their way to Devil's Tower in Wyoming when he was eleven. He didn't remember if those little guys were quick or not. All they had ever done was pop their head out of their hole, look around, and disappear again.

I'll probably be up against the same thing today.

He settled into a comfortable spot at the very edge of the wooded area, put his back against a tree and observed.

Initially, all he saw were holes and mounds.

I wonder if they felt the vibrations of my feet as I approached and went to ground. Some animals are hyper-sensitive to vibrations like that. It would help if I knew more about these creatures, but I can't exactly call up Wikipedia to read up on them now.

He craned his neck a little to get a better view. He remembered prairie dog holes to be only a few inches wide, but these were much bigger. Intended, of course, for much wider bodies.

Alex sat patiently for five minutes, ten. His quiet was eventually rewarded when a single head popped up out of one of the far holes. Its movements did seem to be surprisingly quick. It whipped its head around until it spotted Alex. It gave him the stink-eye for a few seconds, then disappeared back down the hole.

Alex reached into his backpack and pulled out some of the pemmican he had brought with him. He drank a little water, chewed on the pemmican—which he had come to like very much—and waited. After the challenges of the previous two days, he was glad for the rest.

Eventually, another desma-ta poked its head out of a hole a little nearer to the trees. Alex couldn't tell if it was the same one or not. Regardless, it gave him the same distrustful look for a few seconds, then disappeared.

Alex continued to sit and relax, doing his best to show he was just a lonely traveler and not someone who had come to capture one of their number.

While he waited, he considered his options. He could pull some vines and wind them into a cord, then try to lasso one. He soon rejected that idea. That seemed like something that worked much better in movies than in real life. He had dressed up as a cowboy for Halloween long ago, but he had no actual rope skills.

He glanced around and found some good-sized rocks. He might be able to throw it hard enough to knock one out.

He picked a promising rock and gave it a toss to gauge its heft. It was the size of a softball, but with ragged edges and a more oblong shape. He picked out a bush about twenty paces away, wound up and threw. The rock sailed wide of its intended target by five feet.

Not sure that's gonna work, either. What then? Chasing after them, leaping from hole to hole trying to play Whack-a-Mole sure isn't going to work. This needs more brainpower and less horsepower.

Alex put the rest of the pemmican back in his pack, and grabbed a few of the nuts and berries that Malen-eh had given him. He ate a few of the round red berries that most resembled huckleberries to him.

Of course.

He walked closer to the edge of the cleared space. A desma-ta that had been watching him dropped down into the safety of its hole. Alex approached still closer, until he was standing on dirt.

He sat down and waited.

Nothing moved for what felt like a long time. Then, the routine he had shared with the rodents a few minutes before began again, with one new addition. This time, when the first one popped its head up from a safe distance, it didn't just look at him—it barked. The noise was surprisingly loud and made Alex jump. That seemed to satisfy the desma-ta and it disappeared down the hole.

Didn't know they did that. Okay, now I'm ready for it.

Alex waited quietly. Several more times, one or another of the denizens of the community poked its head above ground to glare or bark at him. Alex waited and watched the sun and clouds move across the sky.

Eventually, he stood, stretched, and moved right into the middle of the clearing.

Again, he saw no activity at all for a long time, but eventually the furry brown creatures began popping up in the far corners to chastise him for invading their territory.

Alex waited until one popped up ten yards away and threw one of the red berries at it. It landed in front of the hole, but the desma-ta dropped down. All was quiet in the little clearing for what felt like forever to Alex.

This is a long game. Can't be in a hurry.

Eventually, one popped its head up and sniffed toward the berry. After a thorough examination, it gobbled the berry and retreated to its hole. It didn't drop all the way down though. It popped its head back out and stared at Alex.

Alex grinned. He tossed another of the berries so that it landed a little farther away from the hole.

The desma-ta glared at him, but snuck tentatively out of its hole, sniffed and ate it before retreating.

Alex repeated this exercise again and again, luring the creature out of its hole a little further each time. Finally, it came within five feet of him.

Still too far. If I dive for it, it'll be back down the hole before I get close. Then it will never trust me.

Alex reached into his bag and gathered up all his remaining fruit and nuts. He held it out to the rodent in both hands.

The desma-ta barked at him in frustration.

Alex shrugged and dropped the treasure back into his bag.

The overgrown prairie dog, who Alex estimated was two and a half feet tall, barked at him again.

Alex waited a long moment, staring calmly into the eyes of his opponent. Finally, he reached back into the bag and offered it again.

The desma-ta moved forward almost imperceptibly.

Come on, come on.

It came two steps closer, sniffing the air like a dog on a scent. It stopped and stared at Alex from there.

"I'm not throwing anymore," Alex said.

His voice did not startle it, but it did bark back, albeit quieter than normal.

The standoff continued. Alex refused to throw any more, the desma-ta refused to come any closer.

My dad taught me one thing about negotiating. Whoever can say goodbye and walk away wins.

For the second time, Alex moved to drop the food back into his pack.

The desma-ta reached out with its front paw as if to say, *Wait, don't be so hasty.*

Alex raised his eyebrows but held the food out in front of him again.

The rodent took one tentative step closer then paused. Alex didn't move.

Finally, the desma-ta gave in to its stomach and took the final steps to reach the food. It plucked out a fat, juicy berry and moved back slightly. Its eyes never left Alex's as it chewed the berry. It leaned forward to reach a nut.

Alex struck, snapping his left hand out to grab the rodent by the fur of its throat.

He anticipated a struggle but not the all-hell's-breaking-loose furor that happened next. The desma-ta kicked and bucked like a cyclone while simultaneously lashing out with its claws and doing its best to contort and bite the hand that held it.

It did manage to get its hind claw against Alex's bare arm, and it tore roughly down it, leaving bloody claw marks in its wake.

Alex reached around behind it and grabbed it by the scruff of the neck, hoping it would calm it like it did when he had grabbed his kitten that way back home.

It did not work that way.

The rodent redoubled its efforts to free itself, twisting, gnashing its teeth and trying its best to dig its claws into Alex again.

Alex considered banging its head into the solid ground to stun it or knock it out, but he couldn't bring himself to do it. The furry thing hadn't done anything wrong except to trust him not to hurt it.

Instead, he kept his hold firm and continued to wrestle with it. He knew his stamina was greater than the desma-ta. At least he hoped so.

As he thrashed around with it, the rest of its friends began poking their heads out of their burrows and barking wildly at him. As the fight continued, it sounded like he was in a kennel with dozens of angry dogs.

Alex paid them no mind. He knew they wouldn't come at him, no matter how furious they were. Again, at least he hoped so. He thought he was winning the battle with the rapidly tiring prairie dog, but didn't like his odds against a dozen or more of them.

Just at the point where Alex's arms ached so badly he thought he might lose his grip, the desma-ta gave up and hung loosely, defeated.

It gave a few last feeble kicks, but it was done for. It stared at Alex with hate in its eyes.

Alex continued to hold it by the scruff with his right hand and grabbed the bag he intended to stuff the creature into.

That was when the fight started again. It twisted, turned and fought with renewed vigor, not wanting to go into the bag.

Alex had held a vision in his head of opening the bag and slipping the exhausted animal smoothly inside. Instead, it turned out to be like trying to put toothpaste back in the tube—if the toothpaste was fighting tooth and claw.

Being so close, Alex was not going to give up, and eventually he prevailed. He got the live desma-ta tucked inside the bag, pulled the cord tight, and tied it.

He plopped down on the ground, so exhausted he wasn't sure he would be able to lift the bag to get it over his shoulders to carry home.

The cacophony of the barking prairie dogs continued.

Until it didn't.

Like a light switch, every one of them dropped down into their burrows and silence overtook the plain.

That's not good.

Chapter Sixteen
Letting Go

Alex had been so intent on his conquest of the desma-ta that he had let his vigilance slip. It wasn't until sudden silence came to the meadow that he realized his possibly fatal error.

He let the bag sag to the ground. Tied as tightly as it was, there was no way for the desma-ta to escape.

His right hand fell on the handle of the too-large cudgel that was the only weapon he had. His eyes scanned the horizon, trying to see what the prairie dogs had sensed.

The first thing he noticed was that the sun was near the horizon. It would be dark before long. He caught a furtive piece of movement in his peripheral vision to his left. He snapped his head, but it was already gone.

He used his training. He turned his body in the direction of where he had seen the glimpse of motion, then held his head still. He widened his eyes, looked straight ahead, and waited.

And there it was. Mottled gray fur slipping between a bush and a tree. Then another, and another.

Finally, emboldened, they gave up their hiding spot and stepped out into the open.

At first, Alex thought it was a pack of dogs. Then he realized how similar they all looked. Triangular ears. Long, narrow snouts. Tails held low.

Coyotes.

It was Kragdon-ah, so they were not the typical twenty- or twenty-five-pound specimens he was used to back home. These were still lean and hungry looking, but they were taller than any coyote he had ever seen. As they slowly appeared and stalked him, Alex counted their number.

Eight.

Even as exhausted as I am, I could likely handle a couple of them. But eight? No way.

Three coyotes padded around him at a safe distance and took up a position behind him. No matter how Alex turned, he had at least two of the mangy killers at his back.

They were in no hurry to go for the kill. Each time Alex turned and feinted at them with his club, they skittered away out of reach. They knew what the end result of this would be—a big meal to be shared by all of them.

Alex's mind raced, looking for a solution.

Coyotes can't climb. If I can get to the trees, I can at least jump up and try to outwait them. They'll tear that desma-ta apart as a consolation prize if I do.

Alex feinted again at the two coyotes that stood between him and the trees. They jumped back a step, but then squared up on him and the two behind him closed. One got close enough to bite the back of his leg before he swung the club down, catching it with a glancing blow. It cried out, then jumped back into position.

Alex saw the next few moves in his mind and knew he wouldn't survive them.

Amy will never know what happened to me. She will think I deserted her.

He swung the club with increasing desperation, but he had been exhausted when the fight had started. Now, he felt like the desma-ta had at the end of the fight. His spirit was willing, but his flesh was weak.

An arrow whizzed across the prairie and struck the coyote directly in front of Alex. At the same moment, a short spear sank into the side of another. Both shrieked in pain and surprise and turned to see what was attacking them. The others raised their hackles and went from a hunting posture to a defensive one. As a unit, they began to back away from Alex and move in the opposite direction from where they had come.

Alex gaped. Standing among the trees of the forest were Doken-ak, Janta-ak and Sekun-ak. Janta-ak held a bow with another arrow already notched. Doken-ak was fitting another short spear into his atlatl and Sekun-ak held a heavy spear ready to throw.

"What are you guys doing here?" Alex asked, then stopped, realizing he was speaking in English. He also realized he was so exhausted he could barely stand. The last three days had more than taken their toll.

Alex focused on his limited knowledge of Winten-ah and asked again, "Why are you here?"

Speaking slowly, enunciating each word, Doken-ak said, "Saving your skin."

"I thought no help for me," Alex said in pidgin-Winten-ah.

"No help with task," Sekun-ak said. "Help staying alive."

Alex kneeled for a moment to recover—from his exhaustion, from his surprise, from his survival, which had seemed a distant dream only a few moments before.

The three men approached him but stood casually around as though they were at a barbecue, not exposed in the land where everything wanted to kill you.

After a moment's rest, Alex did his best to lift the bag onto his shoulder to carry home.

Sekun-ak lifted his hand. "Desma-ta?"

Alex nodded. "Desma-ta."

Sekun-ak extended his hand. Alex handed the bag over. Sekun-ak untied the knot, held the bag at full arm's-length and turned it upside down. The desma-ta fell out of the bag and laid on its back for two long seconds, either playing dead or shocked at its sudden change of circumstance. Then it sprang to its feet and scrambled away. It ran to the nearest hole and turned and barked viciously at the men.

Alex tipped it a salute, glad that Sekun-ak had verified the result of the test here, so he didn't have to carry the little beast all the way back to the cliffside.

AND SO, MANTA-AK, BORN long ago as Alex Hawk, became a hunter for the Winten-ah.

There was no hunt scheduled immediately after Alex's completion of his three tasks, so he was able to rest and recuperate from his ordeals. The wounds he had received—the bad scrape on his leg, the deep scratches from the desma-ta—had time to heal.

Two weeks went by and he grew bored and anxious. He was never one to sit around and while away his days. He did what he could to make himself useful around camp. He discovered that the old people who sat in the uppermost chamber were unable to climb the ladders that high themselves, so a personal sling system had been developed.

When they woke in the morning, they needed to be carried, one at a time, up to their communal room. In the evenings, the process was reversed.

Alex volunteered for that job. The elders were taller than him but seemed to almost be fading away and weighed much less than he thought. Aided by the sling on his back, Alex was easily able to carry them.

No need for weightlifting or a gym when you've got people to carry.

Hard work is often its own reward, but carrying the elders had other benefits. They took a shine to him and shared stories, history and secrets Alex might not have ever learned any other way.

He also worked on training Monda-ak, who was growing so quickly it was almost frightening. Now that he was one of the tribe's hunters, he didn't worry about the food the dog went through every day. He knew he would help to replace it soon enough. Still, the dog's appetite was prodigious.

The little runt who had been half the size of his brother was now bigger than him, and the gap seemed to grow every day. Several times a week Alex and Tontu-ak, the man who was training the other dog from the same litter, met in the open space in front of the cliffs. They let the two brothers wrestle, fight and growl at each other. It wore the dogs out a little and brought them a little peace. Also, Tontu-ak was a deft trainer and he taught Alex so that Monda-ak would also be properly trained.

One afternoon, Tontu-ak and Alex were standing in the afternoon sunshine watching the two dogs tumble over each other, snapping and yowling when Sekun-ak approached.

Although Sekun-ak had not seemed to want Alex as a member of his hunting party, now that he had qualified, he treated Alex the same as any of the others. That is to say, abrupt.

"Come with me," Sekun-ak said to Alex.

Alex turned to Tontu-ak. "Will you watch Monda-ak? I'll find you."

Tontu-ak touched his forehead with two fingers, which was a Winten-ah way of nodding.

Alex followed Sekun-ak back to the armory, hoping he was about to be told his first hunting expedition would be soon.

Instead, when he entered the recessed room in the rock, he saw his belongings laid out on the table.

His stomach lurched. The sight of his rifle, his pistol, his clips and other trappings of civilization almost made him dizzy. The longer he was here, the more real Kragdon-ah seemed and the more dream-like twenty-first century Oregon felt.

"Time to destroy them."

Mixed feelings swirled inside Alex. Intellectually, he had already agreed to dispose of them, but now, faced with destroying what felt like his last link to his former life, he hesitated.

Still, he knew he was committed.

Sekun-ak bundled the remnants of technology in a thick cloth and handed it to Alex.

He was careful not to touch any of it. The dread of what technology brings runs so deep here.

Sekun-ak signaled for Alex to follow him again and made his way up the trails and ladders until they emerged in the large chamber where the egg ceremony had been held.

This time, instead of many smaller fires, there was one large bonfire burning in the middle. It was so large and hot that it threatened to overwhelm the natural ventilation system as smoke hung against the ceiling.

The room was not crowded. There were a dozen tribe members seated against the far wall. Sekun-ak left Alex and took the only empty chair.

Alex felt alone and unsure, but when he looked to his left, Dan was there.

"It's simple. All you have to do is drop that bundle in the fire. Then you're done. You've fulfilled your oath."

"That's crazy. I can't drop my clips into a fire. It could kill someone."

Dan nodded, anticipating the question. "I told them about that. They asked me to dispose of the ammunition, which I did. I made sure there wasn't one in the chamber of your pistol and checked everything over to make sure nothing will happen." He paused, looked at the bundle Alex was holding. "It's a shame. Those are beautiful guns."

Alex remembered the warrior in the forest doing his best to destroy the rifle.

"They were. They might be disappointed, though. As hot as that fire is, it's not going to melt the guns."

"Told them that too. It's a symbolic thing to them. Tomorrow, after the fire has burned out, I'm to take anything left and throw it off a bluff into the deepest part of the river. No one will ever find them again."

Alex's shoulders sagged, but he nodded. "Okay. I gave them my word."

Since it was a ceremony, Alex didn't want to just hurry up to the fire, toss the bundle in and walk away. That felt disrespectful to him.

Instead, he approached the fire slowly, stopped in front of it and stared into the flames for several long moments. He solemnly held the bundle in front of him and positioned it as close to the middle of the fire as he could get without singeing his eyebrows.

He dropped the last vestiges of his previous life into the fire. The flames leaped so high he could not see what remained of his former life.

PART TWO

Chapter Seventeen
The Hunt

Alex Hawk sprinted across the open plain. His moccasined feet pounded out a steady rhythm and his breath puffed visibly in the chill air. He was not cold, though—his buckskin overshirt and pants saw to that. Monda-ak loped easily alongside him.

Alex held his long, heavy spear low, knowing he could move it to the throwing position in a split-second. He scanned to his left and called to a tall hunter loping a few yards away, "Domit na sloda!" which was Winten-ah for "Look, it's tiring!" After three years, he spoke the language as well as Dan Hadaller.

Thirty yards ahead of Alex, a black-tailed buck ran on, but as Alex had noted, it was flagging. An arrow sunk into its hindquarter bounced as it ran, but that wasn't what was slowing it.

When Alex became a Winten-ah hunter, he learned an entirely new way to hunt. As a boy, Alex and his father had sat in a blind and waited for a buck to come within firing distance of their guns. He had taken his first buck—and cut its throat, as tradition demanded of a first kill—when he was fourteen years old.

Those hunting methods did not work in Kragdon-ah. Very few animals were unwary enough to wander within range of a bow and arrow or atlatl spear. If they relied on the element of surprise, the Winten-ah would have been forced to become vegetarians.

Instead, they used the natural physical advantages that humans had. A black-tail deer was faster than a human. Much faster. But a human was mostly hairless—which allowed it to sweat, and thus cool down, even as it ran. Humans also had greater stamina than animals that relied on sprinting speed to stay alive.

The Winten-ah hunting method, then, was to send a group of trackers out hours ahead of the main expedition, find a target and follow it, but not too closely. They sent a runner back to the hunters, who led them to where the trackers were.

The hunters would run at the animal, shrieking, waving clubs and firing a few arrows. That made for a fearsome sight, but it was intentionally ineffective. They only wanted to spook the deer—or the elk or whatever they were hunting—raise its fear levels, its heartbeat, its entire metabolism.

The deer would sprint away, easily leaving the hunters behind. They would follow at a fast but maintainable pace, using the trackers again if they got too far behind. Each time they drew near, the deer would jump away again, but each time it ran a shorter distance before being winded and overheated. Its fur covering, so necessary to withstand the vagaries of weather, was its own undoing, as it never got a chance to cool down.

Eventually, it wore down, which was what was happening now. The hunting party had been chasing this buck for almost five hours. The warriors were tired as well but were getting their second wind. They knew the end of the hunt was near.

Finally, as it always did, the buck overheated to a point it could not run any more. It slowed to a trot, then stood still, even as the hunters ran at it. It had given everything it had to give. It stamped its feet and shook its antlers at the oncoming hunters, but it was for naught.

From twenty yards away, Alex raised the heavy spear that had become his primary hunting weapon. He bunched the muscles of his right arm and threw as he ran.

The spear flew straight and true, piercing the heart of the massive buck, which fell, dead before it hit the ground.

Alex and the other warriors screamed their victory to the skies. They were the ultimate predator—at least if Godat-ta was not in the vicinity—and they screamed their supremacy.

Alex Hawk now looked like any other Winten-ah warrior. His hair was long and held back by a leather tie. He was leaner than he had been when he stepped through the door three years earlier, but he was more finely muscled. He spent so many hours in the sun, his skin had bronzed. If he hadn't been a head shorter than all the other hunters and hadn't had blue eyes, he might have passed for a Winten-ah.

After taking a few minutes to rehydrate and rest after the chase, most of the hunters set up a perimeter around the animal. Meanwhile, two of the hunters kneeled over the carcass of the buck. They lowered their head and chanted, thanking it for the sacrifice of its life and giving them its strength.

After a moment of silence passed, the two men laid out their tools and began field dressing the buck. They were experienced and skilled. Within an hour, they had finished.

The tribe had a use for almost all parts of the animals the hunters killed. The few parts that had no use to the tribe were left for the scavengers.

The meat, the hooves, the hide and the antlers were divided up and carried back to their cliffside home. The meat would be eaten, either fresh, salted, or turned into pemmican. The hooves would be hollowed and turned into receptacles for drinking or storing powders and liquids. The antlers would be ground into a paste that Niten-eh, the medicine woman, would use in her potions.

On this day, the deer had run west, so they were farther from camp than normal and would not make it home until after dark. It was not optimal, but they had flint to start a fire and torches to light. The strength of their numbers and animals' natural fear of fire kept them safe as they hiked.

They finally made it through the forest that surrounded Winten-ah long after dark. The dazzling field of stars and near-full moon allowed them to snuff their torches as they emerged from the forest.

When they reached the cliffside, a dozen women waited for them there. The hunters' return meant they had completed their job and were relieved of all further responsibilities. The women's tasks were just beginning, and they would work through the night, butchering and preparing the meat so it wouldn't spoil.

The hunters would only be able to rest for one day before they launched another hunt. A single buck—even one as big as the one they had taken down—wouldn't feed the tribe for long, and winter was coming. Winter was always coming.

After three years, Monda-ak in no way resembled the pitiful, dying furball that Alex had first met. His shoulder now reached almost to Alex's chin. If he stood and rested his paws on Alex's shoulders, it nearly drove Alex to his knees. He had never been weighed, but it was possible he was twice as heavy as Alex. Around the tribal home, he was as mellow as a summer breeze. He loved to play and romp with the children in the field in front of the caves. He wasn't quite as big as a pony, but the children rode him as if he were.

In a hunt, though, his primal instincts loomed large. There were a number of hunts in the previous three years where the hunters didn't strike the killing blow because Monda-ak got there first.

As to backing Alex up in a fight, he was an unknown. Anyone who might have been tempted to pick a fight with Alex quickly changed their mind when they saw Monda-ak at his side.

Dan had not been exaggerating when he told Alex how intelligent the dogs were. Over the years, Alex had trained Monda-ak to not only recognize hand signals, but some rudimentary sign language. Alex often had long conversations with him, and he believed that he understood. He was the only animal in Kragdon-ah who understood and responded to commands in English as well as Winten-ah.

Alex and Monda-ak were inseparable. They ate together—though the dog consumed the vast majority of the food—slept together, and spent all day, every day, together.

Three years earlier, on the third day of his tests to become a hunter, Alex had told Monda-ak that would be the last time he left him. They hadn't been separated for more than a few minutes at a time since.

The first time the trader who had sold Monda-ak to the tribe returned with another litter, he gawked at the dog.

"That cannot be the same animal."

Alex had smiled at him but said nothing. He was satisfied enough with the look of regret the trader had on his face. Trading a single basket for Monda-ak had become a legendary trade in the history of the tribe. After three years, Ganku-eh and Banda-ak had still not asked Alex to fulfill his part of that bargain, but he knew it was coming someday.

As other tribe members asked to become hunters, Alex learned that Sekun-ak did indeed give them the same challenges he had been given—with a few minor exceptions. The younger tribe members were only required to bring back a pinecone and piece of limb from the sugar pine with no size requirements. That meant they didn't have to climb as high as Alex did and didn't have to face the worst of the winds, not to mention the wrath of the eagle.

Also, no rattler ever appeared when they ran to the river. It was just a test of stamina, not how to outwit a giant rattlesnake.

One thing remained constant, though. When the hopeful hunter-to-be went to capture the desma-ta, three armed hunters trailed along behind him and kept him from being killed while he concentrated on the task at hand.

That prairie dog challenge was where most apprentice hunters failed. As a rule, they could climb anything and run distances easily. But capturing the giant prairie dogs took brainpower instead of quick reflexes and strong muscles.

After three years, Alex still thought of Amy every day. He marked the annual anniversary of his arrival in Kragdon-ah not because of himself, but because it was her birthday. He knew how fast she grew, and spent many hours trying to age her forward in his mind. He dreamed of her often, but she never spoke to him in any of those dreams. She always remained at a distance, elusive and silent.

He was an accomplished hunter now and had a much better idea of the dangers and survival techniques of this world, but he still didn't believe he had any chance of making it back to the door. No single hunter or warrior from the Winten-ah would ever attempt to cross the open plain on their own.

He had asked to go with the expedition to retrieve karak-ta eggs each time they went. Each time he was turned down. Ganku-eh, who was still chief of the tribe, gave Alex his freedom in everything but this.

When he asked why, she said it was because he was too old to run with the younger men, but Alex noticed that Doken-ak still went, and he was an old man.

The most painful thought to Alex was what he would do if he *did* make it back to the ocean and the door was gone. Until that happened, at least he still had hope. If he arrived at that spot and the door was gone, he would know Amy was lost to him forever.

Alex made many friends within the tribe. His first friend had been Doken-ak, and though the old man did not speak much, he and

Alex spent many hours together in companionable silence. Doken-ak had shown Alex how to make a fishing rod and hooks and they made regular trips to a lake that was within walking distance. Silence and fishing went together.

Dan Hadaller remained his best friend, aside from Monda-ak. They shared a common background that no one else in this world could relate to or begin to understand. Alex had lived in that world forty years after Dan had stepped through the door, but they rarely discussed those intervening years, with one exception. Dan was a baseball fan and he pumped Alex for information on how his fa-vorite team, the San Francisco Giants, had done.

Alex was not a big sports fan, but he did remember that the Gi-ants had won several World Series, which made Dan happy to an un-likely degree.

Everything else—the Challenger Explosion, the fall of the twin towers, the advent of the Internet and other technologies—remained a mystery to Dan. He was happiest that way. He only remembered the simpler times of the 1970s.

Chapter Eighteen
Stama

Several days after the hunt where Alex brought down the black-tailed deer, he, Doken-ak and Dan Hadaller sat around a fire in one of the common rooms, talking. More accurately, Dan and Alex were talking, and Doken-ak was staring at the fire. Monda-eh sat a few feet away, tongue lolling, his eyes never leaving Alex.

It was midway between the summer and winter solstice. Daylight grew shorter and the later afternoons had begun to turn colder.

Life in Kragdon-ah consisted of long stretches of quiet broken by occasional moments of sheer panic. A few weeks earlier, a Ronit-ta—a dire wolf—had run into the open field in front of the cliff. One of the guards in the blind had seen it, but it had been too far away for him to do anything but sound his horn.

Everyone in the field scrambled to safety and Sekun-ak and his hunters had quickly dispatched it, but it was a good reminder that there was no such thing as real safety in a world so wild.

Ganku-eh was afraid that the wolf's attack might have been caused by sickness, so they had carried it to the open plain and left it there for the scavengers.

Since then, it had been quiet.

Until it wasn't.

Alex, Dan and Doken-ak's conversation was disturbed by the sound of a lookout's horn blowing.

Three blasts of the horn—two long, one short—told them some-one was approaching, but it wasn't a war party.

Alex and Dan peered down to see what—or who—was coming. It was unusual for visitors to arrive during non-trading times.

A procession of six people walked into the clearing and waited. Like the traders that often appeared, they looked like Winten-ah with certain small exceptions in dress and jewelry.

Women hurried out to the clearing and removed the curious children who were eyeing the visitors. Moments later, Ganku-eh and Banda-ak emerged from the cliffside and approached the strangers.

In Kragdon-ah, people did not shake hands. Instead, they each extended their right arm and rested it on the left shoulder of the person they greeted. The Winten-ah chieftain and her husband greeted each of the visitors in turn.

Ganku-eh turned and spoke to a nearby woman who disappeared up into the caves.

The group was too far below them for Dan and Alex to hear, so they had to make do with guesses based on body language.

Doken-ak had not moved from his spot by the fire, but he uttered a single word: "Stama."

Alex and Dan turned to look at him. 'Stama' was a word rarely used by the Winten-ah. The mere mention of it caused old women to spit on the ground and turn away. Its meaning was complex, but it spoke of both magic and technology. It was one element all tribes within a thousand miles could agree on. Stama was bad.

"What do you mean, 'stama'?" Alex asked.

Doken-ak said nothing more, but just continued to watch the dancing flames.

Far below, tribe members had brought chairs to the meadow. The eight of them sat in a tight circle.

They sat together for more than an hour, then food was brought out to them, and they shared a meat stew made partially with the deer the hunters had just killed. They continued talking until after the sun was down.

Outsiders were never brought up into the cliffside under any circumstance, but on this evening, sleeping mattresses and covers were brought down and laid at the edge of the meadow for them. It would have been barbaric to send the visitors out into a cold, dangerous Kragdon-ah night.

The Winten-ah were not barbarians.

While the beds were being set up, the meeting continued.

Although there was no communication method in the cliffs beyond mouth to ear, word of the visitors' purpose spread through the entire community before they had finished their stew.

Doken-ak had been correct.

The group had come to warn of another tribe, the Denta-ah, who were going against the universally agreed-upon covenant against stama.

It was heresy. It was against ancient tribal agreements.

It could lead to war.

There were stories passed down over the generations about tribes who had committed this heresy. Each time, all the other tribes had banded together and destroyed them. It was the price for breaking the one inviolate law of the land.

That was all Dan and Alex were able to glean. They were not on the council of the Winten-ah. They were not even officially tribe members. They would have to wait to learn more. They returned to the fire and engaged in one of mankind's favorite sports: speculation and formulating wild theories.

As it turned out, they didn't have to wait long. A runner appeared and told Alex and Dan they were summoned to the gathering below.

Darkness had fallen and a fire pit had been built where they were meeting, along with a row of torches to chase away the darkness.

Alex and Dan approached the group but did not speak.

The visitors considered the two men for long moments. Finally, a man dressed in a long calfskin robe spoke in the universal language of Kragdon-ah.

"Yes. Like them."

Alex glanced at Dan, who stared diffidently down into the fire.

"Go to the council room," Ganku-eh said in English, knowing no one else would understand her. "I'll meet you there."

For some reason, Alex felt like saluting, but he fought the urge. Instead, he and Dan climbed back up the cliffside and went to the room where all official Winten-eh business was conducted.

They had more information now but were still confused.

"Like us?" Alex asked. "What does that mean? Is there someone else who stepped through the door? Or, are there other doors?"

Dan shook his head. "No way to know."

After Alex and Dan had chased their own tails for half an hour, Ganku-eh, Banda-ak, and Sekun-ak climbed the ladder into the room. Their faces were uniformly grim.

The three of them joined Alex and Dan around the fire.

"It is bad news," Ganku-eh said. "Our way of life is threatened. The Denta-ah are breaking our most sacred law. Those who came today claim to have seen this with their own eyes. I have known Yosta-ak for many years and never known him to be untruthful. Still, for something of this importance, we must be sure."

"Why were we summoned to the meeting?" Dan asked.

"There is a rumor that another like you has joined with the Denta-ah. Again, Yosta-ak says he has seen him with his own eyes. He says this man brought many ideas with him. Instead of killing him as they should, the Denta-ah have welcomed him. Together, they are determined to recreate the stama that once destroyed our world. If it is true, both the Denta-ah and this man must be destroyed."

Beside her, both Banta-ak and Sekun-ak touched two fingers to their forehead in agreement.

"We have decided the best course is to travel and see the truth for ourselves. We have a group setting out at first light. Manta-ak, you will accompany them."

It was not a request.

Alex's eyebrows rose in surprise. He was perpetually ready for an adventure and he had hoped to see more of what Kragdon-ah was like, but he had not expected to go on a mission that seemed so important.

"Of course," was all he said. His heart beat faster at the thought of heading out into the wilderness of this strange world.

"I understand your surprise," Ganku-eh said. "Normally, I would not send you. But, if there is someone like you and you have a chance to see or meet him, I would like your perceptions of him."

Alex lifted two fingers to his forehead to agree. "How many of us are going?"

"We will join with Yosta-ak and his party. You, Sekun-ak and Doken-ak will be going with them."

At first, Alex wondered why Doken-ak would go. Why send someone so old? Then he remembered how wise Doken-ak was on those occasions he did speak and that he was part of all the expeditions to the ocean. He was older, but he had the strength and stamina of a younger man. He was also among the best in the tribe at surviving outside the confines of the cliff. He could fish, and his knowledge of what berries and roots were safe was surpassed only by Niten-ah.

Ganku-eh dismissed Alex and Dan with a wave and fell into deep conversation with Sekun-ak and Banda-ak.

As they climbed down, Dan said, "You're not going to sleep tonight, are you?"

"What do you think?"

"I think your head and heart are already out in the open space, hoping for adventure."

"I can't say you don't know me."

"All right. Let's get you ready to go. If I were you, I'd carry a second water bag in your pack. There are times where it's a long way between water sources."

Alex nodded. "Good. What else?"

"Load up on pemmican. I know it can get monotonous, but it's packed with fat and protein. You can pick up berries and things on the trail. Just check with Doken-ak before you eat anything."

"What about weapons?"

"You can take your spear, but I'm not sure I would. It's heavy and awkward. If it comes down to a fight, it might only take out one person. If it was me on a journey like this, I think I'd go with my club attached to my belt on one side and a rock hammer on the other. I've seen you with those tools, and you're dangerous. Of course, your best weapon is Monda-ak."

The dog, who had been laying with its massive head between its gigantic paws, looked up at the sound of his name.

"I can't carry enough food to feed him on the trail. Should I leave him behind?"

"No. He might not survive it. Once these dogs bind themselves to someone, they almost can't be separated. Don't worry, he'll be able to help provide on the trail. His breed can find a surprising amount of food on their own."

"I guess that's it, then."

Alex moved up and down the cliff gathering what he needed for the journey. When he had completed that task, he and Monda-ak sat at the edge of one of the caves. Alex dangled his legs over the side, stared at the stars, and waited for light.

Chapter Nineteen
Stipa-ah

Alex adjusted the pack so it was more comfortable. They had been on the march for almost four hours and he had learned long ago that when something chafes, it never improves on its own.

The nine humans had not stopped to even empty their bladders since they left Winten-Ah. Except for Monda-ak, of course, who did that whenever he liked.

For the most part, the group walked in silence, preferring to stay constantly vigilant. Neither Sekun-ak nor Doken-ak were much when it came to talking, and the other six tended to speak in their own language, which Alex couldn't understand.

Alex had watched the six strangers as they walked, and he had concluded that Yosta-ak wasn't just the leader of the group, but the others were primarily there to keep him safe. That sat well with Alex. He wasn't sure what value Yosta-ak would bring in a tense situation, but the others were heavily armed and seemed comfortable with their weapons.

Several times, Monda-ak had proven Dan's prediction right by leaving the trail they were on and returning a few minutes later with a piece of fur or feathers stuck to his fangs. He seemed to think the whole trek was one big wildlife buffet.

They had left that part of the country that Alex was familiar with. Or, more accurately, they had left the area behind that Alex was familiar with *in this time frame*. There was a time or two that Alex saw a geographic landmark that rang memory chimes for him. It was incredibly difficult to equate a wild area, overgrown with trees and bushes, and match it with a memory of a small town he had passed through in his earlier life.

There was nothing like a road system in Kragdon-ah, but there were a series of paths that seemed familiar to Yosta-ak. He navigated them as sure-footedly as a long-haul trucker who had long-since memorized every turn on his route. Each time the group came to a fork in the road, or when a path began to peter out, he knew which way to go.

It had been cloudy and cold since they left Winten-ah, but in early afternoon, it also began to rain. It wasn't a heavy rain, but the typical unending sprinkles that Alex was so familiar with.

Yosta-ak, who had been in the lead since the beginning, said something to the man behind him. It was in Yosta-ak's language, so Alex could not follow. Yosta-ak dropped back to the rear, where the three Winten-ahs marched.

"There is a rock overhang just ahead. We will stop there and eat. We can't stop long, though. I know of a spot where we will be safe overnight, but it is still far away."

Five minutes later, they found the rock overhang. All the men—even Doken-ak, by far the oldest in the group—sat easily on their haunches and pulled food from their packs. Alex gave Monda-ak a hand signal that set him free to hunt for his own lunch.

To the men of Kragdon-ah, they were on a sacred mission, one that would protect their beliefs and way of life.

As for Alex, as much as he had blended into Winten-ah, he still had no fear of technology. It certainly wasn't magic to him. In his three years living in the caves on the cliff, he had found he didn't miss all that he had left behind. He had put his cell phone on his workbench before he walked through the door. He hadn't thought of it since.

He didn't miss television, the Internet, or even his truck.

He only missed Amy.

Yosta-ak ended Alex's daydreams by standing and putting on his pack. He pointed ahead to a long, green hill that rose in elevation until the peak got lost in low-lying fog.

"Now, we climb," Yosta-ak said, and Alex gave one short whistle. Monda-ak burst through the underbrush and took his place padding alongside Alex.

Dan says they become completely dependent on us emotionally, but I admit, I feel a lot better when he's right beside me, too.

Yosta-ak held up a hand. "One other thing. Rutan-ta lives in these hills. I don't believe she will bother us, but it is good to stay alert. If she does attack, it will always be from behind."

Alex felt a small tingle run up the back of his neck. Rutan-ta was the Kragdon-ah equivalent of a mountain lion. Like everything, Rutan-ta was much bigger than it had been in the twenty-first century.

Alex had no idea how or why the creatures in Kragdon-ah were so huge. He and Dan had many conversations about it, but neither of them were scientists. They also didn't have any realistic idea how far into the future they had gone when they stepped through the door.

They didn't know if it had been long enough that it was just evolution, or if something else was at work. Alex had a theory that because civilization had been gone for so long, a lot of the damage it had done to the environment was also gone. He thought that might cause a higher oxygen content, which might lead to animals growing larger. In the end, it was only a conversation, though they returned to it again and again to pass the time. Whatever their theories, the reality was the reality.

At the moment, that reality included a cougar that was likely the size of a brown bear that might be stalking them that afternoon.

Alex's head was always on a swivel when he was outside the safety of the cliffside, but knowing a big cat might be watching him increased his wariness.

The hill they climbed was deceptively steep. There were parts where the path took switchbacks to facilitate the climb. Still, they ended up cutting branches for makeshift walking sticks.

Monda-ak needed no such thing. As big as he was, he was agile and climbed every obstacle easily. If not for his coloring, he might have been mistaken for a shambling bear himself.

Yosta-ak said that there was a cave ahead where they could stop for the night, but at this time of year, the sun set early and darkness wasn't far behind. On many rainy days in autumn, it could feel like it never got fully light at all, even at apex.

They finally reached the peak of the hill after several hours of hard climbing. For just a moment, the rain ceased, and the last of the sun's rays poked through the clouds. They stood in a clearing and looked out over a scene Alex would never forget.

A small river wound its way lazily through a valley filled with green trees that seemed to roll on forever. The golden light of the unexpected sunshine bouncing off the clouds added an ethereal element that made the whole picture feel almost supernatural.

This is what this same scene might have looked like a million years ago. The Earth is healing itself from whatever damage we inflicted on it.

Beautiful as the view was, they did not linger. Sunshine notwithstanding, it would be dark soon enough.

They walked down the hill, making sure to angle themselves and use their walking sticks to slow down. The hill was steep enough that if they weren't careful, they could find themselves hurtling down at an unstoppable speed.

Monda-ak, who had been occupying himself with small forays into the surrounding forest stayed near Alex's side. He bumped his head into Alex's hip, then stopped.

"Hold up," Alex called in the universal language. "He sees or smells something."

The men stopped, gathered into a knot and listened.

Monda-ak stood stiffly alert, tail out, ears up. He turned his head slowly, smelling the air. He took one, two, three, tentative steps forward, then paused again. He was completely still for two beats then barked. It started low in his cavernous chest, then exploded. He pointed his nose up at a tree just off the trail.

What I wouldn't give for my flashlight.

All nine men squinted into the gathering dusk. Then they saw it. A cat so huge that Alex wondered if it was a lion, not a cougar. Even that wasn't adequate. It hunkered on a branch like a cat might sit on a windowsill.

Having alerted Alex, Monda-ak stopped barking, but still growled deep in his chest—a resonant, menacing sound.

The big cat didn't seem bothered in the least that it had been spotted. It jumped easily down from the tree, landing silently. It stared at them with wide, golden eyes for a long moment.

The men had produced their weapons but held them at their sides. They showed no interest in taking the conflict to the cat. They waited to see if it would come at them.

Rutan-ta stared them down like the predator she was, but eventually dropped her head slightly and moved away. It moved sideways, so it never exposed itself. Eventually, it dropped out of sight ahead of them.

Gone, but definitely not forgotten.

Yosta-ak turned to the group. "Just making sure we knew she was here. They rarely attack people. There are so many easier animals to kill that can't fight back. Come. Let's hurry on."

They increased their pace but were still forced to complete the hill in almost pitch darkness.

Near the bottom, they found the promised cave. It was nothing like the caves of Winten-ah, which were light and open to the air. This cave was dark and dank, with bones scattered on the ground and it smelled like rotting meat.

They were thankful for it.

It was out of the rain, they could build a fire, and they only had a single entrance to defend.

Alex volunteered to take the first watch. He hadn't slept at all the night before, and hoped that after his watch he could grab a few hours of uninterrupted sleep.

While Alex stood guard, the others gathered wood. The surrounding area would have nearly qualified as a rainforest, though, so dry wood was sparse. They managed to get a fire going, but it sputtered and barely burned. It gave off almost no heat.

Alex and the others ate again from their backpacks.

When they had started, Alex had no idea how far they were going, but guessed it was likely two or three days. He had been wrong.

On the seventh morning after they left Winten-ah, he ate the last bit of pemmican from his bag and scraped around to find the last of his berries and nuts. He had been conserving his food for days, but even that had not been enough.

Yosta-ak gathered them around their latest accommodations—a rock overhang that kept them dry but not much else.

"Today, we will arrive at Stipa-ah. That means we are only a day's walk from Denta-ah. They are friends and they are the nearest tribe to Denta-ah. We will be able to learn what they know, and they will resupply us."

That's good. I was about to compete with Monda-ak for some of his prey, and I think he's a much better hunter than I am.

Alex shouldered his pack, which was much lighter than when they had set out, and they were off and walking at the same steady pace before the sun was up.

All villages or tribes in Kragdon-ah needed to be built with certain advantages in order to survive. It was difficult for a tribe to establish a home in the middle of an open prairie, for instance. Winten-ah was in an almost perfect location, with the cliff walls and surrounding forest to protect them.

Stipa-ah had another such location. They had built their community on a small island in the middle of a lake. The island was too small to sustain them, but its position in the lake made it easy to defend. Very few humans or animals were interested in swimming out to attack them.

At the same time, the Stipa-ah needed to get off their island to hunt and gather. They had spent years building up a rock pathway from the shore to their community. The rock path was only wide enough for one person to walk at a time, again giving them an easy-to-defend access.

The group pushed on, but the path they followed was level—a relief after the hills and valleys they had climbed in the previous week.

At mid-day, Yosta-ak stopped and pointed. "Smoke from their fires. We are close. We can dry our clothes and revive ourselves."

Alex looked in the direction Yosta-ak had pointed.

"They must have big fires there. That's a lot of smoke."

After half a mile more, they hiked around a bend, and the lake spread out in front of them.

The smoke was not from hearth fires. The village was burning.

The group of nine stepped off the path and blended into the surrounding woods.

Stipa-ah consisted of a series of low-slung buildings and lean-tos. At least half of them were still smoldering.

Alex stepped forward a bit to look for activity—any sign of life. There was none.

Doken-ak spoke for the first time in several days.

"I'll go first."

"I'm with you," Alex said.

The two men and Monda-ak approached the village slowly. Doken-ak let each footfall rest a moment before taking the next, constantly watching for any sign of movement.

Aside from the sounds of the fire, the village was quiet. There were no sounds of the wounded crying for help. No animals bleating. Just the fire, crackling.

From the edge of the lake, it was clear that it was the buildings on the perimeter of the village that were most badly damaged.

Doken-ak and Alex crossed the stone footpath to the island unmolested.

Doken-ak pointed to the ground where the footpath met the island. It was dark and stained with blood, but there were no bodies.

They hurried to the first of the buildings—a lean-to that looked like it had housed animals. It was deserted. They did a quick sweep of the surrounding buildings and found the same.

It looked like the Stipa-ah had set their own buildings ablaze and walked away.

Alex pointed to the roofs of the buildings. It was obvious the fire had started there and spread. In fact, all the roofs had collapsed down into the buildings.

Further into the village, the buildings—simple dwellings for sleeping and food storage were undamaged, but empty.

In the very heart of the village was an open square.

The bodies of dozens of Stipa-ah were piled in the middle of the square.

Chapter Twenty
Denta-ah

A cursory search of the rest of the island showed that the bodies piled in the square were the only remaining sign of the Stipa-ah.

Alex hurried back to the pathway and whistled sharply twice. The remaining members of the party emerged from the woods and hurried across to the village.

"Come," Alex said, gesturing to Yosta-ak. He led them to the village square, where Doken-ak was pulling bodies from the heap and laying them out side by side.

Yosta-ak approached the body of one of the men and pointed. "Henda-ak. He was the chief of the Stipa-ah."

Alex went about the grisly business of counting the bodies. Finally, he said, "Forty-two. Is that the whole tribe, or were there more?"

"There were many more. There were at least two hundred living here."

"Would they give up?" Alex asked. "If things looked hopeless?" Alex wanted to ask if they would surrender, but there was no word for that in either Winten-ah or the universal language of Kragdon-ah.

"Give up?" Yosta-ak said. "Let themselves be taken? I can't imagine such a thing."

"But the village is empty. They must be somewhere."

Yosta-ak looked at the sun. "It will be dark before too many more hours. We do not want to arrive at Denta-ah in the dark. Let us stay here tonight. There are many buildings which are undamaged. We can sleep in them, then start early in the morning. Maybe some of the Stipa-ah will come back. Until then, we can do the right thing with the bodies of the dead."

That meant digging a long pit on the edge of the island and carrying the bodies there, then filling it in. It was hard, dirty work, even though the soil was easy to turn. It was long past dark when the last of the Stipa-ah had been buried.

Yosta-ak stood over the mass grave and chanted, but it was in his own language, so Alex could not understand.

All nine men were bone-tired from their labors and the emotional toll it took. They found a bunkhouse toward the middle of the village that was undisturbed.

Another unusual thing about Stipa-ah was that, although its people had apparently abandoned it, they had left much of value behind. Their weapons were gone, but there were still stores of food that showed they had been prepared for the winter to come.

Before they bedded down for the night, the group filled their bags with food, then settled in to sleep. Their work of the afternoon had stolen their appetites for the moment.

Sleep also eluded most of them, including Alex. Laying in the beds of those who had either died or deserted their home made for an uncomfortable night.

They were all awake and moving around long before first light.

Alex and Monda-ak brought up the rear as they walked single-file across the pathway off the island. A heavy rain began to fall, and the wood of the buildings, which had still been smoldering, was finally put out. Alex pulled the hood of his overshirt over his head.

Dawn came, but the skies stayed a steel gray that the sun could not break through. Being this close to Denta-ah, they did not take any breaks. After the mystery of Stipa-ah, they were more anxious than ever to get there.

After several hours of hiking through steady rain, Yosta-ak signaled to the small group to leave the main trail and follow a small game trail to the right. Almost immediately, the trail climbed in elevation. After a short hike, however, it opened onto a small clearing on the side of the hill.

From there, the whole of Denta-ah spread out below them.

Denta-ah had another near-perfect location. It was built inside a box canyon with high, rugged hills on three sides. That funneled all attackers into a single pressure point.

"See what they have done," Yosta-ak said, pointing down at the village.

Where the opening into the village was, a tremendous blockade had been built. It was made from thick trees which had been stripped of their bark and sunk deep into the ground. The end of the trees that pointed toward the sky were sharpened into a point. There was no space between the trees, making for a formidable obstacle. In three locations, there were small buildings that Alex identified as guardhouses.

Alex squinted across the distance and could make out what looked like a gate that was slightly ajar.

I can't imagine what kind of manpower it would take to build a structure like that. I'm sure there's a platform running behind it that men can stand and fire from.

"HAS IT ALWAYS BEEN like this?" Alex asked Yosta-ak.

"No. They had obstacles. Fallen trees piled high, mounds of dirt, a few guard stations, but nothing like that."

Still, it doesn't prove anything. They've improved their defenses against the world. That's a good idea in a world where gigantic bears and dire wolves roam.

The men stood in the clearing, watching the activity in the town far below.

Technology's not all bad. If I had my field binoculars, I might know what's going on down there.

From their distant viewpoint, all that could be seen was a steady stream of people flooding in and out of the gate.

Yosta-ak turned to the three Winten-ah members. "I know that this new defense does not prove anything. I just wanted you to see it before we got too close."

Alex looked at Sekun-ak and Doken-ak, and saw that they weren't going to say anything.

Maybe Ganku-eh should have sent tribe members who actually spoke. Or, maybe that's why she sent me.

"What now?" Alex said.

Yosta-ak looked down at Alex. "Now, we approach them as friends and ask to be admitted as such."

Alex didn't like the idea of walking up to a fortress just to say hello, but it wasn't his party. He was just an invited guest.

The group hiked down the hill and got back on the original path. Ten minutes later, they stepped into the clearing that led to Denta-ah. From that perspective, they could see a forest of stumps off to their right.

Guess we can see where the wood for this project came from. The forest would have offered protection, too, but not as stout as what they've built here.

As they approached the barricade, they saw a few men and women off to the left. Their backs were bent as they busily turned soil. Alex counted a dozen of them, with two men standing over them like guards.

Those guards had an odd-shaped weapon that didn't look like anything Alex had seen on Kragdon-ah. They were too distant for him to be able to make out what they were.

As the group approached the barrier, the gate slowly swung closed. The people who were outside did not seem distressed to be locked out, but continued with whatever task they were focusing on.

Undeterred, Yosta-ak and the others walked to within twenty yards. Up close, they could see how tall the massive fence was. Alex estimated it was at least thirty-five feet.

"Greetings," Yosta-ak called in the universal language.

There was no response.

"Greetings," he said again. "We wish to meet with Frema-ak."

After another long silence, a man poked his head over the top of the wall. "What is your business?"

"We wish to meet with Frema-ah," Yosta-ak repeated.

"What is your business?" the man atop the wall also repeated.

This could go on all day.

"There are rumors that a tribe is breaking the covenant and is using stama. We would like to talk with him about it."

I guess that will lay our cards on the table.

Alex stared at the man's face who stared down at them. He did not seem perturbed at the mention of a broken covenant. In fact, he did not seem perturbed by anything. Instead, he smirked.

"Frema-ah is ill. He cannot meet with anyone."

"We are sorry to hear that. Who is the chief in his place?"

"I am," the man on the fence said, the smirk never leaving his face.

Yosta-ak touched two fingers to his forehead, apparently acknowledging the truth of that statement.

"Very well. I am Yosta-ak of the Treda-ah." He gestured at Do-ken-ak and Sekun-ak. "These are from Winten-ah. We have walked for many days to meet with you. Will you allow us entrance?"

The man's head disappeared behind the wall. As it did, a line of twenty men appeared on the top of the wall. They all held crossbows.

Alex turned to Doken-ak and quietly said, "Have you ever seen one of those before?"

"Kel," Doken-ak said, equally quietly. *No.*

The smirking man reappeared in his position above the gate. Beside him, a much smaller man's head appeared, struggling to see over the pointed tips of the logs. He stared down at the group of nine men. His eyes swept over them and settled on Alex.

The small man appeared to step up onto something so he could see better. He pointed a finger at Alex, then spoke to the man beside him, gesturing at the others in the group with a sweep of his hand.

The tall man said, "You are in Denta-ah. You are not welcome here. We consider your presence an act of war."

Alex reached out and touched Doken-ak and Sekun-ak on their shoulders.

"We need to leave. *Now.*"

Alex glanced to his left and saw that the two guards who were overseeing the work crew had left their position and were striding toward them. Now that they were closer, Alex could see what he had missed before—they were also carrying crossbows.

Alex gave Monda-ak a hand signal, telling him to stay beside him.

"As an act of war, we are within our rights to execute you as war criminals." In a calm, low voice, he said, "Now."

All twenty of the men loosed their crossbows simultaneously.

Chapter Twenty-One
Enslaved

Short bolts flew like a hailstorm of death.

When the order to fire was given, the Winten-ah trio had been at the back of the group. Thanks to Alex's warning, they had turned to move away and had a few feet of separation when the arrows slammed down.

That saved two lives.

Yosta-ak and his five guards never had a chance to lay a hand on their weapons. They were cut down instantly, each with several of the bolts sticking out of them.

Alex turned to run, knowing he was so badly outnumbered that his only chance at survival was speed.

He glanced over his shoulder and saw that Sekun-ak was with him, although trailing by a few yards.

Doken-ak.

He and Sekun-ak turned at the same moment and ran back toward their attackers.

Doken-ak pitched face forward, a short bolt sticking out the back of his neck. When he hit the ground, two men reached him. The first one raised a heavy stone ax and slammed it down on his head.

Doken-ak!

Sekun-ak took one step toward his fallen tribemate when Alex grabbed his arm and pulled him on.

"He's gone," Alex panted. "We will be too if we don't run now!"

Sekun-ak lingered for one long second before turning toward Alex and Monda-ak. Then they ran.

The gate behind them slowly opened and men poured out, racing toward them. They were well behind, though. Only the two guards were close enough to do immediate damage. One of them attempted to fire his crossbow on the run, which was an ineffective strategy, sending its bolt twenty feet high of its intended target.

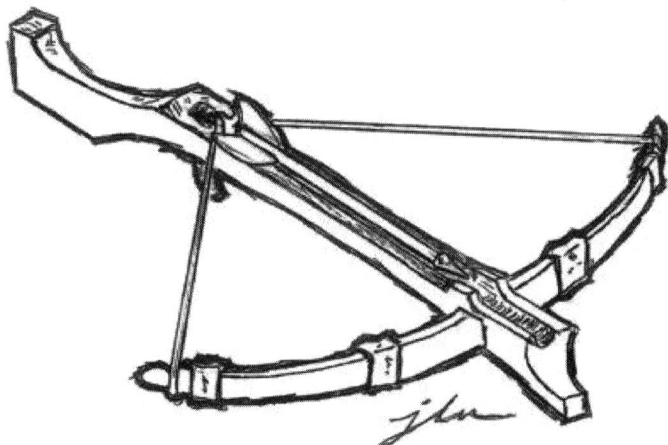

THE SECOND MAN STOPPED, braced his feet and fired. That bolt hit Sekun-ak in the right ear, causing a spurt of blood, but no further damage.

Both Alex and Sekun-ak shed their packs. They knew that anything that slowed them even a second could mean the difference between death and returning home to report what they had found.

They sprinted toward the edge of the field and turned the corner onto the path they had followed.

Alex immediately jumped behind a tree and signaled Sekun-ak to continue on, which he did. Alex flashed a hand signal to Monda-ak, who crouched into an attack position. Alex heard the pounding of feet and held his stone hammer in his right hand. The tree would not hide him completely, but he hoped it would give him a moment's advantage.

As the first man ran around the corner, Alex stepped out and swung his hammer in a low, flat arc. It connected with the man's hip. He fell to the ground, screaming.

The second guard was not as fast and was more cautious—alerted by the first man's screams of pain. He slowed as he rounded the blind corner and raised his reloaded crossbow. He pointed it at Alex.

Before he could release his bolt, a massive blur of fur and teeth leaped from the woods, knocking him flat. The man instinctively pulled the trigger, but the bolt whizzed uselessly into the air.

Monda-ak crushed the man beneath his weight and looked to Alex for his command.

Alex gave the hand signal, and Monda-ak closed his powerful jaws over the man's head and crushed his skull. The man Alex had hit with his hammer lay writhing on the ground. Alex stepped to him and dispatched him the same way that man had killed Doken-ak.

Alex turned to see Sekun-ak behind him with his own ax raised. Their blood was high, but for the moment, there was no one left to fight. In another moment, there would be too many for the three of them to battle.

The two men and Monda-ak turned and ran.

The rest of the pursuing Denta-ah tribesmen came around the same corner and found the two dead men. They left them and chased after their prey, although they ran more cautiously, knowing their prey fought back.

Alex and Sekun-ak ran ahead, wanting nothing more than to put distance between themselves and the Denta-ah. As they ran around another bend in the road, they were stopped by a large tree that had fallen across the trail. Standing behind the tree were six more Denta-ah warriors armed with crossbows.

Alex looked left and right. The Denta-ah had chosen their ambush spot carefully. A steep hill rose to the left, and a large boulder blocked their escape to the right.

Alex flashed a hand signal at Monda-ak, who tore up the hill to their left. One of the crossbowmen turned and unleashed a bolt at him, but he had underestimated how fast the dog could run uphill. The bolt fell short and a moment later, Monda-ak was lost in the trees.

The pursuing warriors caught up, and Alex and Sekun-ak were trapped.

"Weapons on the ground," one of the men said from behind the log.

Alex and Sekun-ak exchanged a glance but knew they were in a helpless situation. They both dropped their clubs and hammers. The warriors who had been chasing them picked up the weapons, and tied their hands behind their backs with cord.

One by one, the bowmen clambered over the log. They surrounded their prisoners and marched them back toward Denta-ah.

When they reached the clearing where they had been ambushed, Alex whistled three times—two short and one long. That told Monda-ak to stay hidden, but nearby. The guard behind Alex cuffed him in the back of the head.

Alex ignored the blow but looked around the open space for Doken-ak. Or, more accurately, Doken-ak's body.

The workers who had been turning sod in the field had been reassigned and were dragging the bodies of the victims of the massacre away. Alex saw Doken-ak's lifeless body being drug carelessly by the heels. His blood boiled, but he knew there was nothing he could do other than get himself killed.

I'm sorry I couldn't save you, my friend.

The guard who had hit Alex pushed him along toward the gate, which was now partially open. Alex and Sekun-ak stepped through and into Denta-ah.

Alex tried to look everywhere at once.

As he had suspected, there was a platform with ladders that were attached to the log wall. Immediately behind the wall was something Alex had seen only in drawings and movies: a trebuchet. A type of catapult, a trebuchet could fling heavy objects across a great distance, causing tremendous damage.

Of course. I should have realized. That's how they destroyed Stipa-ah. They carried it in pieces, assembled it on the lakeshore and lobbed burning projectiles onto the village. They would have no defense against that. If they tried to come off the island to defend themselves, they would face the same problem an attacker would have—they could only do it single file. They were bombed into submission.

IN HIS MIND, ALEX PICTURED them doing the same in Winten-ah. Their caves were not as vulnerable to that sort of attack as Stipa-ah had been, but it would still be the likely end of the tribe. A single burning projectile flung into one of the large caves would kill dozens of Winten-ah.

Alex didn't know the exact population of Winten-ah, but looking at the amount of activity and people moving around in Denta-ah, he estimated that there were five or six of them for every person in his tribe. He guessed that this open area had once been used much like the open space in front of the cliffs at home. Now, it looked more like the headquarters for an army.

The guards continued to push Alex and Sekun-ak along, while Alex dug his heels in to try and get a better look around. He didn't know if he would ever get back to Winten-ah, but if he did, he wanted to have good intelligence to share.

On his left was a long, low lean-to filled with weapons. Back at the cliffside, there was a room he thought of as the armory, but it was mostly to keep weapons for hunting, the guards in the trees, and trips to the ocean for karak-ta eggs. This was something else entirely.

There was row after row of not just heavy spears, atlatls, and cudgels, but crossbows and what looked very much like longbows. Alex had contemplated introducing longbows to the Winten-ah, but there were no yew trees—which make the best longbows—in the area.

When he had broached the idea with Sekun-ak, he had asked why such a thing was needed. Alex hadn't been a good salesman on the idea and so it had languished. Here, though, the idea had found more fertile ground. Alex had read once that elms could be treated to make a good longbow, but he didn't know enough about the process to implement it.

Before Alex could look around anymore, he was pushed into a small building. Inside, there was a guard on either side of the door and a long table serving as a desk. An open window let light in on each side. On the wall beside the window was something Alex hadn't seen since he stepped through the door: a series of maps.

They were nothing like the maps at home, but they were still maps. They appeared to be made on the tanned hide of an animal stretched tight, then sketched on with charcoal. Alex wanted to get closer, to see what was being mapped, but the guards pushed him to stand in front of the table.

The only other person in the room was the man who had given the order to execute the traveling party. He looked at Alex with intense, bright eyes. The eyes of a fanatic.

Aside from that, he looked like any of the people in Kragdon-ah. He was very tall, with dark skin and dark eyes.

He pointed at Sekun-ak. "Take him away. Put him to work in the fields."

One of the guards stepped forward and put an arm around Sekun-ak's neck. He struggled against the guard and struck the man in the face with the back of his head, bringing a spray of blood. The second guard calmly stepped forward and slammed his cudgel into the side of Sekun-ak's head. He dropped in a heap. The guard with the bleeding nose kicked him hard in the ribs, then the two of them hauled him away.

When they left, two more guards stepped through the door and took their place.

"Sit," the man at the desk said. "I am Dunta-ak."

Alex did not feel like sharing social niceties with a man who had just killed his best friend and ordered another one carried away into slavery.

"I know *what* you are. I just do not know your name."

"I am Manta-ak."

"Are you? You do not look like a Winten-ah. You are short. Your skin is an unpleasant color. Your eyes are an ugly color."

Again, Alex stared at him with no answer.

Dunta-ak raised his voice and said, "Doug-ak, come in."

The man who had peered over the wall at him entered. He was a fiftyish man with blond hair combed over to cover a balding head. He wore horn-rimmed glasses, a blue button-down shirt and khakis. He looked soft, a little pudgy. It had been more than three years since Alex had seen anyone overweight.

"Doug-ak, this man says he is Manta-ak."

The man looked at Alex's Winten-ah clothes and long hair. "Gone native, have you?" The man spoke in English. In fact, he had the remnants of an English accent. "Did you think you were the only one? Dear boy, where there's one, there will always be more."

Chapter Twenty-Two
Douglas Winterborne

Alex had known from the beginning of the journey that there was almost certainly someone like this. A man who had found his way to this time and place, and who wanted to change what he found. Still, sitting in front of him—seeing his mode of dress, hearing him speak in a language Alex rarely spoke—was an unsettling experience.

The man walked across the room and sat beside Dunta-ak. He glanced at him, then leaned forward and said, "Don't worry. As long as we speak English, he can't understand a word we say. Forget about all this Doug-ak nonsense, too. I'm Douglas. Douglas Winterborne." He smiled at the man and touched two fingers to his forehead.

Dunta-ak returned the gesture.

"Savages. They're all ignorant savages. Who is afraid of progress? Who doesn't want to make their own lives easier?"

"People who know that stama nearly destroyed the world." It was no accident that Alex chose *stama* instead of *technology,* or *progress.* When he had first arrived in Kragdon-ah, he had felt that the Winten-ah's aversion to using the tools he had brought was stupid and backward. As he had lived with them and watched their lives, he had changed his mind.

He was a guest in their world. Why should he try to change what they believe?

"You really have gone native, haven't you? What's your background? What year was it when you crossed over the threshold?"

Alex considered not answering, but remembered he was a prisoner who could be put to death as easily as Doken-ak had been. If he was dead, then this whole journey had been for nothing and the Winten-ah would be unprepared for whatever was coming next.

"I was in the Army."

"Specialist of some kind?"

"Just a grunt." *No need to tell him more than that.*

Douglas's mouth twitched in obvious disappointment. "Well. I see. What year did you cross?"

"It was April of 2019 when I walked through the door."

"And how long have you been here?"

Alex didn't care for this intense line of questioning but couldn't see any harm in answering.

"Three and a half years ago."

"And what have you accomplished in those years?"

Accomplished? I stayed alive, so I can get home to my daughter.

"I learned the language, the customs. I became a hunter."

"Once a grunt, always a grunt, right?"

"That's what I hear."

Douglas sighed and leaned forward. "When I heard there was someone like me, I was so hopeful. I know many things, but no man knows everything. I was hopeful you would be able to fill in some gaps."

"I've been a disappointment to people all my life."

"Yes," Douglas said, drawing the word out as he contemplated Alex. He turned to Dunta-ak and switched to the universal language.

"This man is of no use to us, aside from his strong back and weak mind. Put him to work in the fields."

Dunta-ak said something Alex could not understand, and the two guards grabbed him from behind and hauled him out of the room.

Alex hoped that they would take him into the village proper so he could get a better idea as to the size and strength of the town, but he was led out to the fields where men and women alike were turning soil using crude shovels. He was relieved to see Sekun-ak bent over a shovel as well. A blood trail ran down his neck, but he seemed to be fine.

The guard handed Alex a shovel and pointed to a row. It wasn't hard for him to decipher what his job was to be. He put his weight on the tool and turned the first of many thousands of shovelfuls of Denta-ah dirt.

As he worked, Alex kept a steady eye on the forest line. Before too long, he saw what he expected—Monda-ak broke out of the trees and ran straight toward him. As he dug, Alex gave two short, sharp whistles he knew would reach the dog's ears. Monda-ak stopped and looked questioningly in Alex's direction. Again, Alex gave the two short whistles.

Monda-ak turned, ran back into the forest and disappeared into the underbrush.

THE LIFE OF A SLAVE laborer in Denta-ah was not a pleasant one. They slept shoulder to shoulder in a lean-to outside the city gates. They were exposed to both the elements of the approaching winter and the possibility of animal attacks. Sekun-ak and Alex organized a rotating sentry detail.

Guards awakened them before first light, and they were only given a weak stew to eat morning and night.

Alex was not allowed back through the city gates for any reason.

The other slaves were primarily from Stipa-ah, and they had only been captured the day before Alex, so they didn't know much more than he did. Some of the others had come from other tribes and had been there longer.

One tall, strong man said his village had been destroyed before the summer solstice, and he had been working ever since. His first job at Denta-ah had been to help cut down the trees that made up the formidable wall. He said that when he first arrived, there was only a small fence that ran in front of the village, and that it had been farther back than the wall that was built. Moving the wall out gave them additional room to work in safety.

The man said both he and his wife had been captured together, but that he had only seen her once since they had arrived. She had told him that she had been put to work creating the bolt shafts that were used by the crossbows. She also said that there were ten more just like her, working all day every day to make various weapons.

Denta-ah was preparing for a war the other tribes would not be ready for.

When they worked in the fields, they were required to be silent, but the first night, Alex found an old man who had been captured at Stipa-ah.

He asked him questions in the universal language of Kragdon-ah.

First, he found that the man thought the trebuchet, which he called the long arm, was magical.

"When they fired the long arm, did they use men to pull it down, or load it with rocks?"

"Men pulled it down. They set heavy stumps on fire, then the long arm threw them into our village."

A traction trebuchet, then. That makes it easier to transport than a counterbalance. Smart.

"Did they just show up and throw fire at you?"

"Our guards saw them as they approached the lake. We watched as they surrounded us and built the long arm. We thought we were safe behind the water. Everyone was inside the village and we knew we could defend the island if they attacked us. We had never seen anything like the long arm, and didn't know what it would do. They did not talk to us. They rained fire on our village."

"How many times did the long arm throw fire at your village?"

"I don't know. Five times, six, seven. It was hard for us to understand what was happening. Our own defense, the water that surrounded us, trapped us. We did not know it was possible for someone to reach us from the land. We thought we were safe. When we realized we were not, it was too late. Our warriors and hunters ran to the battle, but their line was thin. They could only run single file. They were slaughtered as soon as they stepped off the path."

"How did they kill your warriors? Did they fight them hand-to-hand?"

"No. They stayed back. They shot them with short arrows before they stepped off the path. The bodies of our warriors were piled high. We did not kill even one of them. Stama."

"We found the bodies of the dead in the middle of the village."

"They made us carry the dead there and leave them. They said we could carry the bodies or be killed ourselves."

"We buried them, so the animals would not find them."

The old man, who had been losing interest in the conversation, laid his hand on Alex's shoulder. "Thank you. That makes it easier to think about. We all will die, but I didn't like to think about our brave men left to the scavengers."

Each day, as Alex worked, he saw Monda-ak appear at the tree line, look at him, ask for permission to come to him.

As they turned more and more soil, they moved away from the gate to Denta-ah.

On the fifth day, Alex estimated that they were out of range of the crossbowmen who stood atop the gate. That left only the two other guards who watched over them.

That afternoon, when Alex saw Monda-ak appear at the edge of the forest, he whistled one shrill blast.

Monda-ak's ears pricked up and he ran full speed toward Alex.

Alex stood and pointed at Monda-ak. All the workers and guards turned toward him. The first guard raised his crossbow and aimed. As he did, Alex dove across the space that separated them. The second guard wheeled and pointed his crossbow at Alex. As he released the bolt, the old man from Stipa-ah stepped between them.

The bolt from the second guard slammed into the throat of the old man just as Alex swung his shovel, hitting the crossbow of the first guard. The second bolt flew high and over the head of Monda-ak, who never slowed.

As the one standing guard reached for his cudgel, Monda-ak slammed into him, knocking him to the ground in a twisted mess of dog and man.

Alex looked at the old man who had sacrificed himself. He was gurgling blood and could not speak, but waved Alex away.

The guards on the tower saw the fight and unleashed their own bolts, but as Alex had guessed, they were out of range.

Alex whistled at Monda-ak, who dispatched the man and ran to Alex's side. Sekun-ak raised his shovel and brought it down on the second guard's head.

The gate had already been opened to allow workers and guards to go in and out and men poured out of it.

The slaves, who were slaves no more at that moment, scattered and ran for the trees.

Alex, Sekun-ak and Monda-ak did not run for the path they had used originally. Alex was afraid that the tree would still be across the trail and there would be more armed men waiting for them. Instead, they ran for the part of the forest where Monda-ak had sprung. The going would be slow, but that would be true for their pursuers as well.

With everyone running a different direction, it slowed the response. The guards didn't know which of the runners to chase. Eventually, Dunta-ak ran through the gates and directed a group of men to pursue Alex, who was just disappearing into the forest with Sekun-ak and Monda-ak. That gave them a five-minute head start.

As they ran, Alex gave a signal to Monda-ak to lead the way. He was a wide body and protected from the thorns of bushes by his thick coat, so he made an easier path for the humans.

Monda-ak zigged and zagged as he ran, checking over his shoulder to make sure Alex was close behind and slowing down if he needed to. They were breaking a trail as they went, which would make them easy to follow, but it was the only way to keep a distance between them and their armed pursuers.

They broke through into a clearing and heard the sound of rushing water nearby. They moved to the edge of a small cliff and saw a river running below them, heading west.

Behind them, they could hear the crashing of the guards through the trees. Alex looked into the frothing gray water.

He looked at Sekun-ak and shrugged, then gave Monda-ak the signal to follow and jumped.

Chapter Twenty-Three
The Journey Home

Alex had known the river would be cold, but when he hit the water, he had a hard time drawing a breath.

Not going to be able to stay in this water for too long without risking hypothermia.

He finally managed to draw a breath and looked desperately around. Monda-ak had followed closely, because he was swept along not far behind Alex. As heavy as he was, Monda-ak was an excellent swimmer and had the additional advantage of his thick fur.

The Winten-ah were not great swimmers, but Sekun-ak had also taken the plunge. The river represented a better chance at life than staying to face an unknown number of armed men intent on killing him. He splashed his arms and did his best to keep his head above water, but Alex could see the river would not be a long-term strategy for him.

Beyond Sekun-ak, there was nothing but a long stretch of river. None of the guards had wanted to pursue them into the water. Alex had no doubt they would follow them, but they wouldn't be able to move as quickly as the river was carrying him.

Alex called to Monda-ak and turned to swim for the far shore. As long as he didn't try to fight his way back upstream, he made progress toward reaching the opposite bank.

Ahead, he saw a spot where the riverbank sloped gently down into the river. He swam for it, doing his best to give a whistle for Monda-ak to find him. He scrambled ashore, exhausted, but knew he didn't have a moment to waste if he was going to grab Sekun-ak. He looked desperately around for a fallen limb he could extend out into the water, but there was nothing there. When he glanced up, Sekun-ak was already past him.

Alex knew he couldn't run as fast as the river, but he and Monda-ak ran through the thin underbrush alongside the river anyway. He shouted to Sekun-ak that he was coming, and to try to swim to the shore.

He can barely keep his head above water. What are the odds he can manage to swim to the shore?

Alex ran on, heedless of the branches and vines that snagged him. After half a mile of hard running, he came to a pool that had been created when a massive tree had fallen completely across it, creating a natural dam.

His heart sank when he saw Sekun-ak's body bumping lifelessly into the tree, face down in the water. Alex splashed out into the pool and grabbed him under the arms. The pool wasn't deep, but the rocky bottom was slippery and Sekun-ak, even after a week of starvation diet, was heavy. Still, Alex managed to bring him ashore.

Alex touched his carotid artery but couldn't find a pulse. He put his ear against his chest but there was no heartbeat. Alex tilted Sekun-ak's head back and opened his mouth, looking for obstructions in the airway.

He straddled Sekun-ak's waist, placed his hands over his motionless chest and pressed down. When he had been taught CPR, his instructor had used the Bee Gees song *Stayin' Alive* to show the proper rhythm. He compressed the chest in time with the old disco song, then covered Sekun-ak's mouth and blew into his lungs.

It might be hopeless, just the two of us lost a hundred miles from home, hunted by men who want to kill us, with wet clothes and no way to start a fire, but things would be much better with two of us. Come on!

In between compressing Sekun-ak's chest and blowing air into his lungs, Alex glanced up and across the river. Their pursuers had been right behind them when they jumped. How long would it take for them to catch up?

Alex continued the CPR for long minutes. Long enough that he thought all hope had passed.

Then the spark of life returned. Sekun-ak coughed up river water, gasped for air and looked wildly about. Alex had believed that drowning was a peaceful way to die, but seeing Sekun-ak's response to waking up on this side of life's curtain, he reevaluated that.

Alex helped him to sit up and pounded on his back to expel the last of the water from his lungs.

"We need to move away from the bank. We're too exposed here."

Alex helped Sekun-ak to his feet and half-carried him to a hidden spot deep in the trees. They were no more than tucked away than Alex heard the pounding of feet across the river. Monda-ak growled quietly, deep in his chest, but Alex quieted him with a gesture.

There were six men chasing them. Two were armed with crossbows, but the other four carried the typical weapons of Kragdon-ah—long cudgels and hammers.

When they came to the spot opposite Alex, they paused and looked at the bank where he had resuscitated Sekun-ak.

I should have erased any sign of us. Are there drag marks?

The men stared in their direction for a long minute, then continued down the river.

Alex relaxed, but only a little. They were still in a precarious position. Both he and Sekun-ak had already begun to shiver. It would be a cold night spent without a fire. Even if they had the ability to start a blaze, they couldn't risk it for fear of being seen. Their clothes were wet and unlikely to dry in the near-freezing overnight temperatures.

Alex had Monda-ak lie next to Sekun-ak while he explored their immediate area. With their hunters gone past them, they could stay and rest for the night. Surviving it without hypothermia was the challenge.

Alex scouted for anything that would give them shelter from the night's winds and rain, but couldn't find anything resembling a cave or rock overhang. Finally, he found a huge, hollowed-out tree.

Best we're gonna do, I think.

He hustled back to Sekun-ak as the weak light of the afternoon faded into dusk. Alex helped him to his feet, and noticed how beaten-up Sekun-ak had gotten in his trip down the river. He was cut and bruised in a dozen spots. He was also shivering dramatically.

Alex led him back to the tree, put Sekun-ak inside and clambered in behind him. It was a tight squeeze, but he called Monda-ak and arranged him over the top of both of them—a massive breathing, farting comforter. They huddled together and hoped for sleep to arrive.

As Alex dropped off, the last thought that went through his mind was "Even this is better than where we were at the beginning of the day." Then he slept.

Alex awoke in the middle of the night to see two golden eyes staring back at him and Monda-ak growling softly. Rutan-ta had come for a visit. With no weapon other than Monda-ak's claws and fangs, Alex hoped that she was not looking for a midnight snack.

The gigantic cat stared into their hidey-hole for a long minute. Out of the corner of his eye, Alex saw that Sekun-ak was also wide awake and staring back.

Rutan-ta gave them one last sniff, then turned and padded silently away.

Neither man slept again that night.

When the earliest light showed in the east, they untangled themselves from Monda-ak and walked stiffly back to the river. They laid and drank deeply of the cold water. It might be the only thing they had to put in their bellies for the near future.

They were both banged up and sore, but they knew they needed to move if they were going to make it home.

They searched the riverbank until they found stones they could sharpen into a blunt cutting instrument. They cut branches down from a red alder tree, measured them to a proper length and sharpened one end. It made for a crude weapon, but if they were forced to fight, they didn't want to be empty-handed.

Sekun-ak also found thin vines that could be used as cordage, and found a sturdy stick and rock that he could bind together into another basic weapon.

Their clothes had mostly dried overnight, but if they stopped moving for long, the cold seeped into their bones.

Without the trail they had followed on their way to Denta-ah, they were essentially traveling blind. They knew they had traveled east on their journey out, and that the river, although it twisted and turned, eventually flowed west. They decided to do their best to follow the path of the river and hope that Sekun-ak would begin to recognize landmarks when they got closer to Winten-ah.

The underbrush was tangled and difficult to move through, but from time to time they found a game trail they could follow until it inevitably moved away from the river. It made for slow going.

Alex estimated that on the journey to Denta-ah, they had traveled as many as fifteen miles in a single day. He didn't think they were making more than four to five miles traveling through the brush, stopping and listening for their pursuers every hundred yards.

Their stomachs had already been empty when they escaped, as they had never been given enough of the weak stew to do anything but survive. After three more days of burning calories through steady hiking, they were flagging.

Eventually, they came upon another spot that had been dammed. This time it was beavers who had built their home in a spot where the river narrowed. That had formed a pool where the water moved very slowly before crashing over the small dam.

Sekun-ak said, "Wait," and stripped off his buckskin breeches. He waded waist-deep out into the freezing water and stood still for several minutes, then came back to shore and said. "Genta-ta."

Genta-ta was a fish that the Winten-ah often ate, particularly when hunts were unsuccessful. It was much like a trout, but naturally, it was more the size of a salmon.

"How can we catch it? We don't have anything for fishing line or a hook."

Sekun-ak smiled—an expression that touched his face only on the rarest of occasions.

He picked up his crude spear and waded back into the water, where he went completely motionless. He was so quiet, Alex wasn't even sure he was breathing. He posed like a statue, one arm holding his spear slightly above his shoulder.

For long minutes, he didn't move.

Then, lightning quick, his right arm flashed down. He held on to his spear, but only just barely. As big and strong as Sekun-ak was, the genta-ta put up a titanic struggle. Sekun-ak dropped the spear low to keep the fish from wriggling off, then braced his feet and lifted it over his head. Freed from the spear, the fish flew backward onto the bank where it flopped and strained to reach the river.

Alex jumped on the fish and threw it further up the bank. He grabbed the hammer Sekun-ak had made him and bashed the fish on the head, once, twice, three times.

Alex grabbed the fish by the tail and lifted it up, smiling for the first time in many days. He held the tail at eye level and the head reached below his knees.

Wading out of the water, even Sekun-ak gave a satisfied smile.

Sekun-ak kneeled over the fish, chanted his thanks for its life and strength, then found a sharp rock and cut the fish open. He scooped out the entrails and piled them for Monda-ak to eat, who gobbled them in seconds and looked for more. Sekun-ak cut the head off the fish and threw it into the river, then removed the spine. Roughly, he cut two large slabs of meat.

He handed one to Alex who accepted it gratefully. They both sat on the ground and devoured the raw fish. Almost immediately Alex felt strength coursing through his body. Even eating all they could hold, they ate less than a quarter of the meat.

Sekun-ak cut more slabs off then walked into the forest. He reemerged a few minutes later with a handful of leaves the size of a man's chest. He made small holes in the leaves, then used more of the thin vine to sew the leaves into makeshift bags. He divided the meat equally and placed half in each of the bags.

"The meat won't stay good for long, but we can eat it tonight and in the morning."

Alex nodded. *Sekun-ak, you're a good dude to get lost in the woods with.*

Chapter Twenty-Four
Blizzard

The next morning, snow began to fall.

Alex, Sekun-ak and Monda-ak had started hiking along the river just before dawn. By the time the first light showed in the east, fat, heavy flakes fell, sticking almost immediately onto the frozen ground.

They walked on for another mile, ignoring the gathering puffs of fallen snow around their feet. It became apparent that, at least in the short-term, the storm wasn't going to let up. Being stuck in an early winter snowstorm without fire or adequate clothing was a recipe for frostbite or hypothermia.

Alex turned to Sekun-ak and said, "No one is going to be looking for us in this storm. We need to find a place to hole up."

Sekun-ak didn't hesitate but turned away from the river immediately. Monda-ak got the idea and jumped in front again, breaking trail and pushing snow out of the way like an overgrown St. Bernard.

Within minutes, the falling snow increased to near-blizzard conditions, essentially blinding them. A howling wind sprang up, which caused the snow to swirl in small tornados.

Alex began to think it was hopeless and maybe they should return to the river so that at least they wouldn't lose their way in the snow, when they nearly walked into a steep cliff.

Alex shielded his eyes with both hands and looked up the cliff, but there were no friendly caves they could climb up and into.

The face of the cliff stopped them from going any further north, so they turned back toward the west. Both Alex and Sekun-ak kept their right hand against the cliff for balance against the wind. Alex nearly fell over when the cliff seemed to disappear. He stumbled but regained his balance, then reached out to Sekun-ak.

There was a narrow opening into a cave.

Alex whistled for Monda-ak, who had continued on. The two men and the giant dog stepped inside, momentarily out of the swirling snow and whistling wind. Inside the cave, the snowstorm seemed surreal in its ferocity.

All three shook themselves to get the coat of snow off.

Alex turned to see how deep the cave was. The day was so deep and dark that the feeble light didn't reach far back. Alex took one tentative step when a blur of fur, talons and teeth bowled into him, ripping and tearing at his buckskin clothing.

The attack was so sudden that even Monda-ak was caught unaware.

Alex landed on his back, doing his best to fend off the clawing, biting creature. He used his crude spear to throw his attacker off, then scrambled to his feet and got his first look at what was trying to kill him.

It was a giant badger. Pound for pound, one of the meanest animals on the planet, and this badger had a lot more pounds than any Alex had ever seen or heard of.

Alex and Sekun-ak were armed only with their crude spears, which were somewhat ineffective in the narrow space of the cave.

Monda-ak did not suffer from any restrictions and threw himself bravely at the badger. As big as the badger was, Monda-ak outweighed it by a multiple of seven or eight, but the badger had ferocity on its side.

Monda-ak got the shoulder of the badger in his mouth and bit down. The badger made a sound like a growl that turned to an unnerving squeal of pain. Its claws tore at Monda-ak, ripping through his thick coat.

While Monda-ak had the writhing creature held at least partially stable, Sekun-ak managed to get his spear positioned and drove it into the badger's body just behind the opposite leg. That did not quiet it. Instead, the frequency and pitch of its cries increased as it thrashed.

Sekun-ak leaned on his spear, which was only a sharpened branch. As he did, it snapped off, with the pointed end buried deep inside the badger.

Alex lifted his spear high above his head and plunged it down on the badger.

Monda-ak held his grip and shook his head violently, snapping the creature's neck and finally silencing it.

Alex whistled the command to release the badger and Monda-ak dropped it but still growled suspiciously.

Alex and Sekun-ak had come out of the conflict unscathed, but Alex pulled Monda-ak to the better light at the mouth of the cave. Sekun-ak pulled Alex's spear out and explored back into the cave in case there were more predators to be found.

He returned shortly. "That was all that was here."

"Unless it had a family, I don't think anything else could have survived in here with it," Alex said, examining Monda-ak's wound. The badger hadn't been able to sink its teeth into him, but its sharp claws had exposed the flesh above the right shoulder.

"I'll clean this as best I can. I don't think it's too serious." Alex put his arms around the neck of Monda-ak and said, "Your first war wound, buddy. Thank you. I am not sure we could have handled him without you here."

Monda-ak whined an acknowledgment.

Alex stood and looked outside, where the blizzard had only increased.

"We can't go anywhere until this lets up."

"But," Sekun-ak said, holding up his leaf-bag, "the snow will keep genta-ta edible for a few days longer."

"A silver lining in every cloud," Alex agreed. "Do you think we could build a fire here in the opening? It would keep us warm and keep other animals from joining us."

"It's possible," Sekun-ak said. "If you can go find us some dry wood, I will try. Look for dead limbs that are hidden from the snow. I'll get everything else we need."

As soon as Alex took ten steps away from the cave, he shouted, "Don't lose the cave," then continued on to a stand of trees. He searched through the trees until he found what Sekun-ak had asked for—limbs that had died for one reason or another but were not exposed to the wet snow.

He gathered an armful and turned back to the cave. When he got to the cliff, the cave was not there.

Must have gotten off course.

Keeping the cliff to his immediate right, Alex stepped carefully along, searching for the opening. After a hundred yards, he realized he must have been off course in the other direction. He counted his steps back, then turned so the cliff was to his left.

After twenty yards, he found the cave. Monda-ak laid on his uninjured side, playing up his wound for all he was worth, showing Alex sad, mournful eyes.

"I know, buddy. Why did he do that to you? You were only going to snap his neck, right?"

Monda-ak's tail thumped against the cave floor as if to say, *Glad you understand.*

Alex dropped his armful of wood and decided to go for another load. He made it to the copse of trees and back in a direct line this time, but when he returned, Sekun-ak had still not returned.

Alex stood at the mouth of the cave, cupped his hands over his mouth and called for him. The raging wind carried his voice away before it traveled more than a few yards.

Alex had no way of judging the passage of time. He couldn't see the sky, let alone the sun. Still, he judged that Sekun-ak had been gone too long.

What can I do about it, though? Go looking for him? I got lost only going to the trees and back. If I go back out looking for him, it will just mean that we are both lost and separated.

Alex looked at Monda-ak, sleeping now, a round mound of dog.

Could I send you out? Would you do better than me?

Alex was still considering his options when Sekun-ak appeared from out of the storm like a ghost.

"I thought you were lost!" Alex shouted over the wind.

Sekun-ak looked puzzled. "Why would I lose myself?"

Alex shook his head. "Never mind. I brought wood."

Sekun-ak picked through the pile of branches Alex had brought back, picking out the thinnest and driest of the bunch. He stripped the needles off those dry branches, then showed Alex what he had brought back. He opened his hands to show small dark balls of sticky material.

"Pitch! Of course."

Sekun-ak also had a piece of dry, flat wood he had found somewhere in his travels, a short, straight branch no thicker than two of his fingers, and some of the vine he had used to make their leaf bags.

Alex sat back and watched as Sekun-ak built a friction bow out of the small limb, then heaped the dried needles, some dead leaves, and several balls of pitch on top of the flat board. Slowly, he moved the bow back and forth, turning the limb against the flat wood.

It wasn't quick, but after fifteen minutes, a wisp of smoke curled up. Sekun-ak blew on the tinder gently and a small flame was created. He dropped more of the tinder and pitch around the flame and a fire bloomed.

Alex had built a small pile of twigs up near the front of the cave and Sekun-ak moved the fire there. In just a few minutes, they had the best fire they had seen in many weeks. Alex looked at the pile of dry sticks he had brought back and judged that it wasn't enough, so they left Monda-ak and ventured out together to find more wood.

On the return trip, Alex watched Sekun-ak. He tread confidently back toward the cave as if he had a compass built into his head, even through the blinding snow.

That's a handy talent to have.

They made two more trips and felt like they had stripped the immediate area of easily burnable wood, but they had a stack that might burn for a few days.

On the last trip, Sekun-ak found another limb that could replace the spear he had broken off in the badger.

Back in the cave, they built up the fire to chase away a little of the chill and gloom. They stashed most of their fish just outside the cave, under the snow. Before they did, they hacked off a large hunk for each of them, including Monda-ak.

They spitted two of the chunks and tossed the raw piece to the dog.

It grew dark early that afternoon as the snow piled up outside their cave.

The two men and the dog sat quietly, enjoying the warmth and glow of the fire and the feeling of food in their bellies.

They felt better than they had since they had left Winten-ah.

Chapter Twenty-Five
A Leap of Faith

The storm lasted two more days. They finished the rest of the genta-ta the second day, but they weren't too concerned. They'd eaten enough to restore their strength and prepare for the next leg of their journey.

During their days waiting out the weather in the cave, Sekun-ak put his time to good use. He used a burning branch as a torch, and was able to explore the rest of the cave. He found several rocks that he was able to turn into tools to shape other rocks. By the second day, he was able to build them better spears and hammers than they'd had.

Alex asked Sekun-ak if they could eat the badger.

"Yes, but it has to be prepared correctly. We would need to put it in a fast-running river for several days before we could cook it. Far-da-ta"—the Winten-ah name for the badger—"eats anything. If you don't wash it properly, it can make you very sick."

"How about Monda-ak?"

"Him? He is a walking stomach. He can eat anything."

So, while Sekun-ak worked on weapons, Alex used a sharpened rock to gut and clean farda-ta. Monda-ak, who had been on a forced diet, devoured as much of the thing as Alex would give him. He never showed any ill effects, aside from noisier and smellier flatulence than usual.

After one such impressive display, Alex said, "That's it. No more farda-ta for you!"

On the morning of their third day in the cave, water dripped down from the mouth of the cave and onto their fire, causing a small sizzle. The snow had stopped, but there were still drifts as high as their chest—Alex's chest, at least—and walking would be nearly impossible.

They decided to stay one more day.

While they waited, Sekun-ak continued to fashion more tools for them—a stone ax for each of them. Not as good as they had in the armory back in Winten-ah, but more than good enough for the journey.

While Alex paid attention and tried to learn the art of building weapons from nothing, he broached a question.

"Do you ever get lost?"

"That is the second time you have asked me that. Why would I lose myself?"

"No, that's not what I mean. Do you ever get so turned around somewhere that you do not know where you are?"

"Yes, of course."

"So you do get lost."

"No."

"I don't understand what the difference is."

"There are times that I have not known where I was, because I have never been there before, but I am not lost."

"Do you know which direction Winten-ah is?"

Without hesitation, Sekun-ak lifted his arm and pointed.

"No doubt about it?"

"I like you, Manta-ak, but sometimes you ask such odd questions."

"You just know. Always."

"Of course. Don't you?"

"No."

"Ah." A look of intense sympathy crossed Sekun-ak's face. The look of the class genius on meeting the guy who flunked out of first grade. "I did not know it was possible to not know the way home."

They're like carrier pigeons. A sense so natural they aren't aware of it.

"Then we don't need to go back to the river to find our way home."

"Of course not. Is that what we have been doing?"

Alex felt a little embarrassed, but said, "Yes."

"There are good things about following the river. A clean water source. There is often food to be found near water."

"Yes, but if the terrain is easier away from the river..."

"We should take the easier path." Sekun-ak pointed outside. "It is already winter. More storms will come. We need to return to Winten-ah quickly. Every day we are away, Denta-ah is preparing for war, while we are not."

"From now on, you point us in the right direction. I'll follow."

"That is as it should be, now that I know you are *trunti*."

'Trunti' is a difficult word to translate from the Winten-ah. It means 'stupid,' but in a special way. Someone who is trunti is stupid but was born that way and it cannot be changed. To Sekun-ak, Alex was now trunti.

Alex knew that whatever reputation he had built during his three years at Winten-ah would take a blow when they returned home. But the thought of the cliffside, with its comfort, friendly faces and warm fires, was enough that a little humiliation was a small price to pay.

They set out before dawn the next day. The snow wasn't completely melted, but in places where the sun didn't reach in winter, it could be months before that happened.

Where the snow had melted, the ground was now mucky, and mud caked their moccasins before they were a quarter mile from the cave. Soon, that muck spread up their ankles and calves, until they looked like they had walked through a mud river.

They had been fortunate to find a cave in their hour of need but knew that was not likely to happen with regularity, and they were right.

Because of the stated advantages, they often turned back toward the river and followed it for a time, but freely abandoned it when terrain turned rough.

Then they ran into a dead end.

It was on their fourth day out of the cave, and they were exhausted and once again hungry. Sekun-ak had tried each day to spear another genta-ta but had failed. Only Monda-ak, who managed to supply his own food, was eating well.

They saw a range of tall hills ahead, and Alex wondered if this was the same range they had climbed over in their first day out of Winten-ah. His excitement grew until they drew nearer and saw the truth of the situation.

The river flowed through a neat valley it had cut between two of the hills, but there was nothing but a steep drop-off where the river briefly became a waterfall. Alex and Monda-ak climbed a few hundred feet up the hill and peered down to see the river splashing into a lake far below. The hills themselves were built on top of the cliff, so even if they climbed it, they would need to make a leap of faith into the water far below.

Alex scrambled back down the hill to where Sekun-ak waited for him.

"There is a drop on the other side of the hill. I can't see all along the ridge, but it looks like it's the same everywhere. Which way is Winten-ah?"

Like the needle on a compass, Sekun-ak's arm pointed directly at the opening between the two hills, where the river dropped off.

"Of course it is. We have two choices then. We either need to hike along this range of hills until we find a place where we can find a way down, or we go over the waterfall."

Sekun-ak nodded. "That is an easy choice. Let's go." He turned and walked north.

"Wait, wait, wait," Alex called after him. "I don't think that's the right answer. It could take us days to walk to the end of this ridge and we'll be farther away from home than we are now."

"Yes, but that plan does not include jumping off a waterfall. It is a better plan."

"Listen, I know last time we jumped into water, you ended up dead for a little while, but I won't let that happen to you again."

"How can you be sure?"

"Well, I can't. But I'll try to make sure it doesn't happen again."

"We will lose our weapons, my sharpening rocks."

"No, we'll just hold on to them when we go over." Alex had started to say *when we jump* but realized they would not actually be able to jump. The river's current was swift and would simply sweep them away as soon as they stepped into it.

"I will not do it."

"Yes, you will, because you won't leave me alone down there." Alex put on his most confident grin and stepped out into the river. He waded to the middle, so he wouldn't hit the rocks on the side as he went over, then whistled. Monda-ak waded into the water after him.

On the shore, Sekun-ak folded his arms across his chest, the picture of defiance.

Alex let his legs sweep out from under him and float in the fast-running current. He knew that Monda-ak would follow him. He was hopeful Sekun-ak would, too.

Alex's toes scraped against the river bottom, then in an instant it wasn't there. His stomach flip-flopped like he was on a rollercoaster.

He had meant to point his toes and hit the water below like an arrow. Instead, he tumbled around and around in the rush of water as he fell—a pinwheel out of control.

He smashed into the water with his left shoulder and the side of his face absorbing most of the impact. He went deep into the lake but did not touch the bottom. When he finally surfaced, he looked around to see Monda-ak paddling toward him.

Sekun-ak was nowhere in sight.

A piercing war cry came from the top of the waterfall, then a body surged over the edge, tumbling just like Alex had.

Sekun-ak hit the water in an awkward pose, landing on the back of his neck. Alex swam quickly to the spot where he entered the water. By the time he arrived, Sekun-ak poked his head up, gasping and spitting water. He glared at Alex.

"Next time I will just leave you to die."

For some reason, that struck Alex as hilarious and he laughed, which made Sekun-ak glare at him even more, until his face split into a wide grin, too.

"You are still trunti."

Alex laughed some more, but said, "Hold on to Monda-ak. He will help you to shore."

Minutes later, they made it to safety. Alex had managed to hold on to his hammer, but lost his spear, which was now at the bottom of the deep lake. Sekun-ak had done the opposite.

They were soaked through, the temperature was dropping, and they had no idea how far it was to Winten-ah. They were fortunate to have survived to make it this far.

Both men stripped naked in the biting wind and wrung out their clothes as best they could. Monda-ak simply shook himself, starting at his nose and ending at the tip of his tail.

"Let's move. Get our blood circulating," Alex said.

Sekun-ak held up his hand. "Wait. Look."

Alex followed Sekun-ak's pointing finger but didn't see anything. A flat stretch of open land, some trees that gently climbed toward more hills.

"That is Gakan Gate."

"You know this place?"

"I know Gakan Gate. It is the spot where two hills come together to form a valley that dips down and surrounds a small lake."

"How far is it from Winten-ah?"

"Gakan Gate is only a day's walk. There is a path from there to home."

Chapter Twenty-Six
Tidings of War

S ekun-ak led the way as they emerged from the familiar forest and looked at the cliffside caves of Winten-ah.

It was dusk, and the field was empty. Orange fires glowed and shadows danced from every cave.

Alex thought it was the most beautiful thing he had ever seen. Only seeing Amy could have been a more welcome sight to him.

Balta-ak, who had once placed a giant rattlesnake on a rock to thwart Alex, was the first to greet them.

All three of them—even Monda-ak—had lost a tremendous amount of weight. They were bruised, battered, scraped, and cut. Alex's left eye was swollen shut from where he impacted the lake. Sekun-ak still had wounds that hadn't healed from his first ordeal in the river.

Monda-ak limped on the right foreleg where the badger had clawed him.

Alex looked at him with amusement. "Knock it off, you big faker. You haven't been limping in days."

Monda-ak pointedly ignored him and limped on.

"We thought you were lost," Balta-ak said. "We'd nearly given up hope."

"We never doubted we would return," Sekun-ak said, "Correct, Manta-ak?"

Alex realized that Sekun-ak would never tell anyone that he was trunti. It didn't matter in any meaningful way, but it was the final element of the brotherhood they had developed on the journey.

"Come, eat, rest," Balta-ak said.

"We want to report to Ganku-eh. We have news we need to share."

"She sent me to fetch you, feed you, and let you rest until morning. She wants a full report then, but she wants it to be coherent. Is there anything that is so urgent it will be different in the morning?"

Sekun-ak considered that, then said, "No."

Alex had to admit that as badly as he wanted to tell Ganku-eh everything they had seen, a hot meal and a warm sleeping mattress sounded irresistible. They had spent the last three days sleeping in tree limbs, with Monda-ak patrolling below them.

They followed Balta-ak across the open field and up the switchbacks and ladders to an open room where several of the traditional low chairs were set around the fire. As soon as they sat down, friends appeared, bringing them food and drink.

Winten-ah is a take-care-of-yourself society, but on this night, both men and dog were catered to.

As soon as they were done eating, Niten-eh appeared with her bag of herbs and medicines, and began tending to their many wounds. When she finished examining and bandaging the men, she examined Monda-ak's shoulder wound. He put up with the pampering with the quiet dignity that he saved for moments like this.

No one peppered the men with questions. They had been gone for a little more than a month, but they felt slightly outside the tribe—almost as though they needed to be assimilated again.

When dinner was done, both men and Monda-ak collapsed gladly onto a mattress and were asleep immediately.

For the first time since they had set out on their journey, they could let their guard down and truly rest.

WHEN ALEX WOKE UP, he saw that the VIP treatment he had
received the night before had ended. There was no one waiting with
hot water to wash him or feed him breakfast. He was relieved and
glad. All he wanted, for the moment, was to get back to being a normal member of the Winten-ah, and to regain his strength.

A few minutes after he woke up, Sekun-ak found him. "Come.
She will want to hear from you."

Sekun-ak seemed slightly distant and formal now that they were
back in the cliffside. Still, Alex remembered the sly sense of humor
he had shown on their perilous journey and smiled inwardly.

There's no one I would rather have at my back.

They climbed the ladders to the meeting room where Alex had
first pledged to destroy his own technology three and a half years earlier. That had seemed such a foreign idea to him then, but after living
with the Winten-ah, he had come to embrace it.

Only Ganku-eh and her husband, Banda-ak, waited for them.

Ganku-eh signaled for them to sit. Before they had a chance to
say anything, Banda-ak said, "Doken-ak?"

Alex's throat tightened, but it was Sekun-ak who spoke.

"He is gone. We were unable to retrieve his body and give him a
proper resting place. We failed him and the tribe."

Banda-ak bowed his head slightly. "I know if there was any way
for you to have done so, you would have."

Ganku-eh leaned forward. "Start at the beginning. Tell us everything."

Again, Sekun-ak took the lead. In the next half hour, he spoke
more than he had the entire time they were gone. He briefly outlined
their journey until they got to Stipa-ah, then asked Alex to relay what
happened there.

"They used stama to destroy the Stipa-ah," Alex said.

"What form did the stama take?"

Alex contemplated. How do you describe something so outside someone's realm of experience?

"The Denta-ah have stama that can throw large, heavy objects great distances. They carried the stumps of trees to Stipa-ah, set them on fire, then used this stama, which I would call the long arm, to throw them into the buildings. When their village burned, the Stipa-ah warriors tried to run to the fight, but the Denta-ah have more stama that lets them throw small arrows great distances at great speed. They used that to kill the warriors one by one as they stepped off the island."

The cave was silent for long moments, with only the sound of the soft crackling of the fire between them.

"Why do you think they did this?"

"It was strategic. I think it was their first chance to test their long arm and their..." Alex couldn't think of a way to describe the crossbow properly. "...fast bow," he finished. That was as good a description as any. "I think they wanted to see if it would work. Once it did, they used it as an opportunity to eliminate a neighbor that might revolt against them and take slaves so they can make more stama."

"They enslaved the Stipa-ah?"

"Yes," Sekun-ak said. "But not just Stipa-ah. We were enslaved ourselves, and spoke to others from other tribes who had been there working ahead of us."

Ganku-eh sat back in surprise. "You were enslaved?"

Sekun-ak's head dropped, and Alex was surprised to see shame wash over him. Sekun-ak didn't answer but put two fingers to his forehead in affirmation.

"But you escaped," Ganku-eh said, giving Sekun-ak back his dignity.

"Yes. Alex and Monda-ak took care of the guards, and we escaped. This should teach them not to attempt to enslave Winten-ah. We will never be broken."

"How many people are there in Denta-ah?"

"They never let us too far into the city," Alex answered. "I couldn't get an accurate count. Watching food supplies and the activity on the edge of town, I would guess there are twenty of them for each Winten-ah. There could be more, though. They could have sent other raiding parties out to destroy other tribes and take more slaves."

Ganku-eh frowned. "That would be the biggest tribe that has ever been on Kragdon-ah."

Well, recently, anyway. You should have seen New York City or Tokyo back in the day.

"They outnumber us ten or twenty to one, and they are using stama to create weapons to destroy villages and enslave survivors," Ganku-eh summarized.

Both Sekun-ak and Alex touched two fingers to their foreheads.

She looked at Alex. "You have more experience with these situations. What do you advise we do?"

"Fight."

Deciding to fight and being capable of bringing the fight to the enemy are vastly different ideas. Sending a few dozen Winten-ah warriors against a fortified city with heavier armaments would be suicide.

"I love peace," Ganku-eh mused. "But there are times that to maintain peace, you must fight. These are not normal circumstances. This will require an extraordinary response." She stared into the dancing flames for long moments. Finally, she said, "Manta-ak, I would like you to organize and lead this fight. You are the best person for it, even though you are not one of us."

Alex felt overwhelmed. He had been a soldier for a decade, well trained to do his job. But that had been in the twenty-first century, using technology from that era. Drones, long distance strikes, smart bombs. And yet, he had always been a student of warfare. Not just Sun-Tzu, but all the masters of strategy and tactics.

I really am the best suited for this.

"I am willing to do so, and I will do my absolute best to win. But, I want something in return."

Ganku-eh did not appear surprised. She did not say 'Name it,' or anything else equally foolish. Instead she said, "What are your terms?"

"If I lead your—" Alex hesitated here. There was no word for *army* in Winten-ah or the universal language of Kragdon-ah. "—warriors, and if I survive the battle, when we return, I want a group of hunters to accompany me to the ocean. I want to return home. I need to see my daughter."

Ganku-eh bowed her head. "You have been a good friend to us, Manta-ak. You have been a mighty hunter, and you helped Sekun-ak return to us. We have kept you here because of the ancient prophecies. It has been told that a stranger from away will help us in our hour of greatest need."

"Maybe this is that time," Alex mused.

"I agree to your terms. If you will lead our warriors, when you come back, I will have Sekun-ak escort you back to the ocean and your daughter, if that is what you wish."

Alex knew they would have to fight smarter, but that they would also need additional forces.

"How many fighters can we gather to take against Denta-ah?" Alex asked.

Ganku-eh and Banta-ak put their heads together and conferred quietly.

"If we pull everyone we can, we could likely gather four hundred fighters. But, if we did that, many tribes would be exposed to dangers. We would be nearly defenseless. If we send that many men and they fall, all our tribes will fall as well. But, it is worth it. Stama must be contained. If it spreads through our land, it will change everything."

Alex considered. Four hundred was more than he had assumed, but still likely too few to take on Denta-ah.

"How long would it take? Could we gather them here, so I can train them? I have some ideas."

"If we sent runners today, the first could arrive in a week. The others, it could be several months."

"The longer we wait, the more heavily-armed Denta-ah will be. But, planning an attack with too few warriors is worse. We need to send our runners immediately."

Chapter Twenty-Seven
Preparations

Winter had gotten off to a harsh start with the blizzard that Sekun-ak, Alex, and Monda-ak had waited out in the cave. It mellowed after that. There were still freezing temperatures and an occasional dusting of snow, but no more drifts as tall as a dire wolf.

When the runners were dispatched, Alex and Sekun-ak went to work on creating anything that might help them fight against the stama of the Denta-ah. It was a difficult line for Alex. He wanted to build weapons and defenses that would give them the best chance to win the upcoming war, but he had to avoid doing the same thing Douglas Winterborne was doing.

When they sat to discuss options the first time, Sekun-ak said, "If we use stama to fight stama, then we have lost before we start."

Alex thought that was a noble sentiment, but he hated to give away any advantage when he knew his army was going to be out-manned and out-equipped.

Still, he and Sekun-ak went to work designing the prototype of the weapons and defenses Alex envisioned as his army marched into war.

Alex felt tremendous pressure because he knew it truly was *his* army. Ganku-eh had been clear about that. Winten-ah did not have a group of men she could identify as warriors. There had been peace in their part of Kragdon-ah for many years. They had hunters and people who could fight if called upon to defend their home, but nothing close to actual, trained fighters. Certainly no one who had experience in the strategies of war.

Except for Alex. And, to a lesser extent, Dan Hadaller. Dan had once been a trained soldier, but he had never taken to it as Alex had. He'd served the absolute minimum, been shipped to Vietnam, and had returned home.

In the almost four years Alex had been in Kragdon-ah, Dan had begun to show his age. He tended to stick to the easier paths up the cliffside and avoid the ladders to the top more and more. His white hair was thinner, and Alex had found he needed to repeat himself more often because the older man was hard of hearing.

In other words, not an ideal choice for leading an army.

Still, Alex intended to pick his brain for ideas.

The night after the runners left for points unknown, Dan and Alex sat alone in one of the meeting caves. It was the same place they had been sitting with Doken-ak when Yosta-ak had arrived to tell them of the coming storm. Now it was just the two of them and the comforting presence of Doken-ak was much missed.

"So you're the man in charge of this circus-to-be, huh?" Dan asked.

"Doesn't seem to be any way around it. I'd like you to be my right-hand man, if you're up for it."

Dan looked out over the open plain far below. Rain fell gently and dripped off the lip of the opening to the cave.

"I hate to leave you hangin', but I don't know that I'm up for it. I don't know if I'm up for anything anymore. These Winten-ah seem to live forever, but those of us from the twentieth century have an expiration date."

Alex leaned forward. "Ganku-eh promised me that if I lead the army, she'll take me back to the door. I want you to come with me.

We can go through together. It's still your house, as far as I'm concerned, so we can stay there together."

"You're a good man, Alex Manta-ak. I'd like that. I'd like to get back and see my dad before he dies if I can. But first, we've got to get you there and back alive. Let's talk about what kind of weaponry that Doug dude has."

"Pretty basic stuff so far. Crossbows, a trebuchet, I saw what looked like longbows being made, too."

Dan whistled. "Damn. Longbows? That changed the way wars were fought. There's no stama in a long bow. Why don't we make them, too?"

"I plan on trying. In theory, you need yew trees, and there's no yew trees in Oregon."

"How sure are you of that?"

"Are you saying I might find Yews around here?"

Dan Hadaller shrugged. "I might know where a stand of Pacific Yews is. We'll have to be careful not to take too many of them, but there's plenty to make longbows."

"Can you show Sekun-ak where they grow?"

"Of course. He's got weapon makers that can make them for you, but that's not really your problem."

"Oh, great. What's my real problem?"

"The English used to say that to use a longbow effectively, a boy should start with it in his crib. It's something you have to grow into. You'll never be able to train decent longbow archers in a few months."

Alex rocked back and forth, deep in thought. "In some circumstances, I wouldn't need true longbow archers, though. I don't need them to hit the eye of a gnat at two hundred paces. I just need them to be able to fire the damn things. These warriors are seven feet tall. That means our bows can be eight feet. Think of the drive and range from a bow like that. English bowmen could supposedly hit a target at two hundred yards. These archers don't need to be accurate; they just need to be able to all point in one direction and fire at the same time. It will be a rain of arrows. They'll have to hit *something*."

"I'll take Sekun-ak out tomorrow. I'm familiar enough with longbow design. I'll help his weapons man design the first one, then he'll be off and running. How many do you need?"

"I'd like to have two dozen longbowmen, if I could."

"I'll see what I can do. What I'm wondering, though, is why he's sticking with such medieval weapons?"

"What are you thinking of? Swords? Tanks? Submachine guns?" Dan smiled at the ludicrousness of the whole idea. "I guess. I don't know what I was thinking. Just something more advanced than crossbows and catapults, I guess."

Alex nodded. "I'm sure there are a lot of things on the drawing board. But, right now, he's limited by a lack of iron. Without iron, you can't make steel, and you're stuck with technology a few hundred years before our time. That means he's using the most up to date technology he can. But, if he can use that tech to get a leg up, he can build a city-state like he's got started right now. He can expand from there. It's gonna be tough for him, though."

"Why?"

"Two reasons. One, our time used most of the easily available resources of the earth. If it was shallow, if it could be gotten without much effort, we took it. We fracked it, strip-mined it, and used it up. Now all the easy stuff is gone, so it's gonna be tough for him to find anything."

"What's the second reason?"

"Because I'm gonna kill him."

ON THE RARE OCCASIONS that a Winten-ah needed a shield, they typically carried a small, round one that was mostly useful for fending off brute force attacks. For the most part, those shields sat unused in a dusty corner of the armory. When you are hunting game, a shield does nothing but slow you down.

Alex and Sekun-ak designed a special shield that Alex had in mind for the attack on Denta-ah. It was tall enough to protect a Kragdon-ah warrior from the top of their head to their ankles. Considering the size of the average Winten-ah warrior, that meant the shield had to be exceptionally long.

However, they were going to need to be hauled a great distance, so they needed to not be too heavy as well.

Alex's first thought was a classic wooden shield with lots of stopping power. Then he thought of the hill he and Yosta-ak's group had climbed their first day, and tried to imagine hundreds of men doing it with a heavy shield on their back. That was not going to work.

That was when he thought of a composite shield. Building a lightweight frame, then attaching layers of different material. Alex sketched the shape he wanted for the frame in the sandbox, then left it to Noken-ak, his best weapon-maker, to try to recreate it.

Meanwhile, Alex took some dried straw and wove it together into a lightweight material. He found a course fabric that the Winten-ah used for making carry bags. The final layer would be leather. Alex had never actually built a composite shield before, but he had read about them, and that the whole was much stronger than each of the parts.

He and Noken-ak needed to create a model, and use a bow and arrow from close range to see how it would stand up to the force of a crossbow.

The initial reason for the crossbow had been to make a weapon that could neutralize armor by piercing it. Alex decided not to waste any of his valuable time on armor then, but to focus on the shield and stopping the crossbow bolts before they got to his warriors.

By the next day, Noken-ak had created a framework that Alex was happy with. The two of them attached the layers of woven straw, cloth, and thick leather, then hefted the shield.

"Not as light as I'd like it, but better than anything else would be."

Noken-ak looked at Alex. Even among the Winten-ah, he was tall. But, where most of his tribemates were lean, he was thicker. There was no fat on him, but his shoulders, arms and upper legs were heavily muscled. His dark eyes smiled. He picked the shield up with one hand. "Anyone can carry this."

"You're right. Any of our warriors will be able to carry this. But, can we carry it up and down steep hills and across long plains, day after day?"

Noken-ak did not realize Alex was asking a rhetorical question. "I could."

"I believe you could," Alex said, laying a hand on his shoulder. "Give me four hundred more men just like you and we will win this war."

"There is only one Noken-ak."

"Much to our detriment," Alex said, laughing.

It took three days until Alex and Noken-ak had created a working model they were pleased with.

"Now, we need to test it," Alex said. "Sekun-ak, will you do the honors?"

"It is an honor indeed," Sekun-ak said, grabbing his bow. "There has never been a shield like this in Winten-ah."

"I'll set up the shield against a tree, then let's have you stand back about ten paces and fire an arrow at full strength. That will give us an idea of where we stand and what improvements we need to make."

Sekun-ak and Noken-ak exchanged a curious glance.

"I must have misunderstood what the purpose of the shield is," Noken-ak finally said.

"Really? Come on, this is no time to kid around."

"Is the purpose of the shield to protect the trees of the forest?"

"Of course not. But we're not going to put someone behind an untested shield and have someone fire point blank at it. That would be insane."

"What would be insane would be to create a tool and then not properly to test it."

"Wait," Alex said. "Are you seriously saying you want to hold the shield and have Sekun-ak fire at you from ten paces?"

Again, the two exchanged a glance.

"Of course."

Alex opened his mouth to protest, but the two giant men ran from the armory like schoolchildren let out at recess.

Noken-ak picked up the shield as though it was made of balsa, and strode to the middle of the open field.

It was well past the winter solstice, and the day was frigid. As Noken-ak and Sekun-ak walked to the middle of the field with Alex chasing after them, the children of the tribe sniffed out that something was going on.

Within moments, dozens of children had scrambled down from the warmth of the caves and were excitedly dancing around Noken-ak. The shield that he carried was bigger than all of them.

Noken-ak shooed them back, slipped his arm through the leather bindings, and held it out in front of him.

Sekun-ak marked off ten paces, drew his bow and notched an arrow.

"Wait!" Alex shouted. "I'll be lost without Noken-ak. We cannot risk harming him."

The children all booed Alex, who was trying to take away the most exciting thing they'd seen since the first snowstorm.

Sekun-ak shrugged him off and pulled back on his bowstring. There was really no need to aim carefully at such a distance, but he did anyway.

Alex, realizing there was nothing he could do to stop them, didn't know whether to look away or watch how his creation fared. He chose to do both, closing one eye and looking carefully with the other.

Sekun-ak released the arrow in a single, fluid motion. The shaft flew straight and true and the head of the arrow buried itself in the leather outer layer of the shield. The impact was enough to stagger even Noken-ak back a step.

Alex ran to him to see if he had been pierced by the arrow.

He had not.

Noken-ak's face split in a triumphant smile and he patted Alex on the head like a child.

"I had faith in what we made. You should have more faith in us too."

Sekun-ak simply nodded and said, "I thought it was going to go through. You should be proud that you created something that stopped my arrow."

"You thought it was going to go through, but you shot him anyway?"

"We needed to know, didn't we? Now we do."

Ganku-eh and Banda-ak stepped down from the caves.

"What is this?" Ganku-eh asked.

Alex pointed to Noken-ak and said, "We are going to need special tools to combat the stama they are using. Noken-ak and I have been working on making this shield to keep us safe."

Ganku-eh gestured at Noken-ak. "Bring it here."

Like a puppy brought to heel, the massive man carried the bow to the chieftain and handed her the shield.

She slipped an arm through it and held it in front of her in a practiced manner that told Alex immediately that she was no beginner.

"What is this made of? It is not as heavy as it seems it should be."

"I call it a composite shield. It has twisted straw, heavy cloth, and leather on a wooden frame. The whole is greater than the parts. The light weight will allow our warriors to carry the shields long distances."

She ran her fingers over the leather, the arrow buried in the front, and poked at the tightly bound straw at the back, and declared, "There is no stama here."

Alex felt a surge of elation. He hadn't known there was going to be a stama test, but he had passed it, nonetheless.

Ganku-eh handed the shield back to Noken-ak. "Show me."

"Oh," Alex said. "We already tested it. Sekun-ak shot him. It stopped the arrow. We don't need to test it again."

Ganku-eh shut Alex up with a look. She was not to be disobeyed. Quietly, she said, "Show me."

Noken-ak slipped the shield back on and stood to face Sekun-ak.

This time, Sekun-ak only took seven steps away before he turned to face the shield. Alex thought he might have pulled the string with a little more zest this time.

Is he trying *to kill him?*

Sekun-ak released the arrow and it zinged into the shield right next to the first. Again, Noken-ak took a half step back at the impact. Again, he still stood.

"Very good," Ganku-eh said and turned back to the caves.

Banda-ak waited until she had disappeared up the path, then held his hand out to Sekun-ak.

"Give me that bow. Let me try."

Chapter Twenty-Eight
The Fight

Alex was the Henry Ford of Winten-ah. He introduced the assembly line. He wondered at first if Ganku-eh might think it was stama and forbid it, but she discussed it with him and saw that it was just a more efficient way to prepare.

Of course, air travel was more efficient than walking as well, and Ganku-eh would not have taken well to the idea of climbing inside a winged metal cylinder. It's all a matter of degree.

Alex employed the classic idea of each person only having one job and gaining expertise at it. To that end, three men and women were dispatched to the forest each day, responsible for bringing back the proper wood to build the shield frame. More gathered the long, tough grasses, which were handed off to another team to twist together. And so on, and so on.

Winten-ah wasn't exactly cranking out a Model-T every day, but they were making a fair number of shields.

The first of the recruited troops arrived a few weeks later. There were several dozen men and women, all of whom were hunters or warriors in their own tribe. They all looked like typical Kragdon-ah stock—tall, handsome or beautiful, and athletic.

The exception was one bull-necked man built more like Noken-ak than a typical tribesman. He wasn't as tall, but he still towered over Alex, and his biceps were the size of Alex's thigh.

Sekun-ak brought them together in the big field to address them. He and Alex had talked about it and decided it would be better if he spoke first.

"We appreciate the long journey it's taken to get here. We have a sacred task ahead of us. Leading us on that task is Manta-ak."

Sekun-ak stepped aside and revealed Alex behind him. A few questioning looks crossed the faces of the gathered warriors, but the biggest man laughed at the sight of Alex.

"We are going to be going up against an enemy who has us out-numbered, who is already using stama and will be using it against us. We are going to need to train together so we can fight as one single unit. It's our only chance to prevail."

The warriors glanced from one to another. This was obviously not what they had expected or committed to.

The bull-necked man stepped forward, so he was only a few feet from Alex. "I agreed to come and fight. I do not need training. Show me who I need to kill, and I will kill them."

Alex wasn't completely unprepared for this situation.

"What's your name?"

"I am Tinta-ak," the big man said in a voice so deep it sounded like it came from the bottom of a barrel.

Alex took a step forward to lay a hand on Tinta-ak's shoulder in the traditional greeting. Tinta-ak lowered his head, and an expression so fierce came over him that Alex changed his mind.

"I appreciate that you are a great warrior." Alex swept his arm across the field to indicate all two dozen of the warriors. "I'm sure you're all great warriors. That's why you are here. However, if we do not train properly, we will fight bravely and die."

"Show me," Tinta-ak said.

Alex took one step back. "Show you what?"

"Show me what your training can do. Fight me."

The warriors behind Tinta-ak laughed. The idea of the giant man grappling with Alex was so ludicrous as to not be worth considering.

"All right," Alex said, simply. He looked at the warriors. "Make a circle. Let's say the first person to throw the other outside the circle wins."

"What if I just snap your neck? Can I throw your body out of the circle then?"

Alex twisted his head left, then right, popping his neck. "You bet. If you kill me, I've definitely lost the fight."

Tinta-ak looked surprised that Alex agreed to fight him. He scratched at his nose as if there was something he might be missing.

Meanwhile, the warriors, augmented by additional people from Winten-ah, formed a large circle. Winters were quiet and there was so little entertainment. Soon, every person in the tribe joined the circle. Alex's assembly line shut down. Children jumped and laughed, mock-fighting. A sudden holiday from a depressing winter.

Alex started stretching, which was much more a twenty-first century habit than it was in Kragdon-ah. The visiting warriors pointed and laughed.

One said, "It's like he's preparing his own body for burial." Much laughter ensued.

The two men met in the middle of the human ring. Alex was six foot two and weighed 180 pounds. Tinta-ak was seven foot one and weighed 300 pounds—all muscle.

Sekun-ak went to the middle of the ring and laid his hand on Alex's shoulder. Quietly, he said, "He will likely kill you. You don't have to do this. They will listen to you because of what you know. Not because you are a great fighter."

"I do have to do this. Some might listen, but they won't respect me if I don't."

Sekun-ak glanced over his shoulder at Tinta-ak, who was clenching and unclenching his fists.

"I don't think he likes you."

"You didn't like me either, and now you are my brother."

Sekun-ak could not argue with either sentiment, so he placed two fingers to his forehead and stepped back to the edge of the crowd. There would be no referee and no rules.

Alex gave Monda-ak a hand signal to go with Sekun-ak and he obeyed. The last thing Alex wanted was for his most protective friend to jump into the middle of the fight.

Tinta-ak was in no mood to waste time. He lunged, his long arms reaching for Alex's head. Alex sidestepped the obvious move, dancing lightly on his toes.

Tinta-ak grunted his frustration, dropped his hands, and stepped casually toward Alex, who held his ground. When he was within arm's length, Tinta-ak swung his massive sledgehammer fist at Alex's face.

More accurately, he swung at where Alex's face had been a split-second earlier. Alex had danced away again, still moving, keeping his weight evenly distributed.

Tinta-ak had had enough. With a mighty roar, he spread his arms out and rushed toward Alex. There was no time to dance away. Instead, Alex turned slightly sideways and grabbed Tinta-ak's right wrist. He pulled that toward him while bending at the knee. The big man's bulk crashed into Alex, but he was ready for it. He pulled Tinta-ak's wrist down and lifted with his shoulder.

Tinta-ak's momentum carried him completely up and over Alex. He landed on his back with such a resounding crash that people later said they could feel the ground move. He lay stunned for several seconds. Alex could have pressed his attack but continued to just bounce lightly from his left foot to his right, waiting for Tinta-ak to continue.

Looks of shock and surprise passed through the visiting warriors as they whispered among themselves. The Winten-ah were less surprised, having been around Alex for years.

Tinta-ak sucked air back into his lungs, before rolling onto his knees and springing back to his feet. He was surprisingly nimble for such a beast of a man. Nimble, but untrained.

Tinta-ak moved forward more cautiously, jabbing at Alex with his left hand, setting him up for his right. He jabbed once, twice, thrice, then swung his right fist. If it had connected, it would have likely killed Alex.

It did not connect.

Instead, Alex ducked left and again grabbed the giant's wrist with his right hand. This time, instead of pulling it toward him, he snapped his left hand onto Tinta-ak right elbow, trying for an arm bar. Tinta-ak used his far-superior leverage and simply lifted his arm out of it while delivering a blow with his right hand that made Alex see stars.

Okay, that's not gonna work.

Still, Alex felt he had the measure of the man now. Huge, muscled, and athletic. But people had almost certainly feared that size since childhood, so he had never learned to fight.

Time to end this before he tears my head off with a wild swing.

Alex feinted to his left, then struck with a leopard fist just below Tinta-ak's right elbow, hitting the pressure point perfectly.

The giant man's right arm dropped uselessly to his side. He looked at it almost comically, commanding it to rise up and strike Alex. He rotated his shoulder willing his arm to move, but that only caused it to flop like a beached fish.

The crowd surrounding them said, "Ooooooh," in unison. They had never seen magic like this.

Fury spread across Tinta-ak's face. He bunched up his left fist and swung wildly. Alex dodged the blow easily, then struck Tinta-ak's left arm in the same spot as he had the first, again using a leopard fist—folding his first two fingers in and striking with his knuckles.

Tinta-ak's left arm now dangled as helplessly as the first.

I could do the same to his legs, cutting him down to nothing like the Black Knight in a Monty Python movie, but I don't want to do that. I don't want to humiliate him. I'll need him.

Tinta-ak still had weapons at his disposal—his two legs, his shoulders, even his thick head—but he had no idea how to use any of them. For the first time, the big man looked frightened. He was at Alex's mercy, and he knew it. He did not beg, but simply raised his chin and waited for whatever blow would come.

Alex put all his weight on his left leg and gave a simple front kick with his right. He hit Tinta-ak square in the chest. With effectively no arms to find his balance, he stumbled backwards, trying to get his feet under him. It was a losing battle and he fell for a long time—not unlike the giant in Jack and the Beanstalk.

He fell directly toward the crowd of warriors he had come with. They could have caught him, held him up, sent him back into the fight. They did not. They sidestepped him like a matador in the bull ring.

Tinta-ak finally landed on his back, five feet outside of the ring.

He looked up at the cloudy sky, trying to puzzle out what had happened—how his lifetime streak of undefeated fights had come to an end at the hands of such a puny opponent.

Alex, who had been on the receiving end of only a single glancing blow, hurried over to Tinta-ak. He put an arm under him and helped him sit up. The giant's massive arms still hung limply at his side. He looked from one to the other as if they had betrayed him.

"Don't worry, I'll fix this for you." Alex lifted Tinta-ak's right arm and began to massage it in a circular, downward motion from his bicep to below the elbow.

My two hands don't reach all the way around his bicep. What a specimen. If he's trained, he will be a force to be reckoned with.

After Alex massaged the right arm for a few minutes, blood flowed through it and Tinta-ak was able to move his fingers, then rotate his fist. He looked at Alex, who he had tried to kill earlier, with an expression of devotion. He turned his left shoulder toward Alex, who repeated the process on the second arm.

"It's only temporary," Alex said quietly to Tinta-ak. "You might be weaker for a few hours, but I think a weaker Tinta-ak is still stronger than most other men."

Tinta-ak managed to reach two fingers up to his forehead in acknowledgement of that truth.

Alex sprang to his feet and reached a hand out, lifting Tinta-ak to his feet as well.

Alex turned to the assembled crowd and said, "Winten-ah, please return to the warmth of the caves and return to work on building our shields. We are depending on you."

The crowd broke up into small groups and returned to the caves or to the armory to work, murmuring among themselves as they did.

Alex returned his attention to the visiting warriors.

"Now, as I was saying, we are going to be outnumbered and they will have weapons we do not have. We will need to fight as a single unit if we are to win. As we saw, size and strength does not always equal victory."

The man standing next to Tinta-ak laughed a little and poked the bigger man in the ribs. When he looked at Tinta-ak's face, he took two steps away from him.

The other men lifted two fingers to their forehead.

They were believers.

Chapter Twenty-Nine
Basic Training

"What you did to Tinta-ak. Can you teach me that?"

Sekun-ak and Alex were walking back toward the armory to see how production of the shields was progressing.

Alex looked at him with a glint in his eye. "You said he was going to kill me."

"I said he was *likely* to kill you," Sekun-ak corrected him.

"Right, right. Of course I can show you. I will train you and three other men we choose together. Then, they will each take a group of men and train them. The best from each of their groups will train others. By summer, we will have a group that is at least semi-qualified in hand-to-hand combat."

"What did you do to him? What stama was it that made his arms go limp."

"No stama. Just pressure points." Alex reached out and gripped Sekun-ak's elbow in the same spot he had hit Tinta-ak. A look of surprise jumped onto Sekun-ak's face and he leaped backward, flexing his hand.

"See?" Alex said. "No stama. Just pressure points. It's not that hard to learn, although we will have to go through an accelerated course if we are going to have time to train everyone. There's much more we need to pay attention to as well."

"What?"

"We need to learn to act as a unit. To become a band of brothers and sisters. And we need to learn to use our shields."

Sekun-ak squinted. "Don't we already know how to use the shields? We hold it in front of us when they fire at us."

Alex chuckled. "Yes, hopefully. There's more to it, though. We're going to form a shield wall."

Sekun-ak let that term roll around in his head. He was familiar with both words, of course, but had never heard them used in conjunction.

"What is a shield wall?"

"Here. Grab a shield," Alex said, doing so himself.

The shield Sekun-ak picked up fit him perfectly, but Alex felt like a child holding his father's shield. "I've got to remember to have them make me a shield that fits me."

Alex stood on a low bench, so he was approximately the same height as Sekun-ak.

"Come stand next to me and hold your shield as you normally would." Alex was amused to see that the bench made him slightly taller than Sekun-ak, who stretched his neck a bit to close the gap. Alex placed his shield firmly up against Sekun-ak's.

"Now, what do you see?"

"Two shields?"

"Yes, two shields, but more importantly, the beginning of a shield wall. Now, imagine a dozen men walking like this. They would be invulnerable to almost any attack."

"Not a rain of arrows like we saw in Denta-ah. Many of those would fly over the shields and hit us."

"You are correct. But," Alex lifted his shield up and held it over his and Sekun-ak's heads, "what if the warriors behind us hold their shields like this?"

The light went on for Sekun-ak. "But then we will be blind."

"You're right. Just as the turtle is blind but can't be hurt when it is in its shell. We only make the complete shield wall when we are stationary and under attack. If the strong men in front brace themselves, even a wave of attackers throwing themselves at us will bounce off. Like the shields we are making, the strength of the whole is more than just the component parts."

Sekun-ak put his fingers to his forehead, nodding simultaneously. Alex had noticed that he had begun copying some of the gestures Alex had never broken himself of.

"When we need to move, the people behind will keep their shields over our heads to protect us from the rain of crossbow bolts, but we can look around our shields like this." Alex moved his shield a few inches to the left, his head a few inches to the right, and peered through the slit between the shields.

Sekun-ak took a step back and looked at Alex with newfound respect. "I am glad you are on our side, Manta-ak."

"We have to remember, though, that the Denta-ah have another version of me, but he is not constrained. He is spending all the days and nights while we are training, thinking up new weapons to kill us."

"I saw you thrash Tinta-ak like he was a child. I saw the man who the Denta-ah have. He was soft and white, like a slug. I'd rather be with you. You are a hunter and a warrior."

THE WINTEN-AH RUNNERS had done their jobs and survived their perilous journeys. More troops arrived, trickling in groups of six, ten, or a dozen.

Sekun-ak knew it would be their responsibility to feed more than double the normal Winten-ah population, so he took his hunters out day after day after day, not coming home each trip until they had meat with them.

Alex stayed behind, training the new warriors in hand-to-hand combat and other techniques they would need in the upcoming months.

Finally, Sekun-ak declared that they had enough food and that the last of the runners had returned. The people of Winten-ah who were not directly involved with making the shields went to work cutting trees, constructing lean-tos and making sleeping mattresses. The lean-tos were not as secure as sleeping above the ground in the caves, but with hundreds of armed warriors sleeping there and additional guard patrols, even the animals of Kragdon-ah stayed away.

Alex chose Sekun-ak as his second-in-command but picked the rest of his officers from the ranks of the newcomers. He wanted each tribe to have representation. They were risking the well-being of themselves and their tribe just as much as Winten-ah was.

Tinta-ak had become the best public relations man Alex could have hoped for. With each group of new arrivals, he told how he had challenged Alex and what had happened. He always mimed the end of the fight, showing his limp arms and rumbling, bumbling, tumbling exit from the fighting ring.

Alex never grew tired of watching him recreate it.

When the new arrivals saw Tinta-ak's size and heard the story, they all decided not to challenge Alex themselves.

Alex worked tirelessly into the night training Sekun-ak, Tinta-ak and three other men. Then, the six of them each took sixty men and ran them through their paces.

For the first few weeks, all weapons were banished. Alex had taught his lieutenants the basics of jiu-jitsu and the other self-defense arts he had learned in his Special Forces training.

The men grumbled about not having their weapons. Alex thought it was time for another demonstration.

He plucked one of the men at random from the ranks and tossed him a cudgel.

"Hit me with the cudgel," Alex said.

The man reared back and threw it directly at Alex's head. Alex was startled but managed to move his head just far enough and fast enough that it didn't split him open like a melon. The man rushed toward him, but Alex easily stepped aside, thrust a leg out and sent him flying.

"I said, 'Hit me with the cudgel,' not 'throw the damned thing at me.'"

The gathered men tittered a little.

"Now, try and hit me." Alex picked the club up off the ground and tossed it to the man.

The warrior, again almost a foot taller, launched himself at Alex, swinging the club wildly. Alex ducked beneath the whizzing arc of the club and kicked out, hitting the pressure point at the man's knee. He crumpled to the ground.

"Weapons," Alex said, "only help if you know how to use them. And, if you know how to fight both with and without a weapon, you always have the advantage." Alex helped the man up, but this time did not massage the numbness away. Instead, he let the man try to walk away. His right leg wouldn't bear his weight and he tumbled back to the frozen ground.

The warriors bought in again.

After a month of training, Sekun-ak came to Alex and said, "We have enough shields for everyone."

"Good. Tomorrow, have them all brought to the fields. We'll size them up and assign each man his shield. For the rest of their training, I never want them to be more than a few feet away from their shields. When they eat, when they sleep, when they sit around telling lies to each other, I want them to have their shields with them."

The men had come expecting to go to war immediately, so they had already brought their weapons of choice with them—atlatls, spears, bow and arrows, and stone hammers. Once the shields were distributed, their outfitting was nearly complete.

Alex had decided against armor, with one exception. He knew his army was going to have to travel a long distance just to get to the battle. The more and heavier equipment they had to carry, the worse shape they would be in when they arrived. However, if Douglas Winterborne had also decided on creating a shield wall—a real possibility, based on the other weapons he was creating—then there might be a true shield wall clash.

When two shield walls ram into each other, it is a frenzied display of strength and willpower. There are three ways to win when one shield wall meets another. You can use sheer brute strength, knocking the front row of the opposing wall backward until they fall like bowling pins. You can slip a sword or spear through a gap between the shields, injuring the man behind it, which creates an opening. Or, most likely, you can hack down at exposed ankles. A warrior with a spear through their calf is not focusing on the job at hand.

So, Alex had asked that the hides the Winten-ah had stored be cured, soaked, tanned and turned into a stiff leather. One at a time, he had his warriors go into the armory, where they were fitted with a piece of leather that ran from just below their knee to down over the top of their moccasins.

With the shield, their lower-leg armor and whatever weapons they had brought with them, the warriors were equipped.

The makeup of Alex's Army was mostly men, but there was a smattering of women, too. Diversity in all things was popular in Kragdon-ah. Alex trained the women just as he did the men, and one woman—Senta-eh—took to his strategies so quickly that he made her one of his lieutenants, in charge of sixty other men and women.

Senta-eh was unusual, in that her hair was not the jet black of almost everyone else Alex had met. Instead, her hair was dark, but with red streaks that ran through it. Her eyes, instead of being as dark brown as other Kragdon-ah, were gray. She was a striking woman, but there was no sexual harassment in Alex's Army. The women warriors were every bit as tough as the men and were not shy about showing it.

Alex knew time was growing short. He had met with Ganku-eh, Banda-ak, and his lieutenants, and they had decided to march on Denta-ah at the summer solstice. That would give them the maximum amount of daylight to travel each day, and they wouldn't have to worry about cold temperatures.

Dan Hadaller had delivered the yew trees as promised, and Sekun-ak and his weapon maker had managed to create longbows with assistance from Dan. Alex picked out twenty-four warriors who had brought bow and arrows as their weapon of choice, figuring they were already familiar with the basic concepts.

Sekun-ak had only been able to produce four of the bows and a few dozen of the longer arrows so far, but that was enough to begin training.

Alex cleared out the field, which was more than two hundred yards from side to side, then took his four most promising bowmen all the way to one side.

"Don't worry about aiming at anything. Let me just see how they fire. But, let's do it on my command."

The four warriors nodded, notched their longbows, and held them, muscles in their arms straining, but they held the arrows steady.

"Fire!" Alex said. He spoke in the universal language, and *fire* in that language actually meant fire itself, but the meaning was clear. All four bowmen released their arrows with a smooth *snick*.

The arrows climbed in a lovely arc and disappeared in the trees more than two hundred yards away.

"Yes!" Alex cried. "Look at them fly!"

The bowmen themselves stood watching the graceful flight of their arrows like the thing of beauty they were. They looked at each other but didn't give a hint of their excitement. Their expressions said, 'Of course I shot an arrow farther than anyone on Kragdon-ah ever has. I am a *warrior.*'

Alex, meanwhile, offered a ride on Monda-ak to each child who could retrieve one of the practice arrows. Monda-ak didn't really mind, as he liked children, and each of those arrows took time to replace.

Alex assembled the nearly-four-hundred warriors on the same open field the next morning.

He had been working with them on marching, singing cadences his first drill instructor would have been proud of, and learning to act as a unit. For the first time, he had them wear their belted weapons, shields, and lower-leg armor. When they stood at attention, they looked like a formidable force.

Alex pulled Tinta-ak away from his unit, had six men form a shield wall, and told Tinta-ak to break it.

"I don't want to hurt them," Tinta-ak said, flexing his biceps. "They are not me, but we will still need their numbers, right?"

"Right. I don't think you're going to be able to hurt them. I think they are going to knock you down instead."

There was a time when Tinta-ak might have scoffed at Alex, but he had learned the error of his ways.

"Shield wall!" Alex yelled.

The six warriors locked their shields together and braced themselves.

Tinta-ak pawed the ground like a bull, then launched himself across the field. He was swift for a man so big and had momentum by the time he got to the wall. He lowered his shoulder and hit it dead center.

The men he hit staggered ever so slightly, but as Alex had predicted, Tinta-ak once again ended up on his prodigious backside.

There were a few chuckles, but Alex said, "I invite any man who wants to try to break the shield wall to line up."

To Alex's surprise, dozens of warriors from all over Kragdon-ah lined up to try.

Alex turned to Sekun-ak. "Do you never believe your eyes?"

"We believe others have failed, but always think that we will not. That is our way."

Alex watched, amused, then began to send the men in groups of two or three. The shield wall never budged.

"Do you see now that there is more strength in the group than there is in all the individuals?"

The combined cry of the warriors tore through the air.

Alex turned to Sekun-ak.

"We're ready."

Ten days before the main body of the army left, Alex selected an advanced team for a special mission. Their goal was difficult and filled with uncertainty. The possibility of death was perhaps higher than even for the warriors who would follow behind them.

Alex asked for volunteers, and received three-hundred and seventy-six of them—every man and woman in the Manta-ak Army, as the group had taken to calling itself.

With such a broad field to choose from, Alex conferred with his lieutenants, and chose four men and a woman. Janta-ak, who Alex had kept alive on his first day in Kragdon-ah was one of them.

Alex, Janta-ak, and Malen-eh, his wife, had been close friends since that very first day. Both had nursed him through his sickness, and Janta-ak had been his partner on many successful hunting expeditions.

Alex hated to send him on such a dangerous mission, but he also needed someone who he knew had a cool head and would respond well under pressure, because Alex expected a *lot* of pressure on this mission.

Alex briefed all of them on what their mission was, then they left immediately. Since they were a smaller group, they would travel faster and arrive days ahead of everyone else.

Alex burned to be with them—to immediately be moving, doing something, but he knew he was needed with the main group.

He laid his hand on Janta-ak's shoulder in the universal show of affection and said, "Gunta, old friend."

The five set off at a steady pace.

As Alex watched them disappear, he didn't know if he would ever see any of them again.

Chapter Thirty
Janta-ak's Journey

Janta-ak kept a fast pace—almost a steady jog—as he and the other four volunteers moved over the path to Denta-ah. Janta-ak had never been far from Winten-ah, but they still moved unerringly toward their target.

One of the other warriors who Alex had chosen was Prata-eh, from a tribe called the Nekan-ah. Nekan-ah had been friendly neighbors with both Stipa-ah and Denta-ah. With the built-in ability to locate her own home, she was also able to guide them to Denta-ah, which was only half a day's walk further on.

All five of the team members were magnificent physical specimens, but that was true of everyone in Manta-ak's Army. This allowed them to keep up the grueling pace—even over the first mountain and its switchbacks—for most of the trip.

Alex had told them where the rest spots were that he had used when he made the trek with Yosta-ak, but Janta-ak and company did not use them. They were too far ahead of the pace Yosta-ak had set. It didn't matter—they only rested for a few hours each night and did so by climbing trees to sleep.

On the first night, just as they settled in, they heard a slow, snuffling sound. From their perches, they looked down and saw Godat-ta. They had climbed high enough in the trees to avoid all but the best predators, but that did not include Godat-ta.

The giant bear wandered along the path, then stopped below the five warriors. All five held their breath, unwilling to make even that gentle sound.

Godat-ta stopped directly beneath them. Humans have a blunted sense of smell, but bears do not. A bear's nose can be thousands of times more sensitive than a human's. Godat-ta was no exception.

He sat on his haunches and looked straight up into the branches above. A bear's vision is not as keen as its sense of smell, but it was plenty good to see the five warriors perched on the branches above.

All five knew their mission was over, if Godat-ta wished it. He could climb better than they could and a footrace—whether uphill, downhill, or on level ground—was no contest. As with everything Godat-ta saw, if he wanted to kill the warriors he could.

Godat-ta looked around curiously.

The warriors contemplated their mortality, and hoped that Godat-ta was on his way home from a big meal with a full stomach and maybe some heartburn.

His black eyes gleamed in the moonlight as he looked up at them. Finally, he snuffed out a blast of air, fell back onto all fours, and meandered down the path. An inconsequential decision to the bear.

Life and death to the warriors.

Janta-ak looked at Prata-eh and the other warriors.

Prata-eh smiled at Janta-ak and said, "Werta," which meant fate, or joss, in the universal language.

"Werta," Janta-ak agreed.

Figuring that a run-in with Godat-ta was the worst thing that could happen at that moment, Janta-ak wrapped his legs around the trunk of the tree, laid his face against the hard wood and drifted off.

Janta-ak kept up the same grueling pace for the next five days, stopping only to eat some berries and pemmican or jerky, and to grab a few hours of shut-eye before starting again.

The weather was good, though, and aside from the close call with Godat-ta, they had been left alone by other wildlife.

When they approached Stipa-ah, they slowed. They knew from the stories Alex had told them about his journey that Stipa-ah had been destroyed, but they didn't know what its current status was.

Alex had thought it was possible that Doug-ak, as he referred to Douglas Winterborne when speaking to the Winten-ah, had taken it back over and rebuilt it. Expanding armies need space and, unless an opposing army had a trebuchet, Stipa-ah was easily defendable.

Janta-ak and his group stood in the trees and watched the village, much as Yosta-ak had on Alex's journey.

At one point, Prata-eh pointed and said, "Movement." They watched the spot for long minutes, though, and did not see anything.

"It was likely just an animal. If Denta-ah was here, we would have seen them. Still, we need to be cautious."

Janta-ak led the small band over the footbridge to the island. The buildings looked just as Alex had described them—the outer ring was burned out, while the interior simply looked like a ghost town.

"Spread out, see if you can find any sign of life."

Janta-ak walked by the mass grave where the warriors of Stipa-ah were buried. Grass was growing over it, but the mound was still visible.

Janta-ak saw a building that he thought might have food stores. "That would be good to know when we march back home. We will be hungry," he said to himself.

He stepped into the cool darkness of the windowless room and waited for his eyes to adjust.

His ears detected a movement to his right and Janta-ak whirled in that direction. Three bodies bowled into him, slamming a cudgel into his ribs.

Janta-ak rolled with the blow, sprang to his feet and had his own club in his hands. He lifted it to strike and held his weapon at the top of its arc.

He was facing three dirty, scrawny, *children.*

The tallest of them barely reached above his waist.

Janta-ak lowered his weapon and put his hands out, placating them.

"I am a friend."

The children, who looked more feral than human, snarled and ran at him.

"Prata-eh!" Janta-ak yelled. "Help me!"

Janta-ak was more than capable of clubbing the children into unconsciousness, but grabbing them and calming them was more difficult.

Prata-eh and the other warriors ran into the building, weapons at the ready, when they saw it was small children attacking Janta-ak.

Prata-eh did her best to hide her smirk as she said, "Gorka-ah, Renta-ah, grab the children." She reached down and plucked the child up but soon lost her smile. The child fought, kicked, and bit like a cat thrown into a river.

She set the child down so she could get a better grip, and the little girl kicked her ferociously in the leg.

"That's it," Prata-eh said, whirling the child around and wrapping her up in a hug so tight she couldn't budge.

Gorka-ah and Renta-ah did the same to the whirling dervishes in front of them, while Werta-ah, the final member watched with a small smile.

"Just hold them," Janta-ak commanded.

"Easier to order than to carry out," Prata-eh said, "or maybe you didn't notice."

"I noticed," Janta-ak said, rubbing a welt that had risen on his ribs where one of the children had clubbed him.

He kneeled in front of the three captive children. In the universal language said, "We are friends, understand? We are not the Denta-ah, who destroyed this village. We are coming to make war with them. *Kunta.*"

The children quit struggling so much and relaxed, but still eyed him warily.

"Are you Stipa-ah?" Janta-ak asked.

The leader seemed to be the young girl. She answered, "Yes," while touching two fingers to her forehead.

"Have you been alone here since the day Denta-ah destroyed the village?"

She repeated the same gesture.

"How have you survived?"

"When Denta-ah dropped fire on our village, our mothers hid us. They told us not to move, no matter what. We didn't. We stayed in our hiding spot for three days until we got so cold and hungry, we had to come out. Everyone was gone."

"And there's just the three of you?"

In response, the small girl put fingers to her lips and whistled three times.

Over the next minute, four other children came warily into the building.

"How have you survived?"

"The Denta-ah just wanted our people. They did not take our food. We've been eating what was left behind, but it is gone now."

"Let's go outside," Janta-ak said, leading the way.

In the better light, he could see that the children were not just thin, they were emaciated.

"Oh," Janta-ak said. "We will not let you starve." He pulled his bag off his back, took out all his remaining food, and handed it to the little girl. Prata-eh and the others did the same.

"We cannot take you with us yet. We are going to fight the Denta-ah."

"They throw fire," the small girl said.

"We know. That's why we are going to fight them, so they can't do this to other tribes. When we beat them, we will come back to you and make sure you will have food to eat. Understand?"

The children answered in a chorus of, "Yes," but Janta-ak could see they didn't cherish the idea of being alone again for an unknown time.

"We have to go on, but another, much larger, group will be along behind us. They may come and look at the village. If they do, please do not attack them. You can hide, but they are my friends and they are coming to attack the Denta-ah."

Janta-ak wanted to stay, to protect the children, but knew he could not. They still had a mission to accomplish.

Janta-ak and the others walked away from Stipa-ah with lighter carry bags but heavy hearts.

Chapter Thirty-One
Godat-ta

There would be seventeen hours of daylight for their march, and Alex wanted to maximize every minute of it, so he decided there would be no campfires. It was possible that Denta-ah would have spies everywhere. They had enough manpower to do so. A campfire and its smoke can be seen for miles at dusk. That meant there would be no cooking fire, and every person was responsible for carrying their own food.

Again, Sekun-ak had come to the rescue with bountiful hunts. Every warrior in the march started with a shoulder bag full of pemmican, rolled fruits, berries, and nuts. Alex remembered that he had run out of food the day before he had arrived in Denta-ah and so packed more food this time.

Alex had planned for weeks exactly how he wanted his army to march. Most of the men and women carried their shield, but the longbowmen would be firing at a distance and shouldn't need the protection. They carried their bows slung over their shoulder, along with their arrows and other supplies that the group might need for the fight.

Alex had two dozen shield-bearers at the front, then four longbowmen, and kept that ratio until he ran out of bowmen. Alex gave Tinta-ak the honor of leading the march. He knew that the giant man would push them as hard as they could be pushed. Alex and

Sekun-ak marched in the very middle, where they could hear what as many of their warriors were saying as possible.

Before they left, Benka-eh, the priestess, and Lanta-eh, the prophesied savior of Winten-ah stood high on the cliffs in the pre-dawn light and looked down over the assembled warriors. Both spread their arms wide in benediction, and chanted a blessing on both the fighters and their mission.

Finally, in her pure, sweet voice, Lanta-eh said, "I have seen the future and it is good. You are brave and will prevail."

Not exactly 'Win one for the Gipper' as far as inspirational speeches go, but she didn't say we were happily marching to our death, either, so I'll take it.

Ganku-eh and Banda-ak stood with Alex to say goodbye. Banda-ak had desperately wanted to go and fight, but Ganku-eh had forbidden it. Winten-ah was giving more of its warriors to the cause than any other tribe. Banda-ak needed to be home to begin to train the children to fight, in case the Manta-ak Army failed in their mission. They would be all that was left to stand and face Denta-ah if that happened.

As they left the open field, they marched in rhythm. Alex knew it wouldn't add to the distance they covered each day, but he wanted the group to feel like a single unit, and be able to act as such, once they reached Denta-ah.

Monda-ak continued to go where he wanted, when he wanted. He chose not to march in rhythm, but he was rarely far from Alex.

By midday, Alex compared where they were with where they had been when he marched with Yosta-ak. They were behind, and Alex was forced to realize that there was simply no way an army of almost four hundred, no matter how motivated, could move as efficiently as a small group.

Sekun-ak noted the same thing, but said quietly to Alex, "We've waited six months to strike at Denta-ah, one or two more days will not make any difference."

Alex knew the truth of those words, but he still chafed at their pace.

"With almost four hundred people, *somebody* always needs to take a piss."

"We can either stop marching together or take fast breaks more often."

"Which will slow us down in the short run, but maybe move us faster in the long run."

Alex turned to Senta-eh, who was marching behind him. "Tell Tinta-ak to halt."

Senta-eh did not hesitate but fell out of line and ran ahead. Soon the order came back, and they halted.

Alex grabbed his water bag off his belt and drank deeply. The advantage of having made this trip once was that he had some idea where they would pass streams where they could replenish. They could march for days without food, but not without water.

Alex was reattaching his bag when he heard an uproar from ahead in the line.

One panicked word came back to him: Godat-ta.

Alex jumped out of line and sprinted up to the front. When he reached Tinta-ak, he looked ahead on the trail. His bowels felt suddenly watery.

He had seen bears in his life. This was no bear that had ever wandered the earth that he had seen or dreamed of. It was sitting on its back haunches and swiping a paw at a berry bush, pulling it into its mouth and stripping it, thorns and all.

Alex tried to judge its height but gave up. It was at least twice as tall as Tinta-ak, while it was sitting down.

What the hell do we do? There's no way four hundred of us can turn and run.

"Stand down," Alex said quietly. As softly as he had spoken, his words carried on the wind, because Godat-ta slowly turned his head toward him.

Surely, Godat-ta had never seen so many humans grouped together in one place.

Will we look like the buffet table, or will so many of us frighten it away?

In answer, Godat-ta stood on its hind legs and sniffed the air.

The men behind Alex stirred. It wasn't that they wanted to run, but everyone in Kragdon-ah knew one thing for certain. Godat-ta meant death.

The bear dropped back down on all fours and casually walked toward them. Twenty yards away, it stood to its full height and loosed a mighty roar.

"SHIELD WALL," ALEX said. Not that it was a perfect or even good strategy against a bear that size. It was just the only words that hadn't left his head.

Tinta-ak, Alex, and four other warriors clinked and locked their shields, then braced themselves.

To Godat-ta, it may have looked like all the men disappeared, replaced by these odd shapes.

Godat-ta snorted and ran toward them.

Alex and his men were blind, but they knew what was approaching. The sound of the gigantic paws scraping and pounding against the ground was undeniable.

The men directly behind the front shield row put their shields against the men's backs in support.

None of it mattered.

Godat-ta slammed into the shields head first and the men and equipment went flying like bowling pins.

Godat-ta continued on through the line, never slowing or hesitating. Where he passed, he left a tangled heap of arms, legs and torsos. Monda-ak, who many thought resembled a bear himself, launched against Godat-ta, crashing into his hindquarter.

Godat-ta failed to notice.

Eventually, Godat-ta reached the end of the line, ran on for a few yards, then stopped, turned, and looked back over his shoulder at the destruction he had wrought. He shook his head in a circle, then stood and roared.

The ground trembled and birds flew up in a cloud from surrounding trees.

Alex hurried through the line, encouraging everyone who could, to stand. He reached the back of the line, where he found Senta-eh, notching an arrow on her longbow.

"Don't fire unless we need to. I don't think we can take it down," Alex said.

"I'm not going to be run over again while I have my bow in my hand."

Can't argue with that.

Other bowmen—some with regular bows, others with longbows—gathered at the back of the line. They notched arrows, but held.

Godat-ta fell back onto all four and took one menacing step toward the group, then two.

The air was heavy with silence and dread. Alex could hear the slight creak of the bowstrings.

Godat-ta charged.

A dozen arrows flew. Several missed. Most connected, but barely sank into Godat-ta's thick hide, or bounced off completely.

One—fired from the longbow of Senta-eh—pierced the behemoth's left eye.

Godat-ta tumbled to a stop, then righted himself, clawing at the arrow and screaming his agony.

Alex had only a split-second to decide a strategy—try to kill the nearly unkillable beast or run.

He turned to Senta-eh. "Run to the front. Tell Tinta-ak to march us at double time."

An army of nearly four hundred takes time to get underway. While they waited, Alex and a dozen bowmen waited, arrows notched. Every second, more longbows joined them. Alex still didn't like their chances.

Godat-ta managed to grab at the arrow with both paws and pull it out. The giant bear's eyeball came out with it. It tilted its head to the sky and roared—a scream that might have been heard back in Winten-eh.

Alex felt the army behind him moving, and he and the bowmen marched backwards from Godat-ta. The mighty bear continued to paw at its eye socket, then turned and ran straight up a hill.

Alex halted and watched until the lumbering bear disappeared over the hilltop. Only then did he and the archers turn and join the others.

Less than one day out and we've run into the most powerful beast in the world. That's gotta be the worst of it right?

It was not the worst of it.

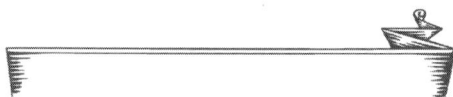

Chapter Thirty-Two
The Plan

J anta-ak and his crew climbed the hill that overlooked Denta-ah and approached the tree line but did not look out. The closer they got to Denta-ah, the more signs of growth and activity they had seen.

Twice, they had passed by crews of men working felling trees and hauling them back. What Alex had described as nothing more than a path was now a road—wide enough for four men to pass abreast. Plenty wide to haul logs back to Denta-ah.

Janta-ak sat in the cool shade of a tall tree and indicated to the others to do the same. It was summer in Kragdon-ah, and the sun beat down mercilessly.

Finally, the air cooled, the sun set, and the diamond-bright starfield came out. The moon was almost full and gave more than enough light to see. And, potentially, to be seen, so they still moved slowly and cautiously.

They crept to the edge of the hill and looked down on Denta-ah. It looked vastly different from what Alex had described.

Where there had once been a stockade across a natural entrance to a dead-end valley, that massive barrier had now been moved out a great distance. They had lost the easy-protection of the hills by doing so, but made up for it by continuing the stockade—built out of the thickest, tallest trees in the surrounding forest. It now looked to Janta-ak as though there was room for an entire community in the space between the beginning of the barrier and where that wall had once stood.

Outside the stockade, a hundred acres of soil had been turned and there were plants of all sorts now springing up in organized rows.

"This is the largest community I've ever seen," Prata-eh said, her voice tinged with awe.

"They will only get bigger and enslave more if we do not do our duty."

The five of them had no food but did not regret feeding the children of Stipa-ah. They knew, if their mission was successful, they would have something to eat soon enough.

"I'll take first watch," Janta-ak said. "Sleep while you can. Prata-eh, I will wake you for next watch."

The four warriors nodded, sat down with their backs resting against a tree and were out almost immediately.

Janta-ak crept back over to the edge of the ridge and watched the activity below. Even at night, there was a buzz of activity everywhere.

The next morning, Janta-ak and the others crept down the side of the hill, moving from one piece of cover to another. When they had nearly reached the bottom, they crept along until they were nearly lined up with the edge of the fortress-in-making.

"Remember the plan," Janta-ak whispered. "And good luck."

The five of them dropped their weapons in the deep grass, then walked to the edge of the barrier and made themselves visible. For long, stomach-churning moments, no one noticed them.

Without warning a crossbow bolt whizzed through the air and into the throat of Renta-ah. The short bolt hit with such ferocity it buried itself almost to the end of the shaft.

Renta-ah scrabbled at the arrow, but it was buried too deeply. His eyes glazed over as he dropped to his knees then pitched forward.

Janta-ak's first instinct was to reach for his fallen comrade. He knew the mission came first. Always the mission.

The remaining four warriors raised their hands in surrender.

Chapter Thirty-Three
The Children of Stipa-ah

The march of Manta-ak's Army felt endless to both Alex and his warriors. The going was slow, and the anticipation of the upcoming battle magnified everything.

They did not run into a threat of the magnitude of Godat-ta again, but that was because there were no other threats in Kragdon-ah that equaled the mighty bear.

After many long days of hiking, the army arrived at Stipa-ah. Alex did not worry about hiding his troops as they approached. If there were Denta-ah there, he knew it would be a small force, easily overwhelmed by his superior numbers.

When he led his army out of the forest that surrounded the lake, he saw an astounding sight. Children stood looking at them at the end of the path. They weren't playing or waving or jumping up and down. They stood silently staring at the army.

Alex turned to Tinta-ak and said, "Keep everyone here. I am going to talk with them. Monda-ak, stay here with Sekun-ak."

Alex removed his weapons, laid them on the ground and crossed the stone pathway to Stipa-ah.

"Gunta," Alex said in one of the few words that translated from Winten-ah to the universal language.

"Gunta," a small girl said. Her hair was knotted and tangled; her face dirty. She looked levelly at him.

Alex kneeled in front of the children, unsure who they were, although the realization was dawning.

The small girl pointed at Alex and said, "You were here before."

"Yes, right after the Denta-ah burned your village. How did you know we weren't the Denta-ah?"

The girl fixed him with a withering look. "We are not stupid. We have survived here alone for many moon cycles." She held out a piece of dried jerky. "Your friend Janta-ak was here. He told us you were coming with a mighty army and not to be afraid." She stared at Tinta-ak and the other men standing in the forest. "Is that your mighty army?"

She sounded doubtful.

"Yes, that is the army." Alex left *mighty* out. It felt presumptuous.

"You and the others buried our dead."

Alex touched two fingers to his forehead.

"Thank you."

The other children around her repeated it—"Thank you."

"We could not have done it, but we would have tried," the girl said. The tiny boy behind her touched his fingers to his forehead and flexed his non-existent muscles in confirmation.

"It was the right thing to do. Did you hide when the Denta-ah came?"

"Yes," the girl confirmed. "We're small, so it was easy for our mothers to hide us." She pointed to a boy who wasn't much more than a toddler. "Grima-ak was scared at first, but he is brave now. We've taken care of him."

Alex shook his head in disbelief, a gesture that didn't translate in Kragdon-ah.

"Can you take us with you? Janta-ak said we had to wait here, but we are tired of waiting. This was our home, but it is not anymore. Our mothers and fathers that weren't killed may be in Denta-ah. We would like to go find them. We can be useful. We're small and can go places you cannot. And, we are brave. Even Grima-ak."

Grima-ak spread his legs wide and puffed his chest out to show his bravery.

"We can't. If your parents are in Denta-ah, we will free them and they will return here for you. If they are not there, we will stop and take you back to Winten-ah."

"What if you die?"

"Well, we won't *all* die. Even if I die, I will tell everyone else that you are here. Someone will come back to get you. I give you my oath."

Even a young girl knew the value of an oath in Kragdon-ah. She didn't like it, but she accepted it.

"What are you eating? How are you surviving?"

"Janta-ak gave us all the food he had. He said they wouldn't need it anymore."

"He was right. One way or the other, they didn't need food from here. Do you have any left?"

"Yes. Do you want it?"

Alex smiled. "No. Show me how much you have."

The girl gestured to the biggest boy, who ran into a nearby hut and emerged with a single bag. She took it and held it open to Alex.

"Stay here."

Alex hurried back to Sekun-ak and spoke briefly. Moments later, he came back with two heavy bags filled with pemmican, hard cheese, nuts, berries, and jerky.

"You're all too skinny. We need to fatten you up before we can take you home." He handed the small girl and boy the bags.

She accepted them solemnly, then tipped her head back and sang a beautiful chant. Her tiny voice soared, and the other children joined in. It brought tears to Alex's eyes.

"There. Now maybe you won't die."

Alex realized with a shock that this young girl was about the same age as Amy. He tried to picture Amy in this situation.

Could she do this? God, I never want to find out.

Alex stuffed deep a desire to hug the little girl. Instead, he laid a hand on her shoulder. She tried to do the same, but her arm only made it a little past Alex's elbow.

Alex spun on his heel and walked back to his army.

They still had half a day's march to get to Denta-ah.

Chapter Thirty-Four
Enslaved II

Janta-ak and his remaining volunteers had been separated. They had not seen what had happened to Renta-ah's body, but they had heard that when slaves died, they just dragged the bodies far out into the forest and let the animals dispose of them.

Each of them had the same assignment from Alex and being split up made that easier.

Janta-ak had been ordered to strip bark off the long trees that the other slaves brought back from deep in the forest. It was monotonous work, and the biggest danger he faced was scraping the skin off his knuckles as he worked.

The biggest danger, that is, unless he was caught fomenting a revolution.

The first day, Janta-ak only watched his surroundings. He watched the guards on the fortification, how and when they changed shifts. He watched people pass through his area and divided people up into three classes—Denta-ah, slaves, and trustees.

It was important that he knew who chafed under the Denta-ah and who had given themselves over and would gladly turn a man in just to curry favor.

Janta-ak was part of a twelve-man operation that stripped three logs at a time. He worked with an older man who never spoke to anyone, and a younger man who showed every sign of being angry.

Janta-ak thought that anger was a good response to being enslaved, but also that it made him a less-than-ideal candidate to confide in initially. He preferred someone who could keep their thoughts to themselves.

They were not allowed to speak as they worked, but at night, they were cycled through a mess area where they were given enough calories to theoretically sustain them for another day. Then they were shuffled off to sleep a few hours before being awakened at dawn to do it all again.

On his second night of captivity, Janta-ak stuck close to the older man and bedded down beside him. There was a guard posted at one end of the lean-to they slept in, but it was a trustee who enjoyed having such a soft job and didn't pay much attention to anyone.

Janta-ak rolled on his side, then whispered, "Where are you from?"

The man didn't move, and his reply was almost inaudible. "Stipa-ah."

Ah. Good, Janta-ak thought.

Janta-ak glanced at the guard, whose eyes were heavy. His head nodded.

"There is an army coming. Kunta for Denta-ah."

The old man did not move or speak, but his eyes were wide open.

"Denta-ah has the stama weapons. They have more people. We need to watch for an opportunity to help when the attack comes."

The old man said one word: "When?"

"They are coming now. Within the next few days. They march from Winten-ah."

The man at Janta-ak's back coughed and the guard's head jerked up. Both Janta-ak and the old man closed their eyes.

Long minutes later, the old man spoke again. "There are not that many Denta-ah. Many are people like me. I know who to trust. I will spread the word."

Janta-ak turned away and closed his eyes. He hoped the others were as successful.

The next morning, Janta-ak was herded out of the sleeping lean-to. Instead of being taken to the area where they would shave the logs, they were taken to an open area where four posts were driven in the ground.

Janta-ak looked around, trying to grab whatever intelligence he could by counting the number of other slaves gathered together. He was trying to not be obvious about his counting, so he wasn't as aware as he normally was. A Denta-ah guard put a forearm into his back, pushed hard, and said, "Move!"

Janta-ak stumbled to one knee. When he stood, he found himself face to face with Prata-eh. Her arms were tied behind her back. She met his eyes for only the briefest of moments, then looked away as though she did not know him.

The guard led her roughly to one of the four poles, then untied and retied her to the pole so she was facing outward, completely vulnerable.

Doug-ak strolled to the front of the gathered slaves. He wore a white broad-brimmed hat, a white cotton shirt, and long pants. To Janta-ak's eyes, he looked ridiculous, barely worth his contempt. Still, he remembered that Manta-ak had told him this man was dangerous.

"We have spies in our midst," he said in the universal language. "Where are the others who were captured with this woman?"

No one moved. Doug-ak walked to Prata-ah and held a long steel blade at her throat. She towered over him, but looked straight ahead, over the top of his head. She was already seeing eternity stretch out before her.

Doug-ak removed the knife with a smile, as though he never intended to do anything so barbaric as slit her throat. He turned to the man Janta-ak recognized as the one who had retrieved him from the field.

"Where are the others?" Doug-ak said quietly.

The man looked around with a hint of desperation. Finally, his eyes fell on Gorka-ah. He pointed at him triumphantly. Doug-ak nodded, and two warriors fell on Gorka-ah and put him on the pole beside Prata-eh.

"There were two more, correct?"

The man nodded and again scanned the crowd.

"Well?" Doug-ak asked, a dangerous edge to his voice.

The man walked into the crowd, searching, searching. Finally, he spotted Werta-ah. He hurried to him with two other guards and pointed at him and the man beside him.

"Here they are, Doug-ak!"

"Excellent. Bring them up."

Janta-ak took a small step. He could not let an innocent man be taken in his place. Suddenly, there was a hand grasped tightly around his wrist. It was the old man he had spoken to the night before. With surprising strength, he tugged Janta-ak back in line.

Janta-ak searched the old man's face, but he remained expressionless.

He is right, of course, Janta-ak thought. *We are all likely to die anyway, but I can still help us before I do. I am sorry.*

Werta-ah and the bewildered man who had been unlucky enough to stand beside him were hauled up and tied to the poles.

"This was a pitiful attempt. I have been expecting exactly this." He nodded at a man at the back and two dozen Denta-ah warriors marched to the front. Six of them lined up in front of each of the poles. They each carried crossbows.

"Now," Doug-ak said laconically.

The sound of crossbow bolts sizzled across the open space as each of the twenty-four arrows slammed home. The three members of Manta-ak's Army and the sacrificial man grunted at the impact, but otherwise died without a sound.

"Back to work!" Doug-ak barked.

Janta-ak went back to work.

Chapter Thirty-Five
Manta-ak's Army

The footpath that led from Stipa-ah to Denta-ah quickly widened. Trees on both sides had been cut down, leaving only stumps. Underbrush had been trampled. Progress was happening in Kragdon-ah.

Alex and Sekun-ak took the lead. They had both been over this trail before and knew where possible pinch points were. Their pace hadn't been fast from Winten-ah to Stipa-ah, but it slowed to a crawl from there.

Halfway to Denta-ah, the front of Manta-ak's Army came around a bend. They walked straight into a work crew from Denta-ah. Two dozen men were hacking at various trees with axes, while five armed guards watched them.

The entire scene was so surreal that both sides stared at each other for two seconds, waiting for things to make sense.

Alex called "Shields up," just before the guards raised their crossbows and fired on them.

Alex had the presence of mind to also say, "Monda-ak. Behind!" The giant dog had no shield and if a stray arrow pierced his lungs or other vital organ, Alex couldn't bear it.

Monda-ak followed the command. He might look at Alex balefully about an order, but he followed it first then complained second.

The bolts slammed home into the composite shields. The bolts stuck, but did not penetrate, the first live-action test of the shields.

Alex felt the impact of two bolts into his own shield, waited one beat, then snuck a peek around the side. The five guards were busy reloading the crossbows. The men who were working stood with axes and ropes in their hands, unsure what was happening.

Alex locked shields with Sekun-ak and said, "Shield wall." Sekun-ak locked with the man beside him and soon they had a wall as wide as ten shields.

The guards had the advantage of an uphill position, but they only had an offensive weapon, designed to keep the workers in line. While the front shield wall absorbed the blows of the crossbows, Alex's longbow group notched and fired from outside of crossbow range.

Their accuracy was not ideal, but they fired enough long arrows up the hill to hit three of the guards on the first pass. Two fell, mortally wounded, and a third tried to remove an arrow from his thigh. All dropped their weapons.

The remaining two guards looked at their dead or dying friends and the force of warriors staring at them and shouted, *Kampa!* — we surrender!

"Throw down your weapons!" Alex yelled.

The two standing guards did so with alacrity.

"Make your wounded comfortable," Alex instructed them.

The unwounded guards walked to the men with arrows through their chests. They said a few words over them in a language Alex did not recognize, then raised their axes and smashed them down on their skulls.

The third wounded man, still struggling with the arrow in his leg, held out his hands and scooted away.

Alex looked at Sekun-ak and said, "This is a tough world."

"They only did what you told them. What did you expect?"

"I don't know. A drink of water, maybe? Asking them if they had any last words to take to their love ones?"

Sekun-ak furrowed his brow. "You are my brother, Manta-ak, but sometimes I do not understand how you think."

Alex saluted him in acknowledgement.

"What do we do with them?" Alex asked Sekun-ak, pointing at the three guards.

"Kill them."

"What? No. They surrendered."

"Yes, they should not have surrendered. Stama has made them weak. Winten-ah would have fought until the last man fell. They are cowards."

"We can't just kill them." Alex walked to a man holding an ax in one hand. "Where are you from?"

"Farga-ah."

"How did you come here?"

"Denta-ah attacked our village. I was wounded in the battle," he pointed to a nasty scar on his left leg, "but they let others in my tribe heal me so I could work."

"Can you tie these men up and guard them?"

"Can I kill them?"

Alex sighed. He was a little out of his element.

"No."

"Yes, I can guard them. I would rather kill them. They have been cruel to us. That one," he said, pointing to the wounded but living man, "came to my village and killed my mother and father. I would like to kill him now."

Alex looked at Sekun-ak, who only stared back as if to say, *See?*

"Just guard them for now. I don't want them following along behind us, or worse, getting there ahead of us and alerting everyone." Alex looked at the guards, who were hanging on every word. "If they try to escape, kill them. Otherwise, just guard them. Can you do that?"

The man was silent. Contemplating. "Yes."

"Good."

Sekun-ak reached into his bag for his flint and handed it to the man beside him. "Build a fire big enough to burn the stama."

"We could use those when we attack," Alex said. "We've got new soldiers here that aren't going to be well trained, but that's the beauty of a crossbow. You don't have to be trained."

"We cannot use that. It is stama. If we use that to stop them, we are the same as them."

Alex pulled another of the workers to him. "Grab their other weapons and distribute them among your men. Travel at the back of our line and stay far enough back that you won't get hurt in the first wave. We have shields. You do not. When the hand-to-hand combat starts, you can come in and have your *kenda*." In the universal language, *kenda* meant a combination of joy, revenge, and satisfaction.

Before he let him go, Alex asked the man, "Do you know if there were other work crews out today?"

"Yes. There are many crews out every day. Some are cutting and gathering logs, some are breaking soil, some are hunting. It is hard to feed such a large tribe."

"Even if they don't feed the workers very much, that's right, I remember. How about other crews who are doing what you are doing?"

"Yes. Two others."

"And you are the farthest out? Are the other crews on this path?" Alex wanted to say *road* instead of path, but there was no language or even concept for what a road was in any of the Kragdon-ah languages.

"Yes. We are the smallest work crew. The other two will be twice our size or more."

Alex turned to Sekun-ak. "Let's take a small group of bow-men—just regular bows, not longbows. Those aren't accurate enough for what I have in mind. If the other work crews are double this size, then they might have as many as ten guards. Let's take twen-ty-four men, march them quietly ahead, and take out the guards like we did here."

"Except we will kill all the guards. Leaving them behind like you are doing here is no good."

Alex considered. *This is war. The mission is all that matters.*

"Yes. Kill the guards. Then have the workers strip them of their weapons—"

"—except for their stama, which we will burn."

I seem to have lost this battle, too.

"—except for their stama, which you can burn. Equip them with whatever other equipment they can take from the guards and have them wait for us there. We'll wait here to give you a head start, then follow along behind you."

Sekun-ak turned immediately, chose his two dozen bowmen and set off at a trot, glad to have a mission to carry out.

The former slaves had tied the guards up and were standing close to them. The one who had asked to kill them urinated, a long, splash-ing arc that spattered all over the guards. He was taking his kenda wherever he could find it.

The men had started a small bonfire and heaped the crossbows on top.

Alex watched them burn.

Chapter Thirty-Six
The End of the Beginning

It had been four days since the execution of Prata-eh and the rest of Janta-ak's team. Because they had also executed an innocent worker, no one was looking for Janta-ak, thinking him already dead. Still, with each passing day, he felt a heavier weight on his shoulders. He knew Manta-ak and his army were on the way—would be there any day in fact—and he didn't feel like he had done enough.

On that morning, Janta-ak became even more concerned. Something was different. Typically, the outer area, which was behind the first barricade, but outside the original wall, was crawling with Denta-ah and slaves alike. On this morning, the slaves were going about their normal chores, but the number of Denta-ah guarding them had fallen considerably.

Janta-ak reported to work stripping the trees down to build more of a new barricade he had heard rumors of, but a guard turned him away.

"Go to the front gate. We're building a large bonfire there. You will chop wood from the trees today instead of stripping them."

Janta-ak kept his eyes downcast and walked toward the outer gate. When he was out of the line of vision of that guard, he picked up an armful of wood and turned back the way he had come. He was careful to avoid the guard who had assigned him to the bonfire,

265

and as long as he was carrying something, no one thought him out of place.

He made it all the way to the spot where the first barricade had been built at the entrance to the dead-end valley.

A heavy hand fell on his shoulder and the tip of a stone spear jabbed him in the ribs.

"What are you doing here?"

He spun around, thinking he'd been caught by the first guard after all. He was relieved to see that it was a different man.

Janta-ak cast his eyes to the ground submissively but lifted up the wood. "I was told to bring this wood to the gate to help build a bonfire."

The guard cuffed him on the head.

"Wrong gate. No wonder we can't get anything done on time. You slaves are dumber than an alecs-ah. Take that wood to the front gate."

Janta-ak mumbled, "Sorry," then hurried toward the front gate. As he did, he counted his steps.

When he got near the front gate, he saw other slaves had already brought armfuls of wood and were stacking them so as to build a huge fire. Janta-ak dropped his wood then blended in with the others.

162 steps from that gate to this one, Janta-ak thought.

As he walked, he had also noticed that preparatory activities throughout the front area were slower. Where normally there was a production line making arrows, crossbow parts and other weapons, those areas were quiet. More workers were wandering around, trying to look busy while not actually doing anything.

And why do they want such a huge fire right here by the gate, he wondered. *What purpose will this serve?*

Janta-ak glanced up to see Doug-ak strolling along, speaking to Dunta-ak, ignoring everyone around them.

Could I kill him right now? Janta-ak wondered. *Smash a piece of wood over his head and kill him? Would it end this, or is it too late? Would it continue without him?*

Janta-ak hefted a heavy stick of wood in his hand as Doug-ak walked by him but let him pass. He knew if he killed Doug-ak he would be killed himself. That thought alone didn't bother him, but he knew he would be needed when the battle began. He wasn't sure if the seeds he had sown since his capture would bloom without him.

The fire was lit and after a few minutes, thick black smoke rose up into the sky.

Janta-ak noticed that the Denta-ah had assembled long, strong pieces of wood into something he had never seen before. Try as he might, he could not puzzle out what purpose it served.

More slaves appeared, dragging a stump covered in black pitch and heaving it on top of the fire. The pitch caught immediately and more smoke boiled forth and flames leaped up from the dried-out hulk of wood.

Janta-ak saw that Doug-ak and Dunta-ak were having a discussion that had grown heated. Janta-ak eased toward them while trying to appear that he wasn't doing that very thing. He carried more pieces of wood and strategically placed them on the pile, straining to hear.

When he finally caught what they were saying, he realized they were speaking Denta-ah, a language Janta-ak barely knew. He casually tossed a piece of wood on the fire, then found the old man who had been his co-conspirator since he arrived in Denta-ah.

Again, without appearing to do so, he leaned over and said, "Can you speak Denta-ah?"

"Yes. They were always our greatest trade partner."

Janta-ak nodded at Doug-ak and Dunta-ak and looked a question at the old man, who nodded and moved toward them. He carried a long stick and poked and prodded at the fire while avoiding the stacks of crossbow bolts and moving toward the two men. When he was near them, he paused, then continued around the bonfire, which was now a mighty blaze.

When he came back to Janta-ak, he said, "They are arguing. Dunta-ak wishes to rain fire down on them. The ugly slug says he wants to trap them."

Trap them how? Janta-ak wondered.

At that moment, a long arrow landed in front of him, barely missing his left foot. He whipped his head around and looked up at the crossbowmen atop the wall. Miraculously, three of them tumbled off their perch and fell to the ground, grasping at arrows buried deep in their throats or chests.

The other crossbowmen ducked low and reloaded. They fired again and again. Moments later, four more tumbled down. There were other bowmen standing by to take their place, but Doug-ak stamped his foot and shouted something that Janta-ak couldn't understand.

The remaining bowmen on the wall hurried down the ladders, happy to be out of harm's way.

Another barrage of long arrows flew over the wall in a graceful arc. Two more of the guards were hit, an arrow landed within three feet of Doug-ak, and the final arrow found the chest of the old man tending the fire.

Janta-ak rushed to him, but the old man didn't say anything. He grimaced, then closed his eyes.

Janta-ak rushed toward the gate. If arrows were going to randomly come over the top, the area at the gate itself was the safest spot.

Doug-ak spoke harshly to Dunta-ak, who barked orders to the gathered crossbowmen. They ran toward the interior gate.

Meanwhile, four Denta-ah soldiers thrust long pieces of wood under the burning stump and carried it to what Janta-ak now recognized as some form of Stama.

A guard saw Janta-ak gawking at what they were doing, said, "None of your business, slave," and slammed his cudgel into Janta-ak's temple.

Janta-ak crumpled to the ground, unconscious.

An unknown length of time later, he came around, stood up and was amazed to see that every Denta-ah guard and warrior was gone. The burning stump was gone. The only people left in the front area were the slaves, who stood around, unsure of what to do. His first thought was to grab some of the weapons and start his uprising.

All the weapons had been hauled away. Every spear, bow, ax, hammer, and crossbow was gone.

Even odder, many of the slaves had been pulled inside. The great open area between the first and second gates was nearly empty. Only a few dozen slaves stood, wondering what to do.

"This is what we have been waiting for. An army is outside, waiting to liberate us and kill every last Denta-ah who enslaved us. Come, help me open the gate!"

A dozen men hurried to him and helped lift and swing the gate outward.

Janta-ak found himself face to face with Manta-ak, Monda-ak, and an army hidden behind shields.

Chapter Thirty-Seven
The End of the Beginning II

Alex dispersed some of the non-essential weapons that his army carried to the men who had been forced to work for Denta-ah. His longbow men and women had a full complement of weapons—axes, clubs, hammers—that they would never use. The longbow contingent was to stand far back and rain death down on the opposition. By the time they got to hand-to-hand combat, there would be weapons abandoned by the dead and dying everywhere.

In the interim, that gave them twenty or so new warriors that could help offset the numerical advantage Denta-ah had in the endgame of a battle.

In most battles, each side fights until they see they can no longer win. At that point, peace might be bargained for.

Not in this case.

Denta-ah would be defending their home. If they lost that, they lost everything.

Alex's Army was fighting for their way of life. They would fight until there was no life left in any of them. In that case, having a few dozen more warriors swinging an ax or hammer might make a difference. If nothing else, it would allow them to die on their feet, fighting, instead of dying of malnutrition and abuse. Every warrior Alex had ever met—in the twenty-first century and in Kragdon-ah—would take that deal.

Alex ordered the men to rest, eat and drink. It would be their last chance before the battle. When he judged he had given Sekun-ak enough of a head start, he had Tinta-ak lead the troop forward.

Alex and Monda-ak stuck to the front.

They marched.

Again, when they came around a bend, they found another work crew. The difference this time was that there were no guards, no crossbows—only workers holding weapons. There was no sight of the guards. Alex could guess what that meant.

Alex counted forty new fighters. Again, they were ill-equipped, but some had the axes they used to bring trees down. Others had weapons acquired from the guards. Again, the longbow men and women shared their striking weapons.

A man with many scars approached Alex.

"Your men came out of nowhere. Our guards were lax and bored. The first time they realized anything was wrong was when arrows struck them. They never even fired their own bows."

"Good. Join us in the back as we march, and the men back there will tell you the plan."

Alex hiked on, his step a little lighter. He had been afraid of a Denta-ah ambush that might cost him warriors on the trek. Instead, they were adding to their numbers.

When Alex knew they were only a short distance from where they would emerge onto the open field that surrounded Denta-ah, he saw Sekun-ak sitting on a stump, waiting for them.

"I thought you had decided to return to Winten-ah." He looked around at all the stumps. "I wouldn't have blamed you. It is ugly here."

"Progress is rarely beautiful," Alex said, then saw that it had gone over Sekun-ak's head. "Never mind. Any trouble with these guards?"

"If the defenders of Denta-ah are as sleepy as these guards were, we will be through the gates before twilight."

"Our bowmen have given up as many weapons as they have."

"I gave them the weapons we retrieved. The others can hang to the back and pick up weapons as we go."

"We are over four hundred strong now," Alex observed.

"But they do not all know the fighting tricks you showed us."

"No, but they can still bash a man's skull with a stone ax."

"When we go around the bend ahead, Denta-ah's guards will be able to see us."

"This far back?"

"They have taken many trees, according to the workers." Sekun-ak didn't want to call the freed men slaves. They had once been, they were no longer.

Alex squinted up at the sun. "It would be better to wait until it is darker. Not full dark, but perhaps dusk?"

Sekun-ak pointed at the new soldiers they had appropriated. "They will be expecting them back soon. When they don't appear, they may not come looking for them, but it will put them on alert."

"Then it is time. As soon as we come out of the forest, we fast march, with each leader separating their own squad. Front row of each squad, shields up from the beginning. Second row, cover the heads of the first. Third row, cover the second and tilt to deflect. We'll know when they think we're in the range of the crossbows, because they'll start hitting the shield. I want every man and woman quiet. All they should hear is the march of our feet."

Sekun-ak had listened patiently. "So, exactly like we practiced it many, many times?"

Alex realized it was just pre-battle jitters. "Yes, sorry."

"No need for sorry. It is good to have it fresh in our heads." Sekun-ak turned and looked back over the assembled men and women. "We are ready."

Alex stepped away from the cover and looked at Denta-ah. Black smoke rose from behind a barrier much further out from where he remembered it being.

"I think they are ready, too."

Alex had run every possible battle scenario through his head as he prepared for this moment. He had thought it would be possible that when they appeared, the Denta-ah would use their superior numbers and bring the battle to them, running out of the gate with shields, crossbows and longbows.

Instead, Alex's Army marched into the open field in crisp formations, formed into their units, and stood stock still, and there was no response from Denta-ah. It appeared their enemy was more than happy to have the army throw themselves against the fortress they had constructed, to hide behind its walls.

Sekun-ak led the first squad, which marched six across and ten deep. For the moment they carried their shields in the relaxed position. They were still hundreds of yards from the enemy and nearly as far out of crossbow range.

Tinta-ak led the second squad, while Balta-ak led the third. They formed up on the immediate left and right flank of Sekun-ak.

Alex and Monda-ak stood in front of Sekun-ak's squad. He would lead all of them because he had seen the crossbows fire and thought he had a good grasp on their power and range. He kept Monda-ak behind him, where he could keep him safe with his shield.

Alex marched forward at a steady pace, followed by his entire army—minus the newest members he had picked up and equipped as best he could. He wanted to keep them hidden as a last-ditch effort if needed. He had left Tontu-ak, who owned the other giant dog—Monda-ak's brother—in charge of that group.

The closer to Denta-ah that Alex got without resistance, the more nervous he became. He had expected a group of longbowmen, crossbowmen, or even slaves armed with more rudimentary weapons to attack them by now. Instead, they marched unimpeded.

Alex held a hand up to shield his eyes from the late-afternoon sun and saw the guards lined up on the fortification, but although they seemed to be looking right at the approaching army, none of them appeared concerned.

Which, of course, concerned Alex.

When an opponent allows you to make a move, it is usually because that is the move they wanted you to make.

As they approached the line Alex had established in his mind as putting them in crossbow range, he held up his arm and said, "Halt."

He took a few steps back to where Sekun-ak stood waiting for orders.

Sekun-ak surveyed the guards atop the fortress. "If they do not attempt to stop us, we can walk right up and fight our way inside."

"I don't like it. Something is off." Alex hesitated. "But what else is there to do? We can't lay siege to them. They've likely got months' worth of supplies in there, while we've got nothing."

"You are thinking too much, little brother. We spent all winter coming up with a plan. Do we want to change it now because they are hiding behind their gate?"

Alex reached out and laid his hand on Sekun-ak's shoulder. "You are correct."

Alex took three steps to the side, sharpened his voice and said, "Squad One, shields up!"

The men and women in Sekun-ak's squad moved together. The front row locked their shields, the trailing rows lifted their shields to cover the rows in front of them.

Alex lowered his voice and spoke to Sekun-ak. "When they begin to shoot at you, hold your shield position and keep moving forward."

Sekun-ak said, "March," and his squad moved as a single organism, marching in time with each other.

"Squad Two and Squad Three, shields up!"

Less than a minute later, all squads marched toward the gate.

Alex kept his shield lowered so he could see the enemy response, but marched behind Sekun-ak's squad.

They were well past what Alex thought was proper crossbow range before the Denta-ah opened fire.

From atop the wall, Alex saw Dunta-ak peering down at them. He raised his arm, then lowered it. A rainstorm of two dozen crossbow bolts flew, whizzing into the shields of Sekun-ak and his squad.

Alex held his breath and waited to see if any warrior screamed or fell.

They did not.

"Hold shield wall, keep marching," Alex instructed both forward and back.

The effect of being fired upon by dozens of crossbows can never be diminished, but Alex thought it was much less intense than he had expected. The aim of the Denta-ah was good, as many of the bolts had buried themselves in the shields of Sekun-ak's squad, but they had no effect.

Alex had thought they might have three to four times the number of crossbowmen on the wall as they did, or at least have others loading and handing the bows up to the men. None of that was happening.

The squads continued to move toward the gate. Every twenty steps, another barrage of bolts hit home, to no effect.

Then hell was unleashed.

A burning mass flew over the wall and directly at Alex's army. His well-trained squads looked up to see a burning comet descending from the heavens directly at them. Discipline and order evaporated in less than a second. The troops scattered, some running to the side, others forward, others backward.

The panic saved a few lives, as a massive, fiery tree trunk landed with a spectacular spray of burning embers. It landed precisely where the fourth squad had been a moment before. It smashed down directly on top of four unfortunate warriors who were crushed by the immense weight. Their death was mercifully quick.

When the stump hit, it bounced, landing on two more warriors, then rolled, overtaking three more. The trail of the stump was marked by sprawled, burning bodies. Uninjured warriors, heedless of their own safety, rushed in to pull the injured and dying from the sudden flames.

Alex raised his voice, pitching it to be heard over the mayhem and screams of the dead and dying.

"Squad leaders! Form up! Shields up, but run toward the gate!"

I don't know if they've got more than one of those damn things, but if we're close to the gate, they won't be able to use it anyway.

"Form up!" Sekun-ak ordered. "Stay with your squad. If the man in front of you is dead, move up and take his place!"

Tinta-ak and the other squad leaders fought down their panic and put their squads back together.

Alex looked at the fourth squad, which had been hurt the worst in the trebuchet attack. "Fourth squad! Move back. Follow the sixth squad now! Senta-ah, make it rain arrows inside the gate."

Alex's longbow archers stopped well outside of both crossbow and trebuchet range, spread out to not present a bunched target and notched an arrow, then waited.

Senta-eh stood slightly behind, notched her own arrow, then said, "Fire."

The longbow arrows flew in a deadly arc, far over the heads of their own troops. Some arrows hit and stuck in the gate. Others flew over the heads of the crossbowmen and into the open area behind them. Four of those arrows, though, hit crossbowmen, who tumbled backwards from their perch, leaving gaps between them.

"Forward," Senta-eh ordered and the longbow archers moved toward the gate. "Halt!" she said after ten steps. The longbow archers notched and held.

"Fire," Senta-eh said, unleashing her own arrow. She followed its parabola and watched with satisfaction as it struck one of the crossbowmen dead center.

Four others fell at the same moment.

All longbow archers notched another arrow and peered out to check their target.

Their targets were gone.

Chapter Thirty-Eight
Trapped

After two rounds of crossbow bolts thunked into the shields of the leading squad, they held for a moment, waiting for a third volley.

It didn't come.

Alex looked around the right edge of his shield and saw that the bowmen who stood on top of the gate were gone. A few of the longbow arrows stuck and vibrated on the wall.

"Hold positions," Alex said, then, holding his shield in front of him, sprinted toward the gate.

The gate slowly rolled open and Alex realized he had been brash.

I might be the first casualty of my own battle plan. Stupid, stupid, stupid.

Alex raised his shield and braced himself for an onslaught that never came.

"Manta-ak?"

Alex was so surprised that he nearly dropped his shield. He looked into the familiar face of Janta-ak.

Monda-ak woofed at seeing an old friend in an unexpected place.

Janta-ak and the dozen men with him put their shoulders into the gate and swung it open.

"When I sent you to prepare the way for us, I didn't expect you to have done all the work when we got here."

"I don't think I did. Your longbows took a few of them down, then they abandoned their posts and ran for the interior gate. But, it was at Doug-ak's command. There was no panic in them. They acted like they were carrying out a plan."

Alex considered that while peering over Janta-ak's shoulder. "Are those all your men?"

"Those are all men who were slaves. They will fight against Denta-ah."

"Do they have weapons?"

"No. Do you have weapons we can equip them with?"

"No. We captured three work crews in the forest and gave them what we had."

"Then we'll do the best we can."

Alex realized he had left his army standing, turtle-like in front of the gate. "Sekun-ak, shields down. Bring your men forward." Alex didn't want to bring all his men in at once, but their goal was to destroy Denta-ah and the only way to do that was to get to the actual village.

Sekun-ak marched his squad forward. They walked through the gate and glanced around, but the only sound was the wind whistling over the logs and a few birds singing.

"How far to the gate? Will we have to fight our way there?"

"I don't think so. It is one hundred and sixty-two strides from this gate to that."

Alex converted that in his head. *Five hundred feet, more or less. A long way to fight against an entrenched enemy, but an easy walk with no resistance.*

Since they were under no apparent time pressure, Alex moved his squads in one by one, pausing between. Soon enough, the entire army was inside the first gate, aside from the freed workers.

Alex took Sekun-ak and Janta-ak aside. "This is too easy. Why would they retreat when we killed a few of their bowmen?"

"I know how we can find out," Sekun-ak answered.

Alex looked at him, surprised. "How?"

"By marching to that gate, burning it down, and killing them all."

Alex sighed and looked at Janta-ak. "Any better ideas?"

"They built that fire to shoot fire at you with their arrows, I think," Janta-ak said, nodding at the blaze. "They will probably still do that."

"Is there water nearby?"

Janta-ak pointed at a series of troughs that had been used to feed the animals used to drag the logs back from the forest.

"Have your men hold their shields under the water and count to ten. I don't know if that will make them fireproof, but it's the best plan I've got."

Sekun-ak told the squad leaders to have their men line up and do as Manta-ak had asked. The first few men had lifted their dripping shields and moved aside when a loud noise came from behind. The men whirled and raised their shields as one, but it wasn't an attack.

The gate was quickly shutting. Before Alex could reach it, it had slammed shut. On the other side, he could hear a heavy log being lifted into place.

They were locked in—trapped like rats in a box.

Then, in rhythm, a new sound came from the walls on both sides of them. A scraping, thumping sound.

Janta-ak realized what the sound meant first. "Ladders," he whispered.

The heads of dozens of bowmen appeared over the walls, surrounding them on three sides.

Chapter Thirty-Nine
The Battle of Denta-ah

A lex reacted immediately, if still too late.

"Shields up! Form into squadrons!"

The men were caught unaware and although most lifted their shields up, they did not have time to form into their units and their shield wall.

The bowmen looking down on them opened fire with devastating effect, then ducked back behind the wall before Alex could return fire. A few moments later, they popped above the wall again and released another withering volley.

Dozens of Alex's men fell, pierced by short bolts.

Alex ran to the middle of the opening, directing his lieutenants, who organized their squads.

Alex held his shield up to cover part of his body, but not all. An arrow whizzed over his right shoulder—it would have been a kill shot if he had been as tall as his warriors—and Alex heard a guttural grunt, followed by a whine.

He looked down to see Monda-ak had been hit in his hindquarter. He tried to stand but couldn't bear his weight and fell. He looked at Alex with terribly sad eyes.

Alex abandoned all pretense of protecting himself, even as the crossbowmen of Denta-ah rained more bolts down on them.

Alex spotted a lean-to that offered some protection from the arrows.

He grabbed Monda-ak by the scruff of his neck and dragged him inside, then shouted at Sekun-ak and his other lieutenants to grab the other wounded and do the same.

As they pulled the injured but not dead into the lean-to, two more of his lieutenants fell.

Alex took over one squad and tapped a man whose name he didn't know to lead the other. The first battlefield promotion in the Battle of Denta-ah. They were forced to leave the downed men who were dead or dying, as the bowmen had seen their strategy. Every time they approached one of their downed men, half a dozen bowmen sent bolts down at them.

Finally, after heavy early losses, the squads were turtled. The bowmen above continued to send bolts down, but the barrage wasn't as heavy, as they just thunked into the shields.

Alex lifted his shield a bit and surveyed the field. Each individual squad looked like a massive porcupine, with bolts quivering as the humans below the shields breathed in and out.

Beyond a few lean-tos, there were no fortifications where he could form his men into an offensive force. All they could do for the moment was hide behind their shields and continue to live.

And what happens if they open the gate at the other end and another force comes running at us? What do we do then? We do what fighting forces have always done—stand, fight, and die.

Alex realized he hadn't heard an arrow bury itself in a shield in a long moment, so took a better look.

The men who had manned the walls on three sides were gone, and there was the sound of a battle raging outside the walls.

He heard the sound of whatever had blocked the second gate lifting and scraping as it opened a crack. One of the men who had been on a work crew that morning said, "Help us open this!"

Two dozen men threw their shoulders into the gate and pushed it wide open.

A full battle was underway, and Alex's last chance army was fully engaged and outnumbered.

Alex shouted orders at each lieutenant, telling them where to take their squads. The former slaves were outnumbered no more. In fact, they had a sudden, overwhelming advantage.

Each squad moved to an area of conflict, shields low, clubs and axes out.

These Denta-ah warriors did not surrender. They fought to the end, but the end was rapid.

When the sound of clubs and axes finally silenced, the field was red with the blood of the fallen.

Alex sent scouts around the perimeter looking for any Denta-ah stragglers but found none. As he was directing triage on his wounded, Senta-eh and the rest of the longbow archers appeared.

"When they engaged in hand-to-hand combat, we had to hold our fire for fear of killing as many of our own as we did theirs."

"That was the right decision. Gather as many of your arrows as you can. We will need you again when we storm the inner gate."

Alex looked at the dead Denta-ah warriors strewn about.

"Everyone who hasn't already, equip yourself with weapons from the dead. This was only the first battle. They thought they had us trapped, but we escaped. Now we will take the battle to them."

Alex left his lieutenants to reorganize their squads and incorporate new warriors where appropriate. He turned and ran back to the lean-to where Monda-ak and the other wounded warriors had been left.

His heart sank as he approached. Monda-ak's head was in the dirt and his eyes were closed.

"Monda-ak!"

As soon as he heard Alex's voice, the dog's huge head lifted up, his eyes opened, and his tongue lolled. He tried to wag his tail, but he whimpered and laid his head down. Alex ran to him to examine his wound and found that another of the wounded men had been ministering to him.

"I am not hurt too badly, so I have been trying to make myself useful. I was able to pull the arrow out and the wound looks clean. It will need to be bandaged, but he will live." He patted Monda-ak on the head and again the tail thumped once, twice, then laid still. "He is magnificent."

"He is my best friend," Alex said simply. The man saluted with two fingers. The bond between these animals and their humans was known all over Kragdon-ah.

Alex laid his hand on Monda-ak's head and asked, "How are the others?"

"Some have died. Some are wounded but will survive. It is the way of war. It is why we don't wage war about anything less than this. Nothing else is worth this price." The man pointed to where he had been pierced by two of the crossbow bolts. "I am not wounded badly. I can fight with you again."

Alex laid a hand on his shoulder. "No. You are more valuable here. Stay here and tend to the men who are wounded." Alex dropped his head low and muzzled Monda-ak. "Stay here. I will be back for you."

He stood and felt his weariness wash away. He held his shield and hammer.

When he turned, Sekun-ak had all the units reorganized and waiting.

The scope of the battle had changed. The warriors of Denta-ah were now contained in a single area, and since more than a hundred former slaves had been freed and equipped, Alex's army was no longer at such a massive disadvantage.

Alex arranged his army so that all his shielded units were up front. Directly behind them, and ordered to hold outside of cross-bow range, was the unit of freed slaves, now fully equipped. Behind them were the longbow archers, ready to rain death from the sky.

This time, as soon as they became visible to the crossbowmen, they took heavy fire. Each Denta-ah warrior fired his bolt then ducked behind the safety of the wall, to be immediately replaced by another archer and so on.

Every single step that Sekun-ak and his men took was marked by the thud and impact of more bolts hitting their shields, adding to the array they had collected when trapped.

Some crossbow archers got smart and realized that shooting into the shields was completely ineffective. Instead, they shot high over their heads, hoping to reach the trailing, unshielded warriors. When that failed, they aimed below the shields, managing to hit several of the lead warriors where their leather armor covered their ankles and feet.

Still, Manta-ak's army marched forward.

Alex stood behind the first squad of men, judging the distance to the gate. He turned and shouted an order to Senta-eh.

She gave the command and her archers released two dozen arrows over the tall gate. Alex stopped and listened. He was pleased to hear the anguished cries of those who had been caught unaware on the other side.

"Again," he shouted.

The arrows flew and again there were screams from the other side, albeit fewer this time.

On the third volley, no sound came from the other side but the sound of the arrows falling onto cobblestones.

Alex ordered the regular archers to move up between the first and second squads. They arrived with arrows notched and aimed at the guards on the gate with unerring accuracy.

Four of the guards fell but were immediately replaced by cross-bowmen who fired back at Alex's vulnerable archers. Three of his archers fell, though the unit in front raised their shields to try to protect them. This allowed the crossbowmen above to take advantage of new targets. Two of his shield-bearers were hit by crossbow bolts.

We can't win like this. If it's a war of attrition, they can wait us out and pick us off.

"Sekun-ak, take your unit all the way to the gate. Turtle up and burn them out."

Sekun-ak and his fifty warriors moved forward under heavy fire until they stood at the base of the gate. They lifted their shields overhead and men dropped to their knees and went to work. Three warriors started to chop at the gate and slowly chipped away a bit of the logs. Three others dug down at the base to create a small hole.

They took the wood chips they had created and piled them in the hole, then added handfuls of pine pitch they had gathered on their march to Denta-ah. They layered wood chips, pine, wood chips, pine.

Sekun-ak removed his flint and bent down to start the fire.

From where Alex was standing, events happened in slow motion, but he still couldn't move quickly enough to stop them. Atop the gate, he saw warriors heft a long trough and tip it over. He watched liquid fall toward his squad and burn everything it touched. He heard the sizzle of burning flesh and the screams of his warriors.

"Squad two, recover those warriors. Drag them out of crossbow range."

He turned to Tinta-ak. "I need you to finish the job. If the wood and pitch is wet, start on a different log."

Tinta-ak did not hesitate. He waited until the first squad had been cleared, then marched forward to carry on.

Sekun-ak did not allow himself to be taken completely out of range, but he was badly burned, with skin already pulling away from his neck, shoulders, and arms. Alex could see that what he had been hit with was not water, but he did not dare touch his wounded friend to see what it was.

"Archers! Move behind squad four. Keep a steady rhythm of fire. Don't all fire at once, but keep arrows in the air at all times."

Alex tilted his head back and shouted, "Senta-eh! Break your archers into four groups. Have one after another fire over the wall. When the last is finished, have the first fire again. Make it dangerous to walk in there!"

As he gave commands, Alex forgot to keep his head on a swivel. He forgot about his shield. His own safety.

A crossbow bolt zipped through the air, knocking Alex to the ground.

Chapter Forty
The Battle of Denta-ah II

Sekun-ak, wincing in pain with every step, ran to Alex, who was face down on the ground and not moving. He ordered the fourth squad to form a shield wall around Alex. Two warriors grabbed him and pulled him away.

As soon as they were out of crossbow range, Alex tried to stand, but Sekun-ak held him down with a hand in his back.

"Stay still. This will hurt." Sekun-ak gripped the shaft of the arrow and pulled. It made a greasy, suctioning sound as it pulled lose.

Alex let out a low, guttural "Uhhhnnnnn"

"Bandages!" Sekun-ak called.

How do I say, 'Your bedside manner could use a little work' in Winten-ah? Never mind. There's no way to express that concept.

Alex stopped struggling and let his face fall back into the bloody dirt.

Janta-ak ran with a bag stuffed full of thin material. Sekun-ak ripped off a small piece, put it on the end of his finger and stuffed it into the hole in Alex's shoulder.

Alex screamed.

"Good. That means you are still alive," Sekun-ak said, wrapping more of the material around and around Alex's arm and shoulder. "We will fix you better when we have run them out of Denta-ah. Look there." Sekun-ak pointed toward the wall.

Tinta-ak and his men had succeeded in building a fire at the base of the wall. Overhead, another group of men hoisted a trough. Before they could tip it over, they were hit with dozens of arrows. They fell backward, taking the boiling liquid with them. Screams of agony could be heard on the other side of the wall.

Meanwhile, smoke began to curl at the base of the gate.

"Help me up," Alex said to Janta-ak.

Tinta-ak's squadron kept their shields up and the smoke thickened.

"Start another spot" Alex yelled. "Archers, protect them!"

Tinta-ak and his crew moved several poles to their right and started the process again. Soon, smoke was curling up from a second spot, then a third.

"Tinta-ak! Pull back! That's enough!"

All squads pulled back out of crossbow range and watched the fires build and spread. Men appeared at the top with another trough, this time undoubtedly filled with water to put the fire out, but they were again taken out by a volley from the longbows.

For the longest time, there was silence, except for the growing crackling of the fire, spreading upward and sideways.

Then, a head appeared. It was Doug-ak, barely able to see over the wall. Smoke curled around him and he waved it away to get a better view.

Longbow archers notched an arrow but held, waiting for Senta-eh or Manta-ak to give the order.

Sunlight glinted off something in Doug-ak's hands and Alex tried to shout a warning. There was no word for 'rifle' in any Kragdon-ah language, though, and for a moment Alex's brain vapor locked.

A sharp crack came from atop the wall and Janta-ak flew backward.

"Longbows, fire!" Alex shouted.

Arrows streaked over the wall where Doug-ak had stood a moment before, but he was gone.

Alex kneeled and saw what he had feared. Janta-ak was shot. A small bullet hole in the forehead and a massive exit wound in the back of his head. He never saw what killed him.

There's no strategic value in killing one of our warriors. He was aiming at me. I should have thought this through. Of course he didn't destroy his weapons like I did. He may have used them to kill the leader of the Denta-ah and put Dunta-ak in his place and kept him there.

Alex looked at the men who surrounded him. Their expressions were blank with shock. They had never seen death dealt so suddenly from so far.

"*That* is stama," Alex said. "He was trying to kill me and missed. Now we will go kill him."

There was still a wall between him and Douglas Winterborne, but it was already smoldering.

The archers stood ready to unleash arrows at anyone who popped their head above the wall, but no one did.

While they waited for the barrier to be consumed by fire, Alex sent a small contingency back to the outer gate to burn that as well. Before he left Denta-ah, he intended to burn it to the ground like an avenging angel.

His friend Janta-ak was dead, another dozens and maybe hundreds of warriors were already dead on the battlefield, and his very best friends, Monda-ak and Sekun-ak were both badly wounded. If he stopped to think about it, he saw only red. As the commander of the army, he couldn't allow himself the twin luxuries of hatred and anger, so he did his best to swallow them down.

The inner gate was fully involved in flames, but still stood. Behind him, where the team was able to build a fire without people firing down on them, dark smoke was already in evidence.

Alex gathered his troops to speak to them. Two healthy warriors lifted Alex up onto the roof of a storage area so he could see over them.

He did his best to stand straight and forget about the throbbing pain in his shoulder.

"We've chased them into their hole and set fire to their gate. Now we will hunt them down and kill every last Denta-ah. By moon-rise tonight, Denta-ah will be no more."

"Kunta" the assembled warriors cried. In case they hadn't been heard on the other side of the wall, they raised their voices louder and cried it again and again: *kunta, kunta, kunta.* Their cries echoed and reverberated on the other side of the wall.

Alex raised his right arm. The assembly quieted.

"This is what we trained for. Remember, your greatest weapon is the warrior to your left and the warrior to your right. Together, we are unbreakable. Leaders, gather your squads. Shield walls first, armed fighters second, longbow archers, stay in the rear. Fire three volleys while there is separation between us, then when we close, join the fray."

That was the moment that the inner gate collapsed forward, slamming to the ground in a spray of embers and ashes.

Hundreds of Denta-ah warriors leaped over, around and through the fire.

They did not come in squads. They came like madmen.

The area where Alex's army stood was wide enough that he had been able to put two squads abreast. The front row of those two squads knew they would absorb the bulk of the initial onslaught.

As the Denta-ah warriors ran, they screamed their battle cries, which had changed very little in many thousands of years. It was rage, primal and pure.

Senta-eh gave the command and her two dozen longbow archers released three shots in fast succession. While she followed the arc of the arrows, she instinctively realized that there was time for more before they reached her army.

"Two more," she shouted, as she pulled her own string back to her ear and released twice.

Denta-ah warriors were not heavily shielded. They relied on strength, mobility, and savagery. Of the one-hundred and twenty arrows released, most flew over the heads of the Denta-ah. A smaller percentage hit home, piercing arms, thighs, and skulls.

A few dozen Denta-ah fell, but the horde did not notice they had been diminished. When they reached the shielded warriors, the first runners did not smash into it, but instead used the shields as a launching pad to jump over and into the squads behind.

Two hundred, three hundred, four hundred, five hundred Denta-ah warriors poured out of the fiery gate and ran at the assembled force of Alex's army.

A shield wall is most effective when it can repel a force from the front. The Denta-ah warriors streamed around and over the shield wall, hacking with axes, probing with spears, slamming with heavy hammers.

The shield wall collapsed, and the battle broke down into small skirmishes.

The army of Manta-ak was better trained and fought with better technique.

The army of Denta-ah tried to overcome that technique with sheer force—in numbers and in attitude.

Alex leaped into the midst of the battles. Adrenaline blocked out the pain of his injury and he knew how to fight without exposing his injured side.

What he couldn't do was hold his shield with his injured arm, so he left it in the dirt and threw himself into the fray holding only his stone axe.

Alex Hawk, who had been born in a small town in Oregon in 1991, was indistinguishable from the men and women of Kragdon-ah.

He dispatched a Denta-ah warrior with a single swing of his hammer and was already ducking an ax blow before the first warrior fell. He feinted left and swung his hammer viciously, connecting with the second man's left arm, shattering it. That warrior fell to his knees and Alex finished him quickly by crushing his skull.

Another Denta-ah a few yards away lifted a heavy spear to throw at Alex's midsection. Before he could let it fly, a three-hundred-pound dog catapulted into the air and knocked him down.

"Monda-ak," Alex cried, exhilarated at the sight of his friend and worried for his safety. Alex ran to Monda-ak and stood beside him, waiting for the battle to come to him.

And he realized there was very little battle left.

Bodies littered the ground, which was slick with the blood and viscera of battle.

The Denta-ah fought hard and bravely. Even when there were only ten of them against hundreds of remaining enemies, they circled together, back to back. When you are the only thing standing between your enemy and your home, you fight until you die.

The archers fired at them. They fell and died.

The army of Manta-ak looked for more enemies to kill, but there were none.

Fifty yards away, Alex saw the diminutive, pudgy figure of Douglas Winterborne, rifle in hand, standing behind the burned-out gate.

He cannot kill all of us, even with that rifle.

Winterborne seemed to come to the same conclusion at the same moment.

He turned and fled.

"Sekun-ak. Stay and help the wounded. Direct the care for them. Make those who are dying comfortable. Tinta-ak? Where are you?"

Tinta-ak emerged from the crowd of warriors. He was covered in blood and gristle. There was a deep slash down his right arm and evidence of an ax blow on his leg that would have devastated a lesser warrior.

He was smiling broadly.

"Yes, Manta-ak?"

"Pick twelve of your best to come with us. Send the rest of your squad into the village. Give the elderly, the women and children the choice to live or die."

Tinta-ak counted off a dozen men and women, all less injured than he was. "You, come with Manta-ak. The rest, do as he says."

Alex, Tinta-ak, and a dozen warriors set off after Douglas Winterborne.

Chapter Forty-One
To Catch a Fugitive

Alex led Tinta-ak and his men across the burning gate and into the inner realm of Denta-ah. There were signs of progress and growth everywhere—pulley systems carrying wooden buckets and other containers from place to place, stacks and stacks of weapons that would never be used, and an aqueduct system that came over the outer wall and filled a deep pool. For the moment, Denta-ah was the most technologically advanced village in Kragdon-ah.

Very soon it would cease to exist except in memory and legend.

Parts of the village looked no different than any other village Alex had seen. Lean-tos and other simple buildings dominated. In the far back corner, though, was something that seemed completely out of place—a log cabin straight out of the American west. It had a pitched roof, shutters over open windows, and a heavy front door. It was placed strategically in the far back corner of the village.

Alex pointed at it. "He'll be in there."

Tinta-ak and the dozen warriors didn't question whether Alex was right or not. They set off at a run toward it.

When they reached the door, Alex knew without trying that it would be locked.

"Tinta-ak. Can you knock that door down?"

Tinta-ak pushed Alex aside, saying, "Of course I can."

The huge man gave it a kick, then another. The door didn't budge. He backed up a few steps and threw his shoulder into it, but again it stood strong.

While Tinta-ak literally beat his head against the door, Alex looked around the village. He spied a stack of logs ready for a project.

He directed the men to pick up the log and use it as a battering ram to knock the door over. Before they could, Alex had to move Tinta-ak away. He was still sure the door was going down any second.

A dozen men ran at the door and slammed the log into the center of it. The log bounced back and the men fell down, but this time the door creaked and rocked in its frame.

"Again!" Alex shouted, helping the men up. They picked the log up, moved back ten paces and attacked the door again.

This time the door splintered inward with a crash, leaving only one small piece standing.

Tinta-ak stepped forward, kicked that piece down and folded his arms across his chest, satisfied that he had done what he said he would.

Alex gathered the men to him. "He is trapped in there. He will have the stick that killed Janta-ak, so we must be careful."

All thirteen men—even Tinta-ak—tapped two fingers against their head. They had all seen Janta-ak fall and felt a superstitious dread that the same fate might befall them.

Alex led the group into the small cabin. It was comprised of one open room, with a fire pit and chimney in the middle. A bed sat in one corner and a workbench—with numerous projects underway—stood in the other.

Douglas Winterborne was nowhere in sight.

Alex and his men spread out and searched everywhere, which took only a few seconds.

"He is somewhere else," Tinta-ak said.

"No. He built this as his last refuge. He wouldn't go anywhere else."

Alex looked desperately around the room, feeling the seconds melt away. His eyes fell on a woven rug in front of the bed. He strode across the room and tried to kick it away. The rug was attached to something.

Alex kneeled and tried to lift it. Finally, he found a wooden handle recessed beneath the rug. He pulled on the handle and the rug and a cutout piece of the floor came up. A damp smell filled the cabin.

There was a tunnel beneath the house. An escape tunnel.

Alex looked at Tinta-ak, then looked at the tunnel. It was too narrow for anyone other than him to fit into it.

"Stay here," he ordered Tinta-ak. "Prepare the village for kunta."

Alex perched on the edge of the tunnel, wished he had a torch, then crawled headfirst into the darkness.

The tunnel was tight. Designed, Alex guessed, to keep people larger than Douglas Winterborne out. Soon, though, it widened, and Alex found he could first crawl on all fours, then walk stooped over, then walk upright. He wondered how many manpower hours it had taken to dig.

The darkness was overwhelming. Alex could not waste time waiting for his eyes to adjust, but it didn't matter. There was no source of light. He moved cautiously ahead, using his right hand in front of him as his eyes.

His mind played tricks on him, making him believe that he heard rushing water, which never appeared, then seeing explosions of color that were not there. He remembered the darkness when he had stepped through the door in his basement and how he had passed out then.

He ignored all these thoughts and sensations and moved on.

After what seemed like hours, but was only a few minutes, Alex saw an unfocused light ahead. The tunnel sloped upward toward the light, which soon revealed itself to be an opening.

Alex approached the opening as quietly as he could, thinking that it was possible that Winterborne would be there, waiting for him to appear, rifle in hand.

Alex listened for any sound, but heard only the slight rustling of the grass moving in the breeze. Slowly, he lifted his head out of the hole, shading his eyes with his good arm and squinting. He had come up in a small clearing. There was no sign of life anywhere.

He climbed out of the hole and grabbed his hammer. It wasn't much against whatever kind of rifle Winterborne might have brought to Kragdon-ah with him, but it was all he had.

Alex looked for any sign of Winterborne and found it easily. It appeared Winterborne was more in a hurry than he was concerned with being tracked.

But where is he going? He can't survive outside by himself, even with his rifle. Not for long, anyway.

An image popped into Alex's head and he knew it was right. It was the image of a dark, shimmering door, standing all alone.

He's trying to go home. He can escape, or reload, resupply himself and try again. Can't let that happen.

Alex followed the tracks, which slowed him down, but soon enough, they ended at a small game trail. He assumed Winterborne had followed the path, which allowed him to increase his pace.

Alex thought of Winterborne—short, pale and pudgy—and tried to imagine him hurrying along the trail, sweating and out of breath. This image helped Alex block out the burning pain in his left shoulder that grew worse with every stride he took.

Every hundred yards, Alex stopped and listened. Listened to see if Winterborne was bumbling through the forest or if he had left the trail and moved in a different direction.

The path petered out, narrowing until it was barely visible. A few yards beyond that, the forest opened onto a wide clearing with tall grass that reminded Alex of the open plain beside Winten-ah.

At the far side of the clearing was a hill that rose up sharply.

Set against the gray of the hill was a black door. Around the exterior of the door, electricity crackled and popped.

Douglas Winterborne was halfway across the clearing, less than fifty yards from the door, but he had come to a stop. His rifle was raised to his shoulder and he was turning left, right, left, in rapid succession.

Alex could see the shoulders of a pack of dire wolves rippling above the grass.

Alex watched in fascination, not even sure what outcome he rooted for as he watched Douglas Winterborne fight for his life.

Winterborne had his rifle.

Kragdon-ah had the dire wolves.

Winterborne sighted in on one of the figures in the grass and pulled the trigger. Blood spattered up from the wolf in a high, arcing spray.

If he had hoped that the noise would frighten the rest of the pack away, he had backed the wrong horse.

Before the body of the first wolf crashed to the ground, five of its brothers and sisters threw themselves into the attack.

Winterborne stayed calm, which impressed Alex. He continued to eject shells and fire. He managed to take down two more before the first wolf launched itself at his backside. The wolf hit him with its front shoulder, knocking him to the ground. The remaining three wolves leaped at the downed man.

Winterborne's screams echoed off the hills. They were terrible, but brief.

Alex turned back toward Denta-ah, but not before he saw that he had been discovered by the alpha female wolf. She raised her head, viscera dripping from her fangs. Her pale-yellow eyes examined Alex without blinking. She looked at him for a long moment, then returned to feeding on Douglas Winterborne.

Chapter Forty-Two
Aftermath

Alex did not push his luck. He turned and ran toward Denta-ah. He followed the game trail back the way he had come, but when he emerged into the small clearing where the tunnel was, he didn't crawl back into it.

No way I make a round trip through there.

He looked up and saw smoke rising from beyond the walls of Denta-ah. He chose to simply run alongside the wall until he came to the front gate again.

When he appeared there, the warrior guarding where the gate had gawked at him. He had seen Alex run toward the dead-end of Denta-ah and now he was here, as if by magic. The man tipped a two-fingered salute to Alex, who returned it.

The gate itself was mostly gone—either burned or still burning. The walls that had formed the outer courtyard were much the same. Unless a sudden downpour appeared to dowse the fire, Denta-ah was done for.

Kunta.

He saw Sekun-ak and hurried toward him. The man's burns, which had looked horrible when fresh, were far worse now. Skin was sloughing off the side of his face, his left shoulder and arm. Still, he walked tall.

"Doug-ak?" Sekun-ak asked.

301

"Doug-ak is dead. I watched Ronit-ta eat him while he screamed."

Sekun-ak considered that. "Likely a better death than I would have given him."

Alex looked around at what had once been the outer courtyard of Denta-ah. The walls were burning, but in the middle, a strip of land had been turned into an emergency hospital and triage. Sekun-ak was a born leader. He had organized a cadre of men and women to search for helpful herbs to make dressings and poultices for the wounded. He had organized healthy men to dig graves for the dead. Those who were capable cared for the wounded, making them as comfortable as possible.

"Where will you dig the graves?"

"Right there," Sekun-ak said, pointing toward a spot where men were already digging a long hole.

"One for the Denta-ah and one for our army?"

A look of amazement crossed Sekun-ak's face. "Why would we do that?"

"To keep the bodies separated? So we know where our men are and where theirs are?"

"I have said before," said Sekun-ak, the man who spoke very little, "there are times I do not understand the way you think. We are all one. Those who were once enemies are no longer enemies in death. We are the conquerors; they are the vanquished. They fought well, and bravely. They are once again my brothers and sisters."

Alex nodded, a habit he still couldn't break. "Where do we go from here?"

With the battle finished, Alex felt more comfortable turning command over to Sekun-ak and his lieutenants. He saw things from a different perspective than Alex, and he was the proper leader for this phase. Not to mention that Alex was as tired as he had ever been.

He wanted nothing more than to let go of all responsibilities, lay down, and sleep for several days.

"After tomorrow, the men who joined us from other tribes will go to their homes. There is no reason for them to return to Winten-ah. They will share the story of our victory in every village they pass."

A sudden pang of guilt struck Alex. "The children of Stipa-ah. I told them we would return for them."

"I have already sent a group of warriors to bring them here. It is safe now, and they can join us for the nanka-tu."

Alex was nearly as fluent in Winten-ah as he was in English, but he had never heard that phrase. "The nanka-tu?"

"Yes, the nanka-tu. The feast to end all feasts where we celebrate those who died and those who lived and begin to tell the stories that will live for many generations."

"Should we maybe hold off on burning the entire village, then? Hard to have a feast when we've burned the village to the ground."

"We are not burning the village itself. Not yet. Just this outer area. I have warriors carrying water to stop the spread of the fire from reaching the village."

"What do we do with the Denta-ah who did not fight? We can't just kill them."

"Why would we do that? They will return with us to Winten-ah. They are no longer Denta-ah. That village is gone forever. They are part of us now." He waved a hand toward the bodies men were carrying to the grave. "It will help us rebuild after those we have lost. We will take care of them and they will be one of us."

"In Kragdon-ah, you are much more civilized about your wars than we are where I come from."

"We are more civilized in everything, I think," Sekun-ak said without a trace of irony.

Alex looked up to see Monda-ak limping toward him as fast as his injured hindquarter would allow. When he got to Alex, he bowled him over, then cleaned Alex's dirty face with his tongue.

"Monda-ak," Alex said, wrapping his one good arm around the dog's neck. "You saved my life today."

Monda-ak looked at him calmly. He already knew that was true.

Alex took in Sekun-ak, who stood firmly erect, but had a slight wobble. "Come, brother. Let someone else organize this now. You are more injured than those you are taking care of."

Alex looked to where the interior gate had once stood and saw a form so massive, it could have only been Tinta-ak.

When he saw Alex, he broke into a run, limping only slightly due to the gash on his leg.

Before he got a chance to ask the question, Alex said, "He's dead. Ronit-ta."

Tinta-ak contemplated that. Like Sekun-ak, it was apparent he thought Doug-ak had gotten off lightly. Alex tried not to think about what they might have had planned for him. Maybe letting the giant red ants feed on him, while the giant cockroaches skittered over him.

"Let's help the injured in to where the village was. We can take better care of them there."

"That includes you," Tinta-ak said softly.

"And you," Alex said. "But let's prioritize those who are badly injured first. Then we can tend to ourselves."

Alex led Sekun-ak to a room with many communal mattresses. He would have liked to put him in Winterborne's log cabin, which was both private and nicer than anything else in the village. He knew instinctively that no one would want to stay there, so he didn't bring it up. Sekun-ak would be happiest where he was among many of his friends. When Alex looked at his skin—covered in what appeared to be second and third-degree burns, he wondered how he had stayed upright for so long.

He designated that particular house as the burn ward and gathered the other warriors who had been damaged by the boiling oil that was poured on them. There would be long, painful days and nights of recovery for all of them and they would wear the scars of their burns until the end of their days. No one would ever have to ask them where they were during the Battle of Denta-ah.

Once Alex got a few other houses set up as medical areas, he submitted to care for himself, leaving Tinta-ak in charge for the rest of the night. One of the women of Denta-ah, who was now a woman of Winten-ah, ministered to him with the same care Niten-eh would have shown him in the caves back home.

She looked at the rough patch job Sekun-ak had done on the battlefield and made disapproving noises. In the universal language, she said, "I am sorry. I am going to have to hurt you before I can make you better." The bandage Sekun-ak had stuffed inside the wound had crusted over and needed to be removed so she could sanitize the wound and put a healing poultice on it.

She gave Alex a piece of wood to bite down on and went to work.

Chapter Forty-Three
Nanka-tu

The next morning, Alex woke to the same woman rolling him over to examine his wound. He tried to sit up, but she pushed him back down, albeit more gently than Sekun-ak had done the day before.

Alex felt like he had a hangover combined with the flu, combined with ten rounds of mixed martial arts fighting.

Senta-eh sat on her haunches a few feet away, petting Monda-ak, who accepted the attention with good grace. He had always liked the attention of women.

"Good morning," Alex said, both to his nurse, Senta-eh, and Monda-ak.

"You look horrible," Senta-eh said.

"And yet you still look as lovely as ever. Maybe I should have been an archer instead of a foot soldier."

"Maybe. I've seen you shoot, though, so probably not."

Alex tried to look over his shoulder at the woman changing his bandages. "I've heard in some armies, the leader gets respect."

"We respect you enough to tell you the truth. And the truth is, you look like the back end of an alecs-ah after a bout of diarrhea."

"You really know how to hurt a guy."

"That is true. I do. All warriors of Winten-ah do. But, that's not the reason I am here. The nanka-tu will be starting soon. We cannot start without you."

"Good enough. I'll be out as soon as my nurse gives me the go-ahead."

Without another word, Senta-eh slipped away.

A few minutes later, with a fresh poultice applied and a new bandage wrap, Alex tried to stand. Again, the nurse held him down.

"One more minute," she said. She rubbed her hands together as if she was trying to start a fire, then cupped them against Alex's lower back. She moved them gently back and forth, warming the whole area. She repeated the process up his spine, carefully avoiding his injured area, then did the same up and down his legs and his right arm.

"There. Now you can go fight the warrior woman if you want and you might have a chance."

Alex stood and stretched, amazed. "I don't know what you just did, but I feel close to being human."

"It has no name now. It was once called a Denta-ah remedy, but Denta-ah no longer exists."

Alex hadn't stopped to consider what life looked like for these refugees from Denta-ah. They had woken up yesterday on top of the world. Now, they were without a country, aside from the one that had forcibly adopted them. As always, in every world, to the victor goes the spoils.

"Will you be part of the nanka-tu?"

The woman looked at Alex as though he had perhaps absorbed a blow to the head the previous day. "Of course. I am Winten-ah."

I've just got to admit that I am out of my element with understanding these things and let it go at that.

"Thank you for taking care of me."

The woman waved him away but smiled as she did.

Outside, Alex squinted in the unexpected brightness. It was obvious that preparations had been underway for hours. A massive slab of meat turned on a spit over a low fire. Everyone hustled around with jobs to do and no one paid Alex any attention.

He headed to the burn unit, but before he could step inside, Sekun-ak came out. He held up his unburned hand and said, "Some of the warriors are burned badly. We should talk out here, so they can rest."

Alex looked at the layers of loose, soft bandages that covered most of Sekun-ak's upper body.

Some of them are burned badly, huh? But not you, right?

"Did you organize all this?"

"A large job divided by many people is easily accomplished."

Or, 'Many hands make light work,' as we would have said.

Sekun-ak nodded at a scene playing out in one end of the courtyard. The children from Stipa-ah were gathered around a small group of people. "They are orphans no more."

"Are those their parents? Are they really that lucky?"

"They are their parents now. I don't know if they gave birth or fathered the children. But, they are from Stipa-ah, which is no more, so now they are all Winten-ah."

"They won't go back to Stipa-ah? Try and start over there again?"

"No. Stipa-ah has been conquered. It is gone forever. Maybe another village will spring up there someday, but not for many years. When we go past it on our way home, we will burn it to the ground, just as we will with Denta-ah when we leave."

Alex thought about it and saw a certain wisdom. Winten-ah had suffered great losses when it spearheaded the effort to eliminate the stama. If either Denta-ah or Stipa-ah were left standing, the tribe members might think longingly of it. Perhaps even attempt to return there. But if the villages are gone, they will only have Winten-ah. Within a generation, those other villages will only be memories passed down through stories and legend.

For the rest of the afternoon, while the massive animal on the spit turned and turned, everything of value that wasn't stama was moved out where it could be divided between the conquerors. Everything from medicine and bandages to food stores and livestock was gathered at the outer edge of the first gate.

The stama—the trebuchet, the crossbows, other things they found scattered around the camp, would be part of the bonfire that would mark the end of Denta-ah.

Alex and Sekun-ak walked along the long grave that the warriors had dug the day before. Almost eight hundred bodies were buried there now, tribes from all over Kragdon-ah sharing their final resting place.

The heaped dirt that marked the grave ran from where the front gate had once stood all the way to Denta-ah proper.

As the sun set, a woman from Denta-ah stood at one end of the grave line, a woman from Winten-ah at the other. They both began a chant in the universal language. The chant mentioned honor, bravery, and coming together when the conflict was over. A crowd lined up alongside them. As they chanted, they moved toward each other. Eventually, they met in the middle, embraced, and raised their hands together.

The last of their chant echoed away as the sun set behind the hills.

Alex, Sekun-ak, Tinta-ak, and Senta-eh walked from the village, each carrying a torch. They stood at the four corners of the pile of stama and touched a torch to it, moving clockwise. When the ring of fire was complete, they tossed their torches onto the pile and watched the flames grow.

The day before, the troughs of Denta-ah had been filled with boiling hot liquid intended to maim and kill their enemy. Today, the troughs were filled with mead.

The flames rose and warriors and former Denta-ah filled their cups with mead and drank their fill again and again. They may have had an injury to their head, leg, or arm, but with a little mead in them, they all seemed capable of doing what Alex thought of as the Kragdon-ah jig.

The beast on the spit was carved and dispersed along with more of the mead. A woman who had been Denta-ah the day before began to sing a song of the battle. When she grew tired, a Winten-ah warrior stood and sang another few verses from his perspective. This went on for more than an hour.

The victors also get to write the history.

Alex watched the whole scene play out in front of him, until Tinta-ak lifted him up onto a small storage shed. He looked out at the gathered throng. Yesterday, they had been both friends and enemies. Today, they were one.

"A great battle was fought here against a brave and tenacious foe. There were many times I thought the outcome could have gone either way. In the end, we were fortunate to have the wind blow in our direction."

The crowd cheered, *Kunta, kunta, kunta* over and over—even the former Denta-ah members.

"Now, I am tired of war. Tired of planning. I only want to think about the next hunt, the next harvest."

The crowd quieted.

An image flew across Alex's brain. Amy, four years older and wondering where her father had gone. "Really, I just want to go home."

The crowd cheered, thinking he meant Winten-ah. Alex, of course, meant something altogether different.

Chapter Forty-Four
The Somber Homecoming

After the massive bacchanal the day and night before, the burning of Denta-ah seemed almost an anticlimax. Everything of value had been stripped from the village. The gates and massive fences had been burned, the same as all signs of stama had burned in the bonfire.

The village was now just a few empty buildings, broken crockery and cookware, and heaps of rubble.

Warriors went to each structure and touched a torch to the thatched roofs, then to another spot ready to be lit.

Ten minutes later, everyone assembled on the same ground where the battle had been fought the day before. There was no marker on the long mass grave. Over time, the mound would settle and nature would reclaim it, as it would the village.

The largest group of warriors headed first toward Stipa-ah, then would move on to Winten-ah.

Smaller gatherings headed in all directions, taking stories of the kunta of Denta-ah with them.

It was hard for Alex to say good-bye to so many warriors who had become friends. It was especially hard to say good-bye to Tinta-ak, because the huge man gripped Alex's good shoulder with his ham-sized fist and wouldn't let go.

"Look at the bright side," Alex said. "You can stop telling people how I thrashed you now."

"You are such a good leader, but are wrong so often. I will take pride in telling people I was badly beaten by the great Manta-ak."

By early afternoon, the large group reached Stipa-ah and repeated what they had done in Denta-ah.

The group was not nearly as large as it had been when it had marched toward Denta-ah, but its makeup was very different. Instead of being almost four hundred warriors marching as one, it was now less than a hundred warriors and many of them were injured—limping, arms in slings, bandages around heads and over eyes.

The rest of the group was comprised of slaves freed from Stipa-ah, who now had no other home to go to, and the displaced former Denta-ah. Everyone who was healthy enough to do so carried a load of some kind with them, either pulling a small wagon or strapped to their back.

Alex had thought they made slow time on the way to the battle. Compared to that, they now moved at a crawl. He wasn't even sure how they would make the trip up the small mountain with the switchback trails. Then he caught himself.

Of course I do. I do know how we'll make it. Together, just like we've done everything else in this impossible mission.

As he walked, Alex let his mind drift to a possibility he had blocked out for years. The chance to go home.

The truth was, Alex Hawk *liked* life in Kragdon-ah. He didn't miss any of the modern conveniences he had left behind. He had never once reached in his pocket for his iPhone or regretted missing a movie or television show. The slower, simpler life agreed with him.

All that was outweighed by Amy. She had turned four on the day he had left. She would be eight now. It was hard for him to age her in his mind. When he had stepped through the door, she hadn't even started preschool yet. Now she would be getting ready to go into third grade.

More than anything else, he worried that she would think that he had simply abandoned her. He couldn't bear that.

On the hike, while others were forming new friendships and bonds, he distanced himself from everyone and was as silent as Do-ken-ak had once been. He knew there were questions ahead.

He glanced down at Monda-ak, limping along beside him. He had chosen him first, but Monda-ak had long since chosen him and bound himself inextricably to him. He knew he couldn't leave him behind, because it would be kinder to simply kill him. At the same time, he didn't know how Monda-ak would adjust to a world with fences, leashes, and automobiles. Not to mention, how would the world react to a dog bigger than anything they'd ever seen?

Monda-ak looked up at Alex with deep brown eyes. As always, those eyes said, *I trust you. You are my human. We will always be together.*

Alex nodded to himself. There was no doubt about it. Monda-ak would always be with him and damn the consequences. With that decision made, and with the possibility of seeing Amy again, Alex's steps grew lighter and quicker. Alex wondered if he could set out for the door the day after they returned. The idea that he could be home in such a short period of time was exhilarating.

Even so, the march dragged on. Between the walking wounded, those who needed to be carried on litters and the various wheeled carts constantly falling apart, it was a long, slow march that ended up taking weeks.

Like all things—even interminable things—it ended eventually. When they had gotten to the forest that ringed Winten-ah, Alex expected to hear cheerful cries of 'Gunta!' from the lookouts.

Instead, the guards in the trees looked like children and were somber. As Alex and the troupe passed guard after guard, a knot grew in his stomach.

Something has happened in Winten-ah. Were they invaded while we were gone and they were almost defenseless?

Alex turned to Sekun-ak, who didn't say anything, but touched his forehead in salute of the obvious truth.

The two men picked up the pace, putting a little distance between themselves and the trailing caravan.

They emerged into the open area. No children were running and playing. It was empty.

There were fires burning inside the cliffside caves, but not the number they would have expected. Ahead, they saw Ganku-eh. She stood with Dan Hadaller, waiting for them.

When they reached her, Alex thought she had aged a dozen years in the time they were gone. Her mouth was pinched and drawn. Worry and sorrow etched her eyes.

"What has happened," Sekun-ak asked.

She answered quietly and without emotion. "Warriors came. Two weeks ago. Banda-ak led the older children and defended Winten-ah. The older warriors who were too sick or infirm to travel with you fought as well. Those who came were well armed and prepared to attack us. We were so badly outnumbered."

Alex wanted to shout, "What happened?" but he held his tongue.

"They were all killed. They are all dead." She pointed to another long grave that ran parallel to the cliffside. Grass was beginning to grow on the mounds of dirt.

Finally, Alex said, "Why?"

Ganku-eh had been staring into the distance. Alex's question snapped her back to reality.

"Lanta-eh. They came for Lanta-eh."

"The little girl?"

"The chosen one."

Chapter Forty-Five
The Oath II

Alex, Ganku-eh, and Sekun-ak sat around the same fire pit where they had sat months before, when they had agreed to go to war with Denta-ah.

There was an empty chair beside the fire—conspicuously empty. Banda-ak, who sat in a position of great authority in the tribe, not to mention being Ganku-eh's husband, was dead.

As Ganku-eh told the story of the attack, he had done everything possible to marshal his limited forces.

"I never thought we would have a sneak attack against us. That's why we have the lookouts in the trees. Somehow, these attackers managed to surprise the lookouts one by one and kill them before they could sound the alarm. I don't know if that's due to the skill of the attackers or the lack of attention by our lookouts. The lookouts were green, but there's no way to know."

"How did it start?" Alex asked, looking for any clue as to who the attackers were.

"The first I knew anything was wrong was when I heard the screams of the children in the field. I didn't let them play in their usual numbers, but it was summer. I couldn't bear to keep them up off the ground all day every day. So, each day, I picked a dozen children and let them run and play in the sunshine. It was good for them, and good for us to see. It brought a sense of normalcy to an abnormal time."

She stared into the small flames, no doubt remembering the scene.

"When I heard the first screams, I rushed to look down. The attackers were running in from the edge of the clearing. It was a terrible position to be in. We couldn't pull the ladders up when the children were in the field, so Banda-ak gathered the small troop he had been training and hurried down to meet them. The attackers had reached the children by then. They killed them, but not all at once. Later, I realized they did that to draw us down."

"Grudu," Sekun-ak said. It was the greatest of the Winten-ah curse words. Alex had only heard it used on two other occasions in his years with the tribe.

Ganku-eh just put two fingers to her forehead in agreement.

"Banda-ak fought as strategically as was possible. He had a few of the shields left from the army and he had been training his apprentices in how to use them. But, other than him, they were too small, too old, too weak. To form a shield wall against a band of warriors with children and the aged was impossible. The invaders overran them. They killed Banda-ak first, because they recognized he was the only warrior among them. I saw what was happening and ordered the ladders pulled up, but I was too late. They were so quick. They were up and killing those I sent on that errand."

Alex and Sekun-ak sat in silence, envisioning what had happened, knowing the horns of the dilemma Ganku-eh had found herself on, not to mention the horror of watching her husband be overrun and killed.

"They shouted again and again, 'Lanta-eh, Lanta-eh!' She was with me and she knew that I would die too before I let them take her. She went to the ladder, ran down it and presented herself to them. 'I am Lanta-eh, what do you want of me?' She was not afraid of them."

Ganku-eh did not need to finish the story. It was obvious what had happened.

"Why would they take her?"

Ganku-eh and Sekun-ak looked at him in surprise.

"Why?" Ganku-eh asked. "Because she is the chosen one. Every tribe in Kragdon-ah would have taken her if they could. She is the prophecy."

"Did everyone know that she was here?" Alex asked. "That she was the prophecy?"

"No. We never told anyone, because we knew this would happen if we did."

"How did they know?"

"It is possible," Sekun-ak said, "that someone who came to fight with us left and took word back to their tribe. They would have known that she was here, and that soon, we would be weakened."

"It was hectic when people first arrived," Alex agreed. "I never saw any of this coming."

"Lanta-eh did, of course. She told me long ago that it would happen. When she was just learning to speak. It was her first prophecy. And now it has come to pass. But there is another prophecy."

"What's that?" Alex asked.

"That you were sent here to bring her home."

Alex bolted upright and walked away from Ganku-eh. He walked to the very edge of the cave and looked down at the field, picturing Banda-ak attempting a shield wall with inexperienced warriors.

He turned back to Ganku-eh. "You told me that if I led your army to victory against Denta-ah, that you would let me return home."

Deep sorrow and pain played out on Ganku-eh's face. "I did. And I meant it, though we would miss you greatly. But, remember Monda-ak."

Alex's heart sank. He did remember how he had been given Monda-ak. He had given Banda-ak an oath. That oath would only die with Alex, not with Banda-ak.

"I am sorry, but I must. I claim the oath you owed my husband. I need you to save Lanta-eh."

To be continued...

Now Available

Book Two of the Alex Hawk Time Travel Adventure Series:[1]

Lost in Kragdon-ah[2]

1. https://www.amazon.com/Lost-Kragdon-ah-Alex-Travel-Adventure-ebook/dp/B086D8YQVZ
2. https://www.amazon.com/Lost-Kragdon-ah-Alex-Travel-Adventure-ebook/dp/B086D8YQVZ

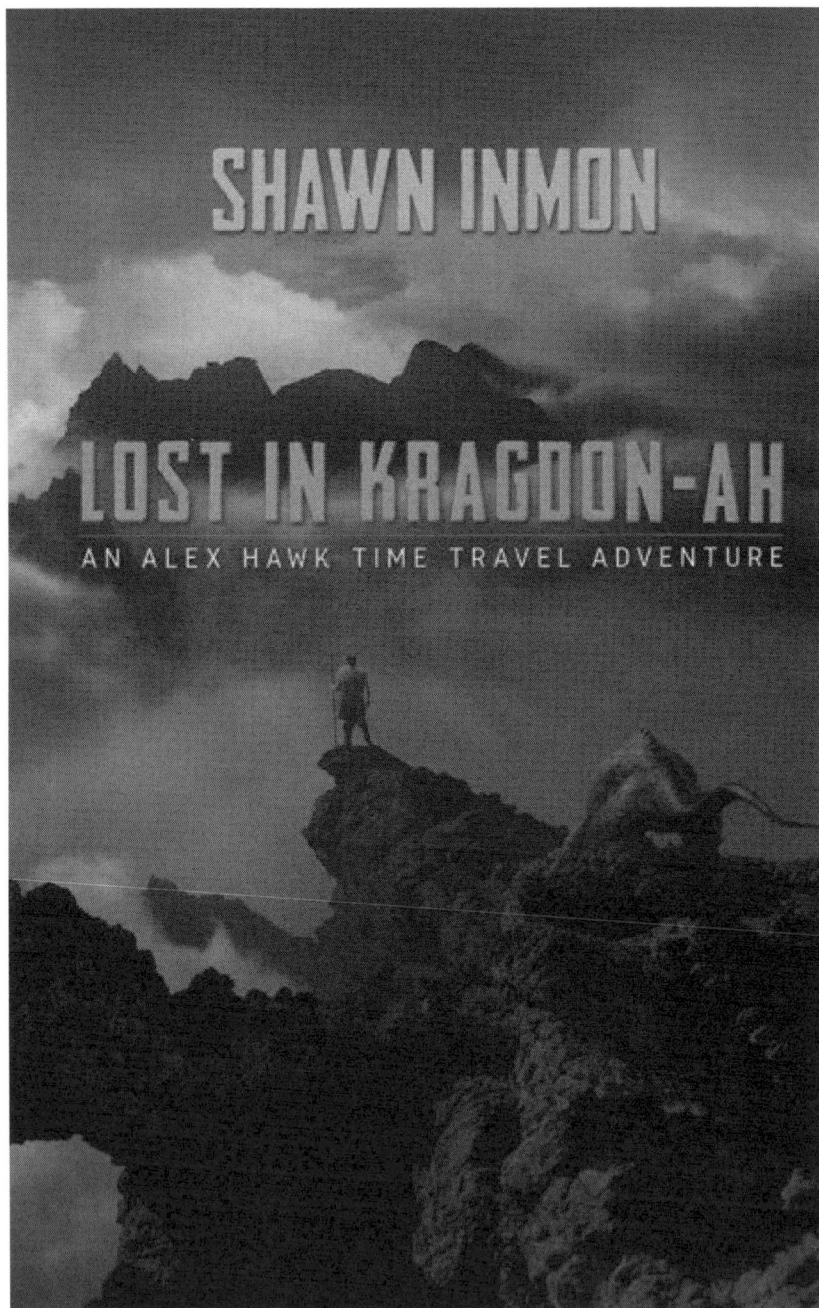

SHAWN INMON

LOST IN KRAGDON-AH

AN ALEX HAWK TIME TRAVEL ADVENTURE

Author's Note

L ike most writers, I was an avid reader as a child. Dr. Seuss's *Green Eggs and Ham* was my entry drug. It was my first literary burning question: why would the guy at least not *try* the green eggs and ham?

By age ten, I discovered Jim Kjelgaard's animal books and sports books. I devoured them by the dozens.

At twelve, I took a step up and looked into the young adult section of the library. That was where I found Edgar Rice Burroughs, Jules Verne, and Robert E. Howard. I knew I was home.

First came the Tarzan books. I really got fired up, though, when I read the stories of *Pellucidar*, the prehistoric world hidden in the earth's core. Then came *Journey to the Center of the Earth* by Jules Verne and Burrough's *John Carter of Mars* books.

These books, which took ordinary men and put them in fantastical situations and extraordinary worlds, fired my imagination. I began to think up my own stories set in their worlds. It was my first tentative step to being a writer.

As an adult, at least in age, if not in temperament, I have gone back and reread those books many times. I still love them, but it's hard to recommend them to modern audiences. They were written, for the most part, more than a hundred years ago. Literary styles change and evolve and even though the stories are still fantastic, they read stilted and dry to modern eyes.

That gave me an idea. Why not write a similar story, but update the style and language?

The question was, how? The heroes reached Pellucidar in a giant mole machine that dug into the center of the Earth. The heroes of

---

3. https://www.amazon.com/Lost-Kragdon-ah-Alex-Travel-Adventure-ebook/dp/ B086D8YQVZ

Journey to the Center of the Earth reached it through a system of caves.

We didn't know as much about the planet then as we do now, but neither of those methods would fly in 2020. However, I've always loved portal fiction. Think C.S. Lewis's *The Lion, the Witch, and the Wardrobe*, or Stephen King's *11/22/63*. Someone walks into a closet, or the back of a storeroom, and voila! They are somewhere else in time and space.

A Door into Time, then, is my own way of combining these two ideas. There is no explanation—or at least none presented in the first book—as to how the door arrived in Alex Hawk's basement. Meanwhile, he is flung into Kragdon-ah, which is my own take on Pellucidar.

In Edgar Rice Burrough's story, Pellucidar is a place where humans and dinosaurs co-exist. I wasn't ready to take my story that far, as I wanted it to be grounded in some form of reality, but I did want fantastic creatures.

So, I set the story far enough in the future that it was possible that evolution had occurred, or even changes in the atmosphere that had led to giant-sized cockroaches, ants, bears and dire wolves.

A Door into Time is set firmly in central Oregon, just many millennia in the future. I researched everything to make sure that the creatures in the book, or at least their ancient relatives, were part of the Oregon landscape.

Each of my books tends to have a single theme. In this one, I wanted to look at the progress the human race has made and examine whether that progress is good or bad. Like all things, I think the answer is somewhere in the middle. I will say I enjoyed these last few months mentally living in Kragdon-ah, where there are no cell phones, internal combustion engines, or Internet. It was soothing to me to step into that world every day, even though I knew dangers lurked around many corners.

Up next will be *Lost in Kragdon-ah*. I am what other writers tend to call a *pantser* because I write *by the seat of my pants*. I prefer the phrase "discovery" writer, in that I discover the story as I go along, never really knowing what is coming around the next bend. That means I only have a few basic ideas of what will happen in *Lost in Kragdon-ah*, but I will admit I am pretty excited by the ideas I do have. If you liked this book at all, I think you will enjoy that one as well.

If you are new to my books, you may not know about this quirky habit I have. For each book, I pick out a single song and listen to it endlessly on repeat during my writing sessions. It becomes like an aural wall against the outside world, and also elicits a Pavlovian response in me. As soon as I hear the opening notes of the song, my brain automatically slips into the world of the story,

For this book, I chose *Hurdy Gurdy Man* by Donovan. If you feel like it, please pull up a copy on YouTube or Spotify and give it a listen. The vibe of the song fits the mood of the book perfectly to me.

Before I thank everyone, I have to share a quick story. I was in third grade in 1969. My family had moved away from the town I grew up in for half the school year, then returned. When I got back to my familiar school, a new kid named Jerry had moved in. We kind of butted heads a little bit—maybe like Sekun-ak and Alex did in this book. But, like them, we soon became fast friends and brothers.

When it rained (which it did a lot in the Spring in Western Washington) our teacher would often let us stay inside and draw or read to ourselves. Jerry and I sat right next to each other and being young boys, we would often draw pictures of war—planes and tanks firing on unfortunate soldiers, that sort of thing.

My drawings were the battle equivalent of stick figures. If you squinted and turned your head, you could kind of tell what they were supposed to be.

Jerry's, on the other hand, were small scale masterpieces. Horrified expressions on the soldiers being killed, intricate detail on the tanks and planes, etc.

As soon as I saw Jerry's drawings, I crumpled up my own and went back to writing stories instead of drawing them. Jerry had a natural-born ability to visualize something, then bring it to life. Over the next eight years, as we stayed best friends, I was continually amazed at the art that flowed from him.

Fast forward quite a few decades to 2020. Jerry and I are still the greatest of friends and brothers. We would do anything for each other and each other's families. We've passed the greatest friendship test of all—our families have gone on vacation together and still loved each other in the end.

As I pondered the inspirations for the story that became *A Door into Time,* I looked through some of my old paperbacks. I noticed that some of them had cool line drawings of scenes from the book.

I called Jerry immediately. I didn't even get the question out of my mouth before he agreed to do it. Before he was done, he had made me the dozen pieces of art that are scattered throughout the book. I feel so blessed that fifty years after we first met, we are continuing not just our friendship, but our creative partnership as well.

I absolutely love what he did for me and I hope you will as well.

A few years ago, Mark Sturgell became one of my proofreaders. For my last two books, he has fulfilled that invaluable role, but has also become my graphics support person. He took all the scanned drawings from Jerry and made them into the files I was able to put into this book. Mark was a triple-threat on this book, though. In addition to proofreading and graphics support, he was also my go-to expert on firearms. He helped me in dozens of ways so that I did not make mistakes that would be obvious to other knowledgeable gun owners. I am grateful for everything he did for me on this book.

Another issue I faced is that Alex Hawk is a military man. I never served, so I was required to write a character who had lived through things I never have. That's where I turned to Diego DeLa Vega. In many ways, he had the same experience as Alex and served as my advisor, not just on weapons and preparedness, but on the mindset Alex might have in many situations. His contributions in advice and aid in helping me understand these things has been invaluable. He turned out to be an excellent proofreader, too!

Debra Galvan has been my proofreader for so long, I can't remember writing a book without her. She has those two critical skills required by every good proofreader—a sharp eye and speed. It's not unusual for Deb to return my proofread manuscript in less than twenty-four hours. Plus, her comments in the margins often crack me up!

Over the years, I have found that various proofreaders catch different things. That is why I have an entire team of proofers, including Aimee Haire, Dan Hilton, and Marta Rubin. They each give so much of their time, energy, and ability that I am in awe of them.

One last thank you goes to Michal Karcz, who designed the cover for this book and each of the books in this series. I found Michal through a friend, who sent me a note saying, "Check out this artwork." As I flipped through Michal's designs, I was completely blown away. I saw so much of my story in his amazing images. One of my happiest days on this project was when Michal agreed to create the covers for me. Typically, a cover designer might make many different possibilities before you come upon the proper design. With Michal, I only have to say "Yes," as soon as he sends me something. I have been blessed to work with an artist of his creativity and vision.

One last thing. If you're a new reader to my work, you might like another series I have written. It is another series of time travel stories, though quite different than this one. It is a twelve-book series called *The Middle Falls Time Travel Series*. The central idea of the series is,

What would it be like if you died, then woke up again, earlier in your life, with all memories intact?

So far, I've found twelve different ways to look at that question and readers keep asking for more, so I will likely return to that series after I finish chronicling Alex's adventures in Kragdon-ah. I'll put a link to them right after this.

As always, more than anything, I owe a thanks to you—my reader. Without you, I would have no reason to make the long trek from my bedroom to my office every day and chain myself to my computer. I appreciate you.

Shawn Inmon
Seaview, WA
March 2020

The Middle Falls Time Travel Series

---

1. http://amzn.to/2aNgrdV

2. http://amzn.to/2wyUfCH

3. http://amzn.to/2yTgHnk

4. http://amzn.to/2z8seyk

5. http://amzn.to/2HkHegL

6. https://amzn.to/2rYBqVh

7. https://amzn.to/2LgxmLq

8. https://amzn.to/2D39mYG

9. https://amzn.to/2SxlzHK

10. https://amzn.to/2Ivx6Yi

11. https://amzn.to/2LBAQZx

12. https://amzn.to/2SewUxA

Printed in Great Britain
by Amazon